Club Crème

We had both started to writhe against each other, Mimi and I, without consciously choosing to do so. For the first time in my life, I felt compelled to make a grab for another woman's crotch. I felt aroused by her much as a man must feel, and began to be drawn towards her intimately and to play a little rough. As I explored this unknown place, I glanced sideways and saw our twin profile in the mirror. I hadn't bargained on two such horny experiences in two days. I felt no embarrassment and no shame. It was going to be an interesting job, working at Club Crème.

Other books by the author:

Country Pleasures

Club Crème
Primula Bond

BLACK LACE

Black Lace books contain sexual fantasies.
In real life, always practise safe sex.

First published in 2004 by
Black Lace
Thames Wharf Studios
Rainville Road
London W6 9HA

Design by Smith & Gilmour, London
Printed and bound by Mackays of Chatham PLC

ISBN 0 352 33907 1

1

There was bubblegum stuck to my shoe. Every other step I took along the grubby pavement was accompanied by stickiness, as if my foot didn't want me to get there. I stopped and leaned against the window of a classy lingerie shop where a headless mannequin in a tightly laced scarlet corset was banging at the window to get out. I frantically scraped the sole of my borrowed, uncomfortable shoe against the sharp edge of the doorstep to get rid of the gum, and wondered how that corset would look worn on its own, with a spiked dog-collar, black leather pencil skirt, bare legs and skyscraper heels.

I earned a glare from the fat lady inside the shop, cerise lips and furrowed brow demanding silently to know if I was coming in to buy. I shook my head and waggled my foot about some more, scraped and kicked, but the gum was still there when I set off again.

I didn't have time to get rid of it. I was late, as usual, and the office was proving impossible to find. I crumpled the newspaper ad into a ball in my pocket as I limped unevenly through Mayfair. I'd forgotten how smart and hushed this part of London was compared to how stressful the city could be; one would always be rushing past even smarter and even more stressed people to get to appointments. Despite the cold weather, sweat was prickling in my armpits as I glanced at all the doorways, some of which had no numbering on them at all.

More than half of me wanted to turn tail and flee. I didn't want a poxy job, here or anywhere else. I wanted to continue living the life of Riley, preferably under permanently blue skies. Whoever Riley was, I wanted to meet him; I wanted him to get me out of this mess. I wanted to forget that I'd run out of money, clothes and a proper working visa, and had nowhere to come but home.

I was rushing past an estate agents' with huge glossy photographs of stately homes in the window, when the name I was searching for flickered out like a tentacle. 'Club Crème' was inscribed in plain black lettering on a neat wooden sign nailed to a little gate. Apart from the luscious name, it could have been an undertakers'. If I'd blinked I'd have missed it.

I came to a halt and the offending shoe flew off. No wonder. Chrissie was several inches shorter and skinnier than me. Her shoes, and the pinstripe trouser suit I had also borrowed, were miles too small. At 28 I was far too young for middle-age spread. Goddam it, I thought I was in pretty good shape. But, trussed up in her miniscule clothes my ribs and toes already felt squashed and bruised, as if they'd done a couple of rounds with Mike Tyson. But I couldn't wear my usual casual clothes to a posh interview, could I? And I needed this job. Any job.

I pushed at the gate and it grudgingly opened with a couple of horror-movie squeaks. I walked up a narrow dark alleyway, all dripping brickwork and distant echoes, and saw a black painted double door ahead. 'Club Crème' was inscribed above this door, too. I pushed, but it was locked. One bell, no label. I rang this and waited. I rang it again, and took out the scrumpled piece of newspaper from my pocket. For the umpteenth time I read its enigmatic request:

> Versatile, energetic and discreet person required
> for varied duties
> Private Gentlemens' Club

Yep, that was me.

2

'How do you know that's you?' Chrissie had snorted the night before, when I read it out to her from the Situations Vacant column, tucked alongside the adverts for cheap flights all over the world, which is what I was saving up for. 'It sounds like an old people's home.'

'Either that, or a massage parlour.' I was already regretting telling her.

'Could be. It's near Shepherd Market, after all. That area used to be a hookers' haunt, you know. Maybe it still is. But with a name like Club Crème, this place could just as easily be a cookery school. But you can't cook, Suki. You can barely type, you've been sacked from virtually every job you've ever had, you've spent the last year doing what, lolling around in the sunshine being bankrolled by some rich prince –'

'He wasn't really a prince, but we all called him that because he looked and acted like one. And I wasn't lolling around all the time. I was helping train his string of horses.'

'Yeah, and I'm the Queen of Sheba.' Chrissie had a great line in barbed comments. 'I suppose that was a step up from modelling trainers in Rio de Janeiro.'

'And swimwear,' I protested. 'They did take pictures of more than just my feet, though it took a lot of persuading, and I wouldn't let them shoot above the shoulders.'

'I don't know why not. It's not such a bad face, when you're scrubbed up, and you'd have made more money that way. Honestly, girl. The only job you haven't been sacked from,' Chrissie went on sternly, 'was mucking out stables at that Lord Whatsit's stately home.'

'And there's a very good reason why I wasn't sacked,' I said preening myself at the memory.

'Why? Shagging the boss, were you? Really, Suki . . .'

'They begged me to stay. I was the best they'd ever had, actually. And you can take that how you like. So there you are!' I interrupted her triumphantly. 'If that catalogue of achievement doesn't make me a versatile person, then I don't know what does.'

'You might call it versatile. I call it unreliable.'

We faced each other over our wine glasses. We were sitting out on her roof terrace, even though it was a cool autumn evening. A plane lifted heavily into the London sky and, as always, I craned my neck to imagine where it was going, who was on board, how hot it would be when they got there . . .

'How about being an air hostess?' I ventured. 'Or flight attendant, as it's called now. That's something I've never tried.' I took a deep slug of wine and wandered across the terrace to peer over the little parapet at the world below. A tube train rumbled out of Earls Court station below us, making the house shake.

'You don't look the part,' Chrissie said as she tilted her head to examine me. 'You'd never fit the bill. Admittedly, I can't remember what colour your hair is naturally –'

'Mouse, I think they call it –'

'But it never used to be so red or so long. No use hiding it under that beret. You look like an onion seller in that tatty T-shirt and torn jeans. You're not on the continent now, you know –'

'Oh, God, Chrissie, I wish I was. I wish I could get this travel bug out of my system,' I sighed, breathing in the city fumes. Then I wagged my finger at her. 'You should have visited me out there. Why didn't you?'

Chrissie pursed her lips, and I wanted to kick her. If I resembled an onion seller, she looked like a Dresden shepherdess: little legs crossed, blonde curls tightly arranged over her small head, perfect fingernails curled round her wine glass – in fact, *she* would make a perfect flight attendant. But the perfume business seemed to suit her. She liked smothering her naturally wicked little face with heavy pink foundation, accentuating her blue eyes with sparkly shadow until she looked innocent, hiding the sharp teeth and sharper tongue under perfectly applied, all-day moisturising lipstick. Most of all, she liked the uniform that the grand department store made her wear for strutting around the fragrant marble floor of her domain.

'You know why,' she replied at last. 'I'm far too busy. I've a career to pursue, and a sexy new fiancé to keep an eye on. Anyway, you were moving in very louche circles. All that champagne, all those pool parties ... I couldn't possibly have visited you, even if I knew where you were. I was worried I'd –'

'Like it too much? You're just jealous that I've been a lady of leisure all this time. Come on, Chrissie, you can take that poker out of your bum and stop looking at me as if I'm something you trod in. I've known you since before you lost your cherry. I was there *when* you lost your cherry, come to think of it, with Sammy Smithson *and* Sammy Smithson's brother. Behind the Odeon, wasn't it? Oh God, I remember now. We'd just been to see *Nine-and-a-half Weeks* and you were gagging for it. Any Tom, Dick or Harry would have done. But you needed both the Smithson brothers to do it.'

'I can barely remember,' she sniffed.

I shook with laughter, and some pigeons flew off the wall and flapped away over the railway line.

'It was better than anything they were showing on screen that day,' I persisted, amused at her discomfort. 'You were so hot. Your PVC miniskirt was up round your waist before you could say "Packet of three" and you were wrapped round Sammy Smithson like he was a lamppost.'

'Well, he was as tall and strong as one,' Chrissie couldn't resist enlightening me. She tugged at her tight skirt. 'And hung like a donkey.'

'His brother and I were supposed to be the lookout, and I couldn't believe it when Tommy Smithson got stuck in there as well. Abandoned his position as lookout, scuttled up and took you from behind, as I recall, while Sammy had you up against the wall. You were known as the Smithson sandwich after that.'

'I never!'

'All lanky legs and arms flailing like a windmill, until you all three crashed over into the dustbins and the manager of the cinema came flying out to see what the commotion was.'

'Flailing like a windmill. That's not very nice,' Chrissie said, desperately trying to retain a stern expression. 'But you would say that. Always ridiculing sex and romance, though I'm sure you're addicted to it really. Actually, I thought it was a very beautiful encounter. All that teen-age cheek and energy. Don't get that these days with Jeremy, sadly. He's always too tired. Ooh, they were like animals, those Smithsons. Wouldn't stop. I didn't want them to stop. They had my feet right off the ground, lifting me like I was a doll. I was weightless. Everything faded away except what they were doing to me. You know. That one little part of me was all I could concentrate on. I *became* that one little part.'

6

Chrissie's eyes were glittering under the sparkling eyeshadow. 'But what a way to go. And there they were, the Smithson brothers; they had me helpless. All I could do was let them shove me back and forth between them with their thrusting while this wild fire built up inside me ...'

'I remember, I remember. God, I wish I hadn't reminded you ...'

'Then the pair of them were grunting in my ears, but I liked it, I liked that they were brutes. And then we were all coming together, hammer and tongs. Wow! My first time.'

'Enough! I shouldn't have started this topic,' I said. I held my hands over my ears. 'A sensational encounter it may have been, but pretty damned acrobatic, too. I never knew a girl had so many orifices.'

Chrissie wriggled on her chair, flushing red.

'Chrissie, you'd love living abroad. That lifestyle is so totally up your alley, and you know it.' I wasn't going to let it go. 'What would your perfume bosses say if they knew how you got a taste for the rough stuff? Their monocles would drop out if they knew what you did when you were bunking off college.'

Chrissie was chilling. I could see a smile tugging at her lips.

'They might congratulate me on having such a sharp business head on my shoulders, even aged twenty,' she replied.

'Yeah,' I smirked. 'More beautiful encounters. Enticing rich men into your mum's house when she was out, promising them a trip to heaven in return for shopping vouchers, never taking cash so you could never call yourself a tart.'

'And they never called themselves punters, did they? I got several wardrobes full of lovely clothes. Holidays.

Cars. Even a job or two. Set me up for life, that did.' Chrissie stretched her legs out in front of her and wiggled her neat ankles. 'In more ways than one.'

'Best not to remind your Jeremy that's how you met,' I ventured and she shot me a filthy look.

'I don't know what you're talking about,' she flashed, lowering her feet again and pouring another glass of wine. 'We're a respectable couple, Jeremy and I.'

'Of course you are,' I soothed. Then I shrugged, teasing her. 'Not that I've met the wonderful Jeremy yet. But still, with that kind of history, you can't criticise me for being restless all the time. You were far more outrageous than me back then.'

'Maybe, but that was back then. All the cheek of the devil at that age. I'm not as adventurous as you, Suki,' Chrissie replied thoughtfully. 'Not really. I know I'm safer in my little world, while you ... you were always the tomboy, always wanting to spread your wings.'

'Back then you were the one that the guys were after,' I said and shrugged. 'They didn't interest me at all. I was too busy looking for a higher tree to climb.'

'I used to think you were gay, you know.' Chrissie paused to give me the chance to confirm or deny. 'Are you?'

I tried to look solemn for a moment, as if she'd struck a chord. What a lark it would be to throw her off the scent, and then try to live up to the lie. But I couldn't.

'I used to wonder about that, too,' I admitted after I'd given up the fight to keep a straight face. 'But it was only because I never fancied any of the boys. I couldn't just spread 'em for any old jock. Not like some people I know.'

'Oi! Less of your cheek. And I'm not like that at all. Go on. After all this time?' Chrissie wanted to know. 'Are you still the tomboy who thinks boys are stupid?'

I drained my glass and looked away over the city. Another tube train rattled and vibrated below us. The sky was inky now, but no stars penetrated the smog. The bright headlights of circling aircraft were the only sparks piercing the thick cloud.

'No. I like boys, don't worry. The prince saw to that. I guess I'm still a bit of a tomboy, yeah. But there's plenty of room for guys in this tomboy's life, I can assure you. Anything goes when you're under the hot, hot sun.'

'No one in particular, though?'

'Nah. It turned out the prince had too many wives already.'

We laughed again.

'We'll have to find you a man now you're back in town.' Chrissie pointed the wine bottle towards me like a microphone, as if she was about to interview me. 'But who? And where?'

Chrissie's phone started to ring. She ran indoors to answer it, while I pondered her question. Who, and where indeed? Compared with where I'd just come from, where all the men, and women, lay about on sun loungers all day or skimmed the blue waves on their monoskis, where everyone was glossy, tanned, bright eyed and rolling in money, London seemed, in the few days I'd spent back here, full of pale, uninteresting, anxious-looking types scurrying along the pavements muffled up in anoraks.

'Sorry about that,' Chrissie called, trotting back to the French window. 'Just work, reminding me that I'm heading up a big perfume buyers' conference and party in some country house on New Year's Eve. Now, where were we?'

'Manhunting.'

'Yeah,' she said. She surveyed me in the doorway, unable to stop her lips pressing disdainfully at the sight.

'I wonder if it would help if we got you out of those clothes? And if you lost that cocky, mannish manner you've had since we were kids?'

'Hasn't stopped me getting what I want out in the Middle East.'

'Maybe not, girl. But it's autumn in England. Remember what that's like? You can't dazzle them with your polka-dot bikini and your horse-breaking skills in the middle of Piccadilly, can you? Men here expect more than that. Because you have to wear more clothes here in London, you need to work it in other ways. Twirl that curl round your finger, stroke your leg as if you love it, make your eyes big and sparkling –'

I raised one eyebrow as she acted out her seduction technique. She frowned, and stopped.

'Come on, Suki. You're capable of being feminine when you put your mind to it. You used to go all fluid and dreamy when you were keen on some older man or other, or when you were listening to music, or planning some new adventure.' She came and sat beside me on the wall. 'But you were always pretty secretive. I was the one who was always going on about sex and boys. You never did.'

'I'll tell you what I got up to out there. One day.'

'It'll be like prizing open a clam. Just like it used to be.'

'Now. Talking about getting me out of these clothes –'

'Don't get saucy now,' Chrissie said and giggled.

'No. I mean getting out of these rags and into something suitable for this interview tomorrow.'

'I must say, I would have expected you to come back from overseas decked out in jewels and finery, not all your old gear from way back,' Chrissie remarked. I could tell she was disappointed that there was to be no more sex talk. I just didn't feel like obliging her. I'd left a pretty wild scene behind me, one pretty wild man in particular, just because I was restless, just because I had itchy feet and just because I'd run out of money. But now I was back in staid old London, I was beginning to regret my hasty decision.

'This gentlemen's club,' I said and sighed, looking again at the piece of paper. 'I need to make an effort, I suppose.'

'Of course you do. Get positive.' Chrissie took a sip of wine, and choked as she started to giggle again. 'Think there'll be any tasty men there?'

'I doubt it. They'll all be old codgers with handlebar moustaches and gout. They'll all be slumped in their leather armchairs, hidden behind the *Telegraph* and demanding port and cigars. Can I hack that? I doubt it. But I just need to earn some money, Chrissie, so I can take off again. Now. Will you help me, or not? I need to borrow some clothes.' I plucked at my frayed Levis. 'What you got, Chris?'

'Just let me toss the salad,' she said, jumping to her feet and going back inside. I remembered that she, at least, could cook. 'Are you staying for supper?'

'In a hurry, but thanks. I'll meet Jeremy another time.' My stomach rumbled. Chrissie was a brilliant cook, and I was dying for a square meal. But I also wanted to be on my own for a while. I was still horribly disorientated, and her perky confidence just made it worse.

It was getting chilly, and I followed her indoors, scooping the wine bottle and glasses off the terrace table.

'Always so restless,' Chrissie complained, energetically chopping some spring onions with violent jerks of her elbow and dropping them into a complicated marinade. I could tell she was pissed off. 'Why the rush?'

There was no reason. I just didn't want to play goose-berry with her and her darling new man.

'Nothing riveting,' I said, truthfully. 'Just need to settle into my lovely bed and breakfast before the dreaded interviews and flat-hunting tomorrow.'

'I've told you. You can stay here. I'm sure Jeremy wouldn't mind.' There was a tiny pause. 'He loves having new people around.'

I hugged her, shaking my head. 'Just take me to your wardrobe, and I'll be gone.'

It didn't take long. We nearly came to blows as she tried to squeeze me firstly into a tomato-coloured sack-shaped dress, and then into a green ensemble which looked like our old school uniform. We were just coming to an uneasy agreement on an outfit when the buzzer went.

'That's Jeremy, warning me of his arrival. He says it's so I can chuck out the toy boys.'

Chrissie patted her already immaculate curls and a pink flush of pleasure went up her neck as she waited for her fiancé to come up in the lift. I grabbed my rucksack and the Harvey Nichols bag stuffed with the borrowed suit. Chrissie had thrown in a silk blouse, some stockings and a pair of shoes. I gave her a kiss on the cheek.

'I'll leave you lovebirds together. I'll be back with the clothes in a day or so, Chrissie.' I pushed my way out of the flat, and took the stairs down to the street.

3

I rang the doorbell of Club Crème once more, keeping my finger impatiently on the little round disc. A taxi rumbled past the alleyway, sending up a dirty spray of puddle water. Still no one came. I turned to go. I was usually willing to try my hand at anything, but Chrissie's remarks about my professional abilities came back to haunt me. I hadn't come all the way back to London just to change old men's catheters, rustle up a mean soufflé or hang about in dingy alleyways.

'Can I help you?'

Someone was pushing open the metal gate at the entrance to the alleyway, which gave another ear-splitting squeak. Stiletto footsteps clacked smartly towards me on the dark tiling. Some murky drops of rain found their way down through the surrounding high walls and started to drum on the top of my beret.

'No, you can't. I'm in the wrong place,' I muttered, squeezing against the dank wall to let her pass.

'Really? So you've not come for an interview? Although now I think about it, you're not our usual type of candidate at all. Could you look at me when I speak to you?'

I jerked my head up like a sulky schoolgirl. The most sensational-looking woman was standing in front of me, dressed from head to foot in what looked like real silver fox fur. She looked as if she should be sweeping into the Savoy, not stamping about in a dank alleyway off Shepherd Market. Then again, after what Chrissie had said, that was exactly the sort of look that would go down a treat at Shepherd Market. She was as tall as me, which was unnerving in itself, and her black hair was piled up on top of her head in that clever way which looks as if it's about to tumble straight down again. Her heavily made-up eyes, ringed in sooty kohl, glittered in the gloom of the alleyway and her big mouth was a slash of scarlet.

'Yes,' I mumbled after a moment, but keeping my eyes on hers. 'I am here for the interview.'

'Good.'

One side of her scarlet mouth curled in what could either have been a sneer or a smile. Holding my gaze, she fingered the lapel of my jacket between finger and thumb, as if checking for dust. Then she smoothed it over my breast, resting her gloved hand there for a moment.

'I'm meant to be seeing Miss –' I checked my scribble on the newspaper cutting '– Miss Sugar?'

My interrogator's head fell back and she let out a throaty chuckle. I could see the sinews in her white throat, the rows of white teeth, and the red, red tongue. She looked like a flamenco dancer about to fling herself into the arms of a matador.

'We love employing people with such hilarious names. You'll see how well it suits her.' She gave me one last, glittering look, then swiped a card key to unlock the door. I followed her, and prepared to hold my breath against the smell of stale cabbage and Elastoplast.

Once inside, I couldn't imagine something as lowly as cabbage ever being cooked inside Club Crème, let alone any ghastly odours being allowed to seep out of the kitchen. (Although it was at that precise moment that the idea of 'school dinners' was hatched, and later, much later, crisp green cabbage was allowed back on to the club menu, lightly tossed in butter, black pepper and a sprinkling of nutmeg . . .)

And instead of peering at chipped linoleum and brooding mahogany, I found myself gazing round a beautiful marble atrium, bathed in a column of light streaming down from a domed skylight above me.

'What is that lovely smell?' I wondered aloud, sniffing the fragrant air. 'Beeswax, and lily of the valley?'

The woman paused beside me and laughed softly.

'Correct. You have sensitive nostrils, like our Miss Sugar,' she replied, obviously amused. She, too, lifted her chin and sniffed. 'The beeswax polish and pot pourri are all her idea, and how right she is. Don't you agree that the first impression to greet you in a new place, or even an old familiar place, is the aroma? Virtually before you've seen anything, or spoken to anyone?'

'Absolutely,' I agreed. 'And how awful it is if you get it wrong. But this is all so right.'

She and I were directly beneath the column of light and I now saw that it illuminated a circular atrium of white marble, with several stained-glass internal doors leading off the hallway and a stone staircase curling upwards. In this cocoon of hushed luxury, it was impossible to imagine the chilly rain falling outside.

'You'll find Miss Sugar through there,' the woman said, waving her hand towards one of the doors. 'I will be fascinated to know what she makes of you. Or you of her, for that matter. Good luck.'

And she was gone, sweeping up the stairs and disappearing into the bright light from the sky.

Miss Sugar was as thin as a pin and looked as if nothing so sweet as an apple, let alone chocolate or puddings, ever passed her lips. Everything about her was grey to the point of see-through. Her eyes, staring behind thick spectacles, her clothes, her skin, all looked as if they belonged to a ghost. She didn't seem to like the bright light and clean marble of the building because she kept her office shuttered and lit by one solitary lamp. Her hair may as well have been grey, but actually it was very pale, silvery blonde, and scraped back into a tight bun. She was the opposite of the voluptuous dark lady. And she was definitely the opposite of me.

'You have done many things in your time.' Miss Sugar stated the obvious, holding my CV up to the lamp light and reading it very slowly. She turned her thick spectacles towards me, and I saw my face distorted there like a fish.

'And I'm not yet thirty,' I interjected. But she didn't smile.

'I can't quite see how all this travelling, modelling and, ah, riding, would fit into the kind of role we are looking to fill here at Club Crème.'

'Well, you didn't ask about my experience when I phoned about the interview, so I figured you were open to allcomers,' I replied, slightly sarcastically. She was taking an age getting to the point, and I could already tell she didn't like me. 'If you could give me a clue what that role entails exactly, I'll tell you how I can fit in. I mean, I can type,' I added, tugging at Chrissie's pinstripe jacket and realising that two of the buttons had already either come undone or snapped off. 'And I know my way round most computer programmes.'

While she bent her head to study my references I undid the other buttons to relieve the burden on the jacket, only to find that the silk blouse was just as taxed trying to cover my big breasts. Irritation began to jab at me as I fiddled with the remaining buttons. The only item of clothing that fitted me today was my bra.

Unbeknownst to Chrissie, or indeed anyone who only encountered me in my usual tomboy mode, beneath my scruffy clothes I always wore exquisite underwear. It was the one legacy I had taken away from my years as the favourite girlfriend. After the first time the prince had unwrapped my body like a precious consignment of contraband, he had trained me to appreciate and dress my body, just as I had trained him to appreciate his horses. To give him his due, he'd brought my body to life under the blazing blue skies, and I had quickly seen why it was important to keep that body in lovely underwear. I particularly treasured my breasts, liked to cosset and look after them. I liked buying something lovely to encase them in. Too bad if I then hid their splendour under sweatshirts and ripped denim.

The prince had set his sights on me after he'd seen me galloping on a silver Arab mare around the pyramids at Giza. Dawn had been breaking; my favourite time of day in a hot country. He had quickly jumped on another horse at the stables – Armani business suit and all – and chased after me. A few hours later, he had offered me a job and we were in his hotel room in the middle of Cairo, drinking Buck's fizz for breakfast to celebrate.

Our conversation had rapidly become less businesslike and more flirtatious, and suddenly room service had appeared with a big box overflowing with silk and lace underwear. The prince had asked me to put it on, and I had been stunned into obeying him.

I'd been in Egypt for precisely 48 hours. I was meant to be passing through. Certainly no thought of men, or sex, or any kind of entanglement, had crossed my mind when I'd set off on my travels. Quite the reverse, in fact. But the prince was different. You'd have to be blind not to be mesmerised by him. Dangerous charm wavered off him like a heat haze. Once he'd got me alone, his eyes were so dark with lust and admiration, so intent on watching me, the champagne so cold and delicious, the underwear so expensive and sexy, that I had done as he asked. I remember shivering uncontrollably as I had pulled off my sweaty T-shirt and jodhpurs.

He had looked calmly at me, not licking his lips or making any comment to embarrass me, and had simply waited, holding out the box of underwear. My head had been swimming by this time with Fuck's bizz (as Chrissie and I always called it), as well as confused excitement. I had returned his gaze and stepped boldly out of my plain vest and pants. Then it was my turn to wait. We had eyed each other in the shuttered cool of the hotel room until he beckoned me over. He had certainly known what he was doing, hooking me tenderly into the various garments, showing me how just wearing a bit of well-designed underwiring, whalebone or even Lycra could alter my posture and my silhouette. As he talked, I had wondered how many other women dotted around the globe were strutting about similarly attired from his generous wallet.

That very first morning he had made me parade round his room like one of his horses in the exercise ring, goading me out of my usual slouch until I was walking tall like a ballerina. Except this prancing pony was sporting a dark-pink basque and matching frilled knickers. My body had felt like a new toy, my limbs swinging, my hips swaying from side to side, my sap rising as the sun blazed down and the cars hooted in the clogged streets outside the hotel.

He had watched me for a while, still sitting on a chair by the window, then he had grabbed me by the hips as I stalked past him and before I could blink he had hitched me onto his lap. He had studied my new, warm cleavage, all raised and ripening under its silky cover, then scooped one breast out of its nest, weighing it like a juicy peach at the market. Dressed – or rather undressed – like this, I felt I was a new person, capable of anything. He was a total stranger. He would eventually flit out of my life as soundlessly as he had flitted in. But I was abroad. No one knew me. No one could stop me. For the first time in my life, I could do what I liked. It had been a great feeling.

I pulled myself back to the present. What a difference five years made. All I had left of the suave but unpredictable prince was the pack of lies we called a reference which he had concocted for me the night before I left.

'It's not exactly typing we're after,' Miss Sugar was saying in answer to my remark, pushing aside the CV. She obviously didn't believe a word of it. I glanced around the gloomy office. There was a computer in the corner and a couple of metal filing cabinets, but no other evidence of secretarial work. When I looked back at her, I saw that she was staring through her spectacles at my bosom. I looked down. The blouse had given up completely, had undone itself to the waist, and my breasts were thrusting out from between the defeated silk folds, encased in cream lace. I tugged the jacket round me, feeling it rip down a back seam, and wondered how soon I could beat a retreat.

'I am very versatile,' I repeated. I'd rehearsed this mantra on the tube coming here. 'Filing, errands, messages, answering the phone, I can spell, I'm good with people, I spent all day being good with people in my last job. I'm good at making coffee – I make a wicked coffee.'

She didn't smile, but looked back at my CV, then waved a hand at the filing cabinets.

'I see you were pretty good with animals in your last job, too. But we don't tend to have thoroughbred horses clamouring to join this club.'

I slowed my breathing down.

'Could you tell me, Miss Sugar, who exactly *does* join this club? Not to mention who exactly works here. I'm afraid I haven't got the picture.'

'Well, it's a very English, very select club. A retreat, if you like, for moneyed, mostly titled people. Aristocrats. Hence the name of the club. We accommodate *la crème de la crème* here.'

She looked me up and down again, obviously placing me firmly below stairs.

'Well,' I announced smartly, unable to resist the opportunity to set her straight, 'I can do aristocrats. I've been working for a prince for the last five years.'

'True,' she said slowly, studying my CV again as if it was an exam paper. 'But I suspect your exotic princes are rather different from our mostly home-grown members. Oh dear. They wouldn't like me describing them as home-grown . . .'

'Quite. It makes them sound as if they live in tweeds and green wellies. Boy! I'm sure my exotic princes could give your aristos a run for their money.' I plonked myself down uninvited in the chair opposite her. 'They're probably far richer, for a start. They'd have far more style. And far more fun.'

'That's where you're wrong.' Miss Sugar's voice cut through the air. I was impressed. Not such a mouse after all. 'I'd be willing to bet that our members could knock your sheikhs into a cocked hat, whatever that expression means.' We both gave tiny puffs of mirth but she kept her face straight and continued, 'Our lot could equal yours in every way, I'm certain. We like to give the impression of an old-fashioned set-up, and that suits the older members. But there's more to Club Crème. Far more.'

'Go on.'

'This is a small establishment. We may have very few clients staying here at any one time, perhaps only a handful, but the ones we do have are our twenty-four hour responsibility, and they pay handsomely for it. Believe me, they can afford it. And our job is to make this place a home from home, in every tiny detail, only infinitely better. They come here to escape from home, in fact: nagging wives, troublesome kids, stressful professions, difficult decisions. But we find that, even when all their extra-curricular problems are sorted out, they still come back here again, and again, and again . . .'

She looked past me dreamily, her voice fading. She obviously lived and breathed this job. I was curious now, eager to know what it was that she did. What it was that she wanted me to do.

'What about the fun?' I badgered. 'You said your members could equal my princes in every way.'

'Fun. Ah yes.' She smiled at me briefly, then seemed to wake up. The smile snapped shut, as if fun was a dirty word, and she folded her hands over my CV. 'I'll come to that. We, which is to say myself, who fixes the nuts and bolts, Miss Breeze, the lady you met in the hallway, who is overall manager, and the vacant position, who will assist her –' here she absently tapped my CV '– we aim to run this establishment like clockwork, but make it seem as if the members are running it. We oversee and create everything from the cooking, the decor and the drinks in the bar, to the design of the bedrooms. We have come to love this building, the very bricks and mortar, and that's what we require of whoever we recruit.'

I nodded. 'I can identify with that. It's a stunning building. But what about the fun element you were going to tell me about?'

Miss Sugar stopped stroking the desk, part of the fixtures and fittings which she obviously loved as much as she loved the bricks.

'Well, our brief extends to planning any entertainment our members enjoy while they're in town. We field their demands. We *anticipate* their demands. At the same time we have to treat them with kid gloves. It's a far more personal service than, ah, *secretarial* work, I can assure you.'

'The less secretarial the better,' I exclaimed, throwing caution to the winds. 'I told you, I can turn my hand to anything. And I came back to London precisely to do that. Everything on my CV is all in the past, Miss Sugar. I am looking for a change now.'

I looked pointedly round her old-fashioned room, remembering the classy design of the rest of the building, the unseen rooms, the bedrooms. The unseen members. Suddenly, I didn't want to wriggle out of this interview after all. I wanted to stay.

Miss Sugar seemed to have calmed down a little. 'We are looking for someone who will be able to meet those demands. Someone slick, and sophisticated, and discreet.'

'Someone who can choose the right pot pourri.'

'Exactly!' she exclaimed and clapped her hands once, then dropped them again. 'Someone who can keep everything ticking over, as I've described, and then, at any time of night or day, act like a hostess, both here and when our members are out and about. Sometimes they require accompanying, you see. Someone with taste, someone who looks expensive, but someone who can blend into the background if required.'

'In other words, the role is hands-on, in every sense. What you're describing here is a cross between a housekeeper and a hooker, right?'

She flapped her hand in front of her face. 'Please, Miss Summers. You've totally misconstrued. Hands-on, certainly. I couldn't have put it better myself. But I'm afraid that you've further convinced me that none of your skills, your colourful experience, nor your particular, ah, style, would be quite right for our discerning —'

'Excuse me, Miss Sugar. Personal service, you said?' I yanked the jacket crossly across my boobs again. It seemed she'd already made up her mind, so what the hell. It was time for shock tactics. 'I can do personal service in spades. But I must say, this place doesn't *look* like a house of ill repute. I couldn't figure it out at first. To think I was expecting it to be an old people's home!'

I thought I heard a snuffle of laughter from the hallway. I twisted to see if the dark lady had heard what I was saying, but instead of Miss Breeze, I saw a tall figure crossing the hall with a slightly shuffling gait, wearing a soaked raincoat and a Sherlock Holmes-style hat. All I could see of his face was greying stubble on his cheeks and chin.

'Afternoon, Sir Simeon.' Miss Sugar was practically curtseying in her chair. I gaped at her, and then at him. He looked like the local tramp, come in for shelter. He paused outside the door. I caught a glimpse of sharp blue eyes above angular cheekbones as he tipped his eccentric hat like an old-fashioned gentleman. He stamped away, and again I noticed the uneven pace of his steps.

Miss Sugar's pale face had two points of pink on each cheekbone. With shaking hands she took off her glasses and pinched the bridge of her nose.

'One of your punters? Sorry, members?' I asked. Miss Sugar shook her head, patted her hair, and handed me back my paper.

'That's the owner of the club: Sir Simeon Symes. Now do you see how wrong your assessment is? I'm dismayed that you thought this unique, refined haven could be a brothel. In fact, it's designed to be quite the opposite. If anything, women are mostly kept out, rather than let in. Wives, girlfriends, mistresses – they are what our members mostly come here to avoid. In fact, there are only three women here on a regular basis. Me, Miss Breeze, and –'

She stopped. Her cheeks were still pink, and her eyes glittering with what looked like angry tears. I wondered who the lucky third woman would eventually be.

'I didn't mean to offend you, Miss Sugar. I get the picture. And it's beginning to sound enticing.' I smiled at her, trying to warm her up a little. 'Three women, Sir Simeon and hordes of dozy gents.'

'That's the way he wants it, yes. Club Crème was his brainchild. He's our boss.'

'He doesn't look like a Sir. He looks like a down and out –' I stopped. Miss Sugar was looking star-struck, and the door was still open. 'So why isn't Sir Simeon interviewing me if he's the boss?' I asked.

'He leaves all that to me. All the admin, finances, back office work, is down to me now. That's why we're looking for someone new for the front-of-house work. The meeting and greeting, the soirées, the parties, the flower arranging, the one-to-one ... Well, now, I wouldn't want to waste any more of your time. I can see the concept of catering to the needs and whims of a group of distinguished gentlemen might clash with your feminist principles. Like I said, I don't think this position would be for you, Miss Summers.'

'On the contrary, Sugar. Forgive me, but I think you're quite mistaken.' The dark lady came in to the room. I could smell a strong perfume sweeping off her, heady like wine. 'I'm surprised that you've failed to spot this candidate's obvious potential. But then again, this is the first interview you've conducted since you became administration manager, or whatever job title you gave yourself, so you are excused a few errors of judgment. As an interview, this session isn't working. Let's all take a break.'

Her hands rested on my shoulders and pressed down. I realised I'd been hunched up in the uncomfortable swivel chair. I also realised she'd been watching us from some hiding place. She pressed until my shoulders were relaxed, and the way she pressed made my head fall back, resting against her stomach.

'Miss Breeze, I'm only concerned about our image. I mean –' Miss Sugar said and glared at me, then stood up and took Miss Breeze by the elbow to steer her to the other side of the room. She lowered her voice a fraction, but I suspected she wanted me to hear every word. 'That filthy beret and that suit that doesn't even fit her properly. Surely that says it all? I can't imagine that any of our members would feel comfortable being greeted by Miss Summers, the way she dresses. Let alone have her pouring cocktails for them, remembering their favourite soap, advising them of the best restaurants to go to, or going with them to the opera. Think of our reputation. It could be ruined in just one evening.'

'*Our* reputation?' Miss Breeze queried, also not bothering to speak quietly. I worked out there and then that it would not do to get on the wrong side of the dark lady. Her voice was like ice cutting through steel. 'Remember you're only an employee here, Sugar. Just like Miss Summers here. It's *my* reputation that's at stake, as *maîtress d'*. And, ultimately, Sir Simeon's reputation. Not yours.'

Miss Sugar's face pinched itself into a series of pained lines, and she groped behind her for her glasses but, just as I was beginning to enjoy her discomfort, the dark woman pulled off my beret and it was Miss Sugar's turn to smirk. My hands flew up to my head, but it was too late. My hair looked like a bird's nest this morning, all tangled and unbrushed. That's why I'd tried to hide it.

'Problem solved!' Miss Breeze exclaimed, tossing the beret accurately into the bin and planting her hands on her hips. 'Now let's take a good look at our candidate.'

'I think I'm the one who was conducting this interview, and I am telling you she isn't right for the job.' Miss Sugar sniffed, patting the papers on her desk, including my CV, into a neat pile. She gave me a pitying look. 'I'm sorry, but I can't see the street urchin look suiting our purposes.'

'Look, as far as I can see, you're only looking for a glorified housemaid. I may not look the part right now, but just because I haven't got the right clothes, doesn't mean you can talk over my head as if I'm not here.' I had had enough. It didn't matter now what I said. 'I did try to smarten myself up to come here today, but I had to borrow this suit from a friend who is much smaller and thinner than me. As you can see from my CV, which I'll have back now, I've been living abroad for a while, where we mostly wore jodhpurs and sarongs.'

'I like the sound of that,' Miss Breeze said huskily, still standing behind me. 'Sarongs and jodhpurs. How free. And how sexy.'

'And when it comes to filthy berets, what about your boss? I thought he was a tramp walking in here just now.' I smacked my lips shut in horror at what I'd just said, but neither of the other women flinched. In fact they both nodded.

'He likes to go about London unrecognised,' Miss Breeze said calmly. 'So you were obviously fooled by his disguise, just like everyone else is.'

'Whatever flicks his switch. But *this* isn't a disguise,' I said. I stretched towards the bin to retrieve my beret. 'This is how I generally look. I've never been any good at putting on the posh, executive style you are obviously looking for. Or would it be some kind of demure uniform? The Mary Poppins look? Floral tea dress and sensible lace-up shoes, perhaps?'

I stood up to go, but Miss Breeze caught me. She smiled her wide red smile right into my eyes. 'It could be whatever you wanted it to be.'

I flushed apologetically, unable to look away. 'I didn't *really* think this place was a knocking shop. Miss Sugar wasn't giving me a chance. I just made that comment because I was feeling sore.'

She held out a red strand of my hair.

'Good. Remember, there's no room for hurt feelings and misunderstandings here. Now look. No tangles.' She brushed the smooth strand against my cheek. 'Let's not beat about the bush any longer. You've got the looks and the body. You've got the attitude, too, with a little bit of refinement. The rest will be easy.' She glanced across at Miss Sugar, then back at me. 'I want you to take the job.'

She had been straightening out my hair without my noticing. There was something intensely sensuous about the thought. How was she to know I loved my hair being played with, or my skull being massaged? The perfume she wore was almost hypnotic, but so were her eyes, glittering and amused. She had taken off the fox fur coat, and wore a long blue velvet dress with a high neck and tight sleeves, buttoned at the wrist. It should have made her look like a spinster governess, but at every curve of her breasts and hips the velvet clung and gave off its own rich light, as if at any moment the velvet would melt away and her body would burst out.

'I can't see Sir Simeon agreeing –' Miss Sugar started to protest.

'It's not down to Sir Simeon. How many times has he told us that he wants to forget the business side of things so he can just enjoy himself? If you can't conduct interviews properly, Sugar, then it's down to me until you've learned how to do it. And I say, forget the interview for today. The decision is made.'

'Forget the interview?' I asked. I didn't understand.

'I'm not sure I like this – this undermining of my position,' Miss Sugar spluttered. I noticed that she had come more and more to life since Miss Breeze had entered the room, had become less and less see-through. Although she was twisting the arms of her glasses in her hands, she'd forgotten to put them back on. I wondered if they were simply an affectation. Her surprisingly attractive grey eyes looked sharp enough to me.

'Miss Sugar is right in one sense.' Miss Breeze was speaking to me as if Miss Sugar hadn't uttered. 'When she uses the word urchin. Today you could be one of those street entertainers, Miss Summers, who tap dance or stand stock-still or dress as Charlie Chaplin. But tomorrow you could be the Queen of Sheba. That's just what we need. Versatility, I think we said in the ad?'

Miss Sugar sighed and held her hands up in surrender. Miss Breeze obviously knew how to soften a chiding with some subtle praise, and the coldness left Miss Sugar's face. She scraped her chair back and came to stand beside Miss Breeze. The two women were like two sides of a photographic negative: one dark and vibrant, the other pale and deathly.

'I don't follow you, Miss Breeze,' Miss Sugar said.

'She's versatility personified,' Miss Breeze explained. She held my face and turned it from side to side. 'Just the way Sir Simeon likes it. You could do anything with this pale sulky face and this crazy hair. It doesn't take X-ray eyes to see that under all this tat there's a beautiful womanly body. You still have a lot to learn about recruitment, Miss Sugar, but never mind. The interview, such as it was, is terminated.'

'You mean I can go?' I asked, ready to put up a fight if they planned to eject me.

'I mean we are offering you the job, so we can drop the formalities. We can take this ugly duckling and make her into whatever kind of swan we choose.'

'I've been called a lot of things, but never a duck,' I joked feebly, looking from one to the other of them as they surveyed me.

Before I could say anything else, let alone accept or turn down the job, Miss Breeze took hold of the jacket, and wrenched it down my arms, ripping the undone silk blouse down with it. My breasts swelled out with shock, the delicate lace of my bra emphasising their size. I had failed dismally to conceal my shape today. The two women gazed knowingly at my breasts until my nipples started to shrink and harden under their scrutiny, the reddening points poking visibly through the cream silk. There was nothing I could do to disguise the signs of arousal.

Miss Breeze turned me to face a full-length mirror. She pulled my hair off my face and twisted it into a knot. Miss Sugar came close on my other side and slid her hands up the sides of my breasts, pushing them up further. I pulled my shoulders back and threw a dark look at the mirror.

'Surprising, that underwear,' Miss Sugar mused, stroking her fingers across the bra. The flesh of my breasts rose higher. 'Very expensive, I can tell. Perhaps there's hope for her, after all.'

Both women smiled at each other across my reflection. 'Today the urchin,' remarked Miss Breeze, 'tomorrow the courtesan.'

Outside the room, those distinctive limping footsteps stopped.

'Did I hear the word thoroughbred earlier on?' demanded a deep voice from the doorway. 'Were we talking about horses, or the pedigree of the club members?'

The two women laughed.

'The former, Sir Simeon. We were talking about horses,' answered Miss Sugar. 'Miss Summers here used to work with horses out in the desert.'

I was surprised that she didn't remove her hands from where they were fingering my underwear. In fact, she pulled my blouse open further so that the full glory of my breasts and underwear was on display. I didn't dare look to see the expression in Sir Simeon's blue eyes.

'And are we hiring Miss Summers to work for us now?' he enquired, not moving from the door.

'That's right.' It was Miss Breeze's turn to speak. 'Although she hasn't actually accepted the post.'

It was a few beats before I realised I was expected to speak. I was too busy enjoying the way the two women were fiddling about with my hair and clothes. For too long I had been the one doing all the touching. I had learned massage in Brazil. I had practised it in Egypt. As an employee, I was used to shaking hands and grooming horses. As a woman, I was constantly fending people off to avoid offending the prince. Now Miss Sugar's hands were dangerously close to my nipples. She half-heartedly disguised the movement by pretending to measure me as if she was a dressmaker. If I moved an inch, her fingertips would make contact. The prince wouldn't have objected to that.

Meanwhile Miss Breeze continued to play with my hair, massaging my head and neck at the same time, so that I was putty in her hands. The more they touched me, the more I realised that, though I could feel myself responding to them, they were only really softening me up for the male attention I needed more.

'Yes, OK.' I broke the busy silence. 'If you think you can smarten me up, and pay me well to "front your house", I'll come and work for you.'

'That's great,' Miss Breeze said and clapped her hands. 'Don't worry, I wasn't serious when I said courtesan. At least, not this time. We just want to find out what you're really like underneath all this polyester.'

I looked at Miss Sugar, for some reason anxious for her approval. Her lips pressed into a thin smile, and she slipped her glasses back up her nose.

Sir Simeon stepped into the room. I could sense the two women standing to attention. I straightened my spine in the chair and let him take my hand to give it a brisk shake. His hand was warm. A faint aroma of cigar smoke and eau de cologne wafted off the tweed jacket he had been wearing under the old raincoat. Above the startling blue eyes, he wore his steely grey hair cropped close, which made him look more like a retired American general than a rich English lord.

'I wonder if I might hijack Miss – Summers, is it – before you set about ripping off too much of the polyester? I need her just as she is. Well, perhaps not in that particular outfit, but unspoiled, certainly. There's a short assignment I have for her back at the ranch.'

'Assignment?' Miss Breeze stopped massaging my head and rested her hands on my shoulders again, partly, I thought, to keep me in my chair. Her voice was suspicious. 'What exactly do you want her to do?'

Miss Sugar gave a dry chuckle, and went back to sit behind her desk.

'A mere trifle, Mimi. Don't worry. It won't take her away for long. Not even a night. I daresay she could do what I have in mind standing on her head.'

I shook Miss Breeze off my shoulders and stood up. Sir Simeon was very tall and upright and exuded a cool mixture of confidence and serenity. I reckoned he was in his late fifties. Unlike a younger man, who would have been unable to keep his eyes off my still-exposed breasts, his eyes were totally unwavering, and they were fixed on my face. I wanted to measure up to him, and rose on tiptoes to equal his height.

'The ranch?' I queried. 'Where's that?'

'My house in the country,' he explained. 'I have some guests arriving there for the weekend and I need someone to prepare the horses for them. Escort them on the hunt, too, if you like.'

'I was hoping to show her the ropes here, Sir Simeon,' Miss Breeze objected, sweeping across to the filing cabinet and getting out some pink files. 'We've got full bookings ahead for the weekend.'

'And you shall have her back before you know it, Mimi. But this way Miss Summers gets to see the stately pile. Call it an initiation. If she's as good with horses as the CV says she is, perhaps we might think about expanding the services of the club one day. After all, several of our members keep horses at their own houses.' There was a pause. Sir Simeon flicked a glance over all three of us. 'Just a thought.'

'Will you not be there to do all that?' I asked him.

He shook his head, and tapped his leg.

'I can't do much of the vigorous stuff with this old injury. Certainly can't ride to hounds with the upper crust bunch. I fractured my femur when I was a young man, in a bit of a state over a woman and galloping about like a madman. Got knocked off my horse by an overhanging branch. If I'd been the horse they'd have shot me.'

'And the horse? Was he all right?'

He laughed, a deep laugh that reverberated round Miss Sugar's panelled office. Miss Sugar started fiddling with a file on her desk. Out of the corner of my eye I could see Mimi looking from Sir Simeon to me and back again.

'Perhaps it's true that you're happier with animals than humans?'

'No,' I said, laughing as well. He was like a sexy uncle, a trifle stern at first, but he already had me eating out of his hand. 'Believe me, I'm good around humans as well.'

'I'm sure you are –' he paused '– because as Mimi and Miss Sugar have told you, that's our business here. Anyway, the horse. Don't you worry about him. He went out to grass, like his owner.'

The three of them were watching me now, and the room was suddenly buzzing with silence.

'So, Miss Summers,' Sir Simeon said quietly, 'a trip to the country. Is that all right with you?'

They all looked at me. I had the odd feeling that they were closing in on me, but instead of feeling trapped I felt liberated and challenged. I felt as if I had been in this room, part of this odd little group, for ever.

'And will you take the job?' added Miss Breeze.

I tore the newspaper ad into tiny pieces and dropped them into Miss Sugar's bin.

'Consider me your "vacant position",' I said, almost saluting them all.

And as the two women pressed up against me again, I thought I heard Sir Simeon say under his breath, 'Oh, she won't be vacant for long.'

4

I zoomed out of London that Saturday morning in a dove-grey MG which had been parked for my use outside the bed and breakfast. As I headed west past Heathrow, I craned my neck at the queue of jets lumbering in to land. I still yearned to be up in the sky, flying towards the sun, but the adventure I was driving towards had potential, too. I folded the map out on my lap and patted my pocket, where a wad of money nestled.

'Sir Simeon said you might need this,' Miss Sugar had sniffed yesterday as she handed me the roll of notes together with the car keys.

'Looks more like some kind of gangster payment,' I had remarked, counting out the money. 'I'd have thought he'd have written me a Coutts cheque instead of handing me a wedge of used tenners.'

'That's all part of his charm. He's a man of many parts,' Miss Sugar had replied sombrely, but when I started to giggle at the double meaning of what she'd said, she allowed herself a tiny curl of one lip. 'As you'll find out, Summers. Do be sure to tell me all about the house when you come back, won't you? I've never been there.'

As I drove under a brick archway smothered in winter ivy, I wondered briefly why Miss Sugar had never seen Sir Simeon's stately pile. But then, as the car bumped over the cobblestones of the cluttered stable yard, I saw why. This was the countryside, complete with mud, rain and animals. Somehow I couldn't see her tiny feet picking their way through this earthy scenario.

On the other hand, as I slammed the car door and went to stroke the long nose of a big bay hunter looking at me from the nearby stable, I felt right at home.

I walked along the row of stables towards the tack room and was surprised to see that most of the horses were already groomed up and ready to go on parade. Sir Simeon had said he needed at least four horses to be available, and that the yard manager would let me know. I suspected that my role today was mainly meeting and greeting, just as it would be at the club.

The rattle of an old engine shattered the early morning peace, and a battered old truck bumped under the arch and into the middle of the stable yard, brakes squealing as the driver pulled up just behind my knees.

'They like you,' said a deep voice as I carried on my inspection of the horses. 'The horses, that is. It's all peace and harmony here this morning.'

I'd heard that deep voice before. Or a very similar one, perhaps a decade or two older. I turned and was pinned to the spot by a pair of bright blue eyes. The man who'd jumped out of the old truck looked like a Native American brave, not a hoary handyman. The black, glossy hair flopping across his eyes and flowing past the collar of his thick lumberjack shirt, the angular cheekbones and full lips were pure Cherokee. A silver earring glinted in one ear. He smelt of horse sweat and the stuff I used to rub down leather saddles with.

'Linseed oil,' he said. He wiped his hands on his torn jeans and gripped my hand in his long, brown fingers, momentarily more like a gentleman than a stable hand. He dropped my fingers abruptly and eased a sugar lump between the eager nibbling lips of the horse I was stroking.

'That's a funny name,' I said, raising my eyebrows.

'That's what you're sniffing. I can tell. Sorry. I haven't had time to get cleaned up or changed into the riding gear yet. The name's Merlin. Which is also a funny name, I admit. Though Linseed would probably suit me better.'

My nostrils were still pricking. The sharp, potent smell coming off him and off the horses was as familiar to me as my own skin. Suddenly, I wasn't sure if I was pleased to be back in my natural habitat or if I would be happier escaping back to London.

'I'm Suki Summers. I've come to meet some of Sir Simeon's friends. He wants me to escort them to the meet this morning, and go out hunting with them if I want, or if they want. Generally look after them, I suppose.'

He dropped my hand. 'No need for you to be here. The meet's right here, up at the house. And they only need two horses. It's all taken care of.' He frowned, and yanked open the tack room door. 'He knows I'm here to do all that. Why doesn't he ever trust me to get the job done?'

'I daresay he just wanted me to do a bit of mingling, then.'

'No need for that either. So he's shipped you down from his new toy in London, has he? One of his glossy new PR types, I suppose. Good at all that sort of thing, are you?' Merlin was chewing his bottom lip with his white teeth.

'Not really, no. I'm new to the club and all the hostessing bit, and he knows it. But that's not why I'm here. I'm actually far more used to working with –'

'So do you actually know one end of a horse from another?'

He didn't wait for a reply, but simply walked off.

Something was bugging him. It had started the minute I said I was sent by Sir Simeon, but I wasn't prepared to take any lip from this yob. I'd better start as I meant to go on, and I had to start as Sir Simeon's representative. Which meant putting some of his other employees in their place.

I followed Merlin in to the tack room, racking my brains for something tough to say. But when I got inside I nearly gasped out loud. He had taken off his jeans and was in the process of pulling off his shirt. It was like walking into a Calvin Klein ad. Despite the miserable English weather this Merlin was showing me a heavenly body. Taut, tanned stomach and cute buttocks clad only in tight black boxers.

'What the hell are you doing?' I asked. I failed to keep the shiver of nervous laughter out of my voice. Was he pulling his clothes off to scare me off, or something? The horses liked me, but he apparently didn't.

'One of us has to get going,' he replied. His voice was muffled as he rummaged in an old leather bag. 'So if you've nothing better to do than gawp at me dressing, you may as well go back to London. You're obviously way out of your depth here.'

'As a matter of fact I'm perfectly *in* my depth,' I said, hoping that raising my voice would replace my confusion with a semblance of authority. 'I've been working with and breaking horses for the last five years.'

'You'll need to get changed.' Now he was bending over with his back to me to pull on a pair of white breeches. Fury began to foment in my chest. He was deliberately ignoring what I'd just told him. Instead, he flung his arm out, still not looking at me, and pointed at two sets of tack hanging on the walls. 'Then you can take those two saddles and those two bridles. The horses' names are labelled above the hooks. We'll each need to ride one horse and lead one up to the house.'

The muscles down his sides rippled as he moved, and

my stomach stirred at the sight of the half naked body in front of me. I was mesmerised at the beauty of it and, before I had time to point out that I wasn't here to take orders from *him*, thank you very much, Merlin swung round, fingers poised to zip up his flies. I clutched the door frame. In the shadows at the back of the room he looked almost sinister. His skin looked even darker brown in the weak winter light, and there was a thin line of hair trickling down the centre of his flat stomach and under the waistband. I could distinctly see a bulge in the crotch, but then any man's tackle bulged when encased in tight breeches. I could swear he was tilting it towards me as he slowly pulled the zipper up, and my stomach stirred like a cauldron.

I shuffled my trainers in the doorway, staring at his stomach. I didn't dare meet his eyes. He didn't seem remotely embarrassed, but I guessed he could sense my reluctant interest in his body. He reached for a crisp white shirt and started to button it up over the tasty midriff. Now I had no more excuses for staring at him.

'I'll get changed then,' I said, backing out of the room, 'and then I'll saddle them up.'

I ran back to the car, which luckily I had parked near an empty stable, and darted into the warm wooden shelter to get dressed. I hadn't worn my formal riding gear for some time and now, like Chrissie's suit, it was very tight. But I was determined to show young Merlin that I knew what I was doing. That these clothes were like a second skin to me. And once I was in my jodhpurs and black leather riding boots, I felt my confidence surging back. I bundled my hair quickly into a net, as always cursing its length and thickness. It would take Mimi days to pull out all the tangles, I thought, smiling at the memory of her hands in my hair.

I ran back to the car to check my reflection in the rear

view mirror. Compared with the healthy glow of Merlin's body, I looked pale. My Egyptian tan had already been peeled away by a few days in the English wind and by the shock of seeing a beautiful male body on display, yet untouchable, in an out of the way, deserted stable yard.

But once I had my riding helmet on, I was myself again. I did up the chin strap and saw a bright green glint jump into my eyes in the shadow of the peak. I allowed myself a knowing grimace. I'll show you, Mr Cherokee upstart.

When Merlin emerged from his horse's stable, I was already mounted on my beautiful chestnut mare and holding the reins of the bay hunter. He looked sensational in his pink jacket. He was knotting the white linen stock tightly at his throat. I glanced at his breeches. I couldn't help it. It was like trying not to look at a ballet dancer's lunch box when you're supposed to be concentrating on *Swan Lake*.

The bulge that I'd seen earlier had mysteriously vanished, quelled into respectability behind the zippered flies and the well-cut jacket. He was an efficient horseman for now, not a sex god. But I knew it was there. I wanted to see it again. My own crotch gave a little twitch of secret intent. I rubbed myself surreptitiously across the smooth seat of my saddle, and a flush of pure satisfaction flowed through me as he literally stopped in his tracks at the sight of me.

'If you're so expert,' he said after a moment, 'you can tie this blasted stock for me.'

Without giving myself time to question why he'd suddenly become incapable, I leaned down from my saddle and flipped the ends of the stiff white material into the requisite cravat round his throat. We were forced to be up close, close enough to sniff each other. Close enough to kiss. I saw his Adam's apple jump as he swallowed, but I refused to catch his eye. I just concentrated on what my fingers were doing.

'All done. Now lead on,' I said, fixing his gold pin and straightening up quickly in my saddle. I was glad I'd left my black jacket undone for the moment. I would button it up when we got up to the house. It was really very tight. I wore a white polo-neck sweater under the jacket. Sitting on the horse forced me to straighten my spine and, as the horse moved so I moved, my bottom sliding on the saddle and my breasts thrusting forwards with each step.

'Mr and Mrs Grey will be impressed,' he remarked, vaulting nimbly on to his horse without bothering to use the stirrups. He looked me up and down again before nudging his horse in front of me. 'They're the guests you're meeting. I must say you look the part.'

'This isn't a part,' I retorted, coming up beside him. 'This is me at my best. And you don't look too bad yourself.'

He glanced at me, his eyes a flash of wicked blue under his riding hat, then he clicked his tongue and we started to trot briskly out of the stable yard and up the long drive.

Already there was a crowd milling about in front of the mellow stone frontage of the big house. A couple of people dressed as footmen were passing round sherry and port on silver trays, and everyone was chattering loudly.

'Merlin? At last. We thought we were going to miss the hunt!'

A woman's voice sailed above the din, and Merlin jerked his head at me to bring the horses up to the front door. Mr and Mrs Grey, for I presumed that was who they were, stood between the pillars which flanked the entrance to the house. They were both dressed in full hunting regalia. From what I could see of her she looked hard-faced and mannish. He looked pleasant and slightly nervous, and kept licking his lips. But apart from that, it was difficult to make out the faces under the paraphernalia of riding helmets and chin straps.

'Avril. Geoff. Meet Suki. She's come down all the way from London to make sure you're enjoying yourselves. Amazing, eh?' Merlin said. He remained on his horse and pointed across at me with his riding whip.

I jumped down from my horse.

'Let me help you, Mrs Grey,' I offered, bending to give her a leg up.

'I can manage, thank you,' she snapped, pushing me out of the way. 'I don't need a young whippersnapper like you to make sure I'm enjoying myself. Sir Simeon has seen to all that already. He's the master at making sure people enjoy themselves.'

'But it was Sir Simeon who asked me to look after you.'

'Nice thought, but can we just get on with the ride, now we're all here?'

The master blew his hunting horn to move off. Avril was up on the horse, and raised her foot to kick into its side. I stepped back to avoid her foot. She was wearing spurs, for God's sake. I made a note to complain to Sir Simeon. I didn't care if her husband was a treasured club member or not. But as I stepped backwards, I slipped on some dung just as my horse raised its hoof enthusiastically at the sight of all its fellows clopping across the gravel, and its weight came crushing down on the top of my foot.

I bit down hard on my lips to stop myself yelping, and shoved the horse off me. I twiddled my toes. I could move them, but already the pain was excruciating.

'Come indoors, Suki. Quick,' said Merlin. 'We have to

get that boot off and ice on before the foot swells up. They'll have to go without their upmarket escort today.'

'I'm not an escort girl. I told you. Sir Simeon told me to look after them.'

But I was already learning that Merlin never stayed still for long. He was busy tying up our two horses securely before leading me slowly into the dark interior of the house, and I didn't bother to repeat myself. I only had time to gain a brief impression of a grand hallway – a lot of fresh flowers, dark panelling and brooding oil paintings – before he pushed through a door at the end of a long corridor. We were in a big modern kitchen. French windows at one end looked over an immaculate formal garden inhabited by topiary figures, which in turn looked over the parkland surrounding the house.

But the parkland could wait. Merlin was kneeling at my feet. He had chucked his hat on to the table. I was looking down at his smooth dark hair. It was all I could do to resist stroking it, but the thought was banished as he eased the tight-fitting boot off my foot and I stifled another yelp as the flesh and bones rearranged themselves.

'This will help. We'll finish the stirrup cup.' To my surprise he laughed as he handed me a large glass of dark red port. The temperature between us had risen from frosty to summery. I started to enjoy his company. On the other hand, he was probably just enjoying seeing me incapacitated. 'Even the staff have got the day off in honour of the hunt. So let the Greys enjoy their ride. I've heard that Mrs Grey always enjoys a good mount.'

Before I could ask him what he meant he was away again, rummaging about in the freezer. He returned with a bag of peas which he pressed on to my foot.

'Not for too long. You'll get frostbite. What say we

explore this place when your ten minutes' ice treatment is up?'

Ten minutes later he was leading me through the house, whispering as if we were burglars. He tiptoed exaggeratedly about and I hobbled after him, up and down staircases and creaking corridors. Upstairs he told me which guests had slept where. Mr and Mrs Grey didn't appear to share a bedroom, but I let that one go. I was more interested in watching the muscles in his strong legs flexing as he moved along in front of me.

There was something illicit and sexy about peeking in to all the guest rooms at the rumpled bedclothes. Most of the rooms had four-posters. I couldn't help thinking of all that red-blooded romping after a long hard gallop and a long night's feasting.

Merlin stopped at the end of the upstairs corridor, all hung with tapestries. We had looked into all the rooms and, suddenly, we were both silent. I felt a crippling shyness stealing over me. The insolent banter we'd shared at the stables and even snooping round the house had been fun, but the grand surroundings were getting to me. Merlin seemed to know the house really well. He'd obviously been up here many times in the course of his working at the stables. But to me it felt like we were trespassing. It was exciting, as well as scary. They could all have come galloping back at any time and found us. Or the butler and maids could have come back early from their day off.

My heart started pounding ridiculously, as did my foot. Merlin flung open the double doors in front of us, as if he owned the place.

'And here we have the master's bedroom. Sir Simeon's quarters.'

Now I really did feel like an intruder. The thought of

Sir Simeon doing something as intimate as undressing and coming to bed here made me blush like a schoolgirl, but I stepped inside nevertheless, unable to resist my curiosity. It was a vast room with a gigantic four-poster bed piled high with quilts and pillows. It was comfortable as well as old-fashioned, with chairs and cushions everywhere, a huge fireplace and, to my surprise, a lovely fire burning there. Huge windows looked down over lawns towards the fields and the stables.

'It looks like those bedchambers one sees when walking round stately homes,' I remarked loudly, to cover my awkwardness. 'Like no one ever sleeps or lives in here. Apart from the fire burning in the grate, there's no real sign of life in here at all.'

I limped over to one of the big windows of the master bedroom and stared out across the misty fields. Down on the gravel drive I could hear our horses stamping their hard feet and rattling the clips where Merlin had tied them up, their breath rising in steamy curls from their impatient nostrils.

'Oh, he sleeps in here all right. He was here last night, in fact.'

'He was here? Then why on earth hasn't he appeared to speak to me?'

The thought of Sir Simeon in this room sent a shiver up my spine. Those eyes alone could drag you to bed ... I could almost hear the bedclothes rumpling as Sir Simeon threw them back, let the thick curtains fall round the mattress, and pulled a mystery woman in there with him ...

'I've no idea. He's probably dodged off again on one of his ploys. Or he might walk back in here any minute. But I'm glad he's not here right now.'

Behind me in the ornate bedroom, I could hear Merlin moving towards me. I could see his reflection in the frosty glass as he came up close. My own face was fixed there like a pale moon, framed by blood-red velvet curtains, his face swimming up beside mine. All of a sudden he looked different. Everything was different. It was being in that grand old room, like naughty children playing hide-and-seek, but we weren't mucking about. He had this serious air about him, like the atmosphere of the house had changed him into someone else. He'd grown in stature, somehow, he was someone big and impressive, someone to be reckoned with, and I liked that.

Our eyes were huge and dark in the reflection, mine especially. He must have felt there was something different about me, too. He couldn't have known that I'd just been fantasising about Sir Simeon. I hadn't got as far as peeling off his silk pyjamas in my imagination, but I wasn't far off. Were those thoughts reflected in my eyes?

Certainly Merlin must have thought I was inviting him, because he reached under my hacking jacket, pulled my thin jumper out from the waistband of my tight jodhpurs and started to brush his warm fingers up and down the ridges of my spine. And did I want to resist? Did I hell.

I had to go through the motions, though, surely. We'd only just met, but everything was pointing to the inevitable. Everything was becoming more and more unreal. I couldn't believe I could be seduced just by the atmosphere of this grand sensuous bedroom in this grand house, or by the shadow of Sir Simeon. I started to walk across the bedroom away from Merlin to see if the action of walking, even the throbbing in my bruised foot, would wake me up. But who was I kidding? There was no blue-eyed shadow seducing me here. There was a living, breathing Cherokee god in the room with me, tugging at my clothes. He was real enough. I'd seen his bum. I'd seen that line of black hair trailing down his stomach. I'd seen the tantalising bulge in his tight white breeches . . .

Merlin stopped me leaving the room. It was no great effort. He just stayed close behind me and wrapped his hand round my waist, under my jumper, flattening it on my stomach. He pulled me back against him, back against that fantastic crotch. Releasing a little moan of surrender I let him take charge.

In all the other rooms the beds were marooned in the centre of the room, miles from the windows or doors. But this one was positioned close to the window so that when you sat on it, you were almost falling out into the fresh open air. Next thing we were sitting on the bed, both staring out at the fields and listening out for the horses and for any returning guests, but all the time he was stroking me, so I wasn't aware of how we'd landed there, and I realised how stiff I was, and cold, but it wasn't out of fear. It was just the nature of the place. Perhaps the house, the bedroom, were haunted, after all, but that only made the atmosphere of what was about to happen that much sexier. Add a voyeur ghost to the feast!

Suddenly, we were on this bed, the house empty, the log fire crackling away, and Merlin had both his hands on me, warming me up.

'I thought you might be cold,' he murmured, illogically explaining why he was undressing me.

His hands were soothing and warm on my skin, as if he was grooming the flanks of one of his horses. His hands were gentle, but strong enough to lift me. And to lay me down on my back, which is what he did next. Down on the bed.

'I'm freezing,' I said. 'Keep doing it.'

As I lay submissively on the rich bedspread and let

him pull the jumper higher and higher up, I wondered lazily how this guy knew I would want him? He'd seen a pretty tough, defensive-looking girl in the stable yard earlier, even if she did scrub up reasonably well in her jodhpurs. But how did he know I wouldn't punch him in the face the minute he laid a hand on me, and yell blue murder?

'You might think you're one of the boys,' he said, reading my mind as accurately as if it had been flashed up on a screen, 'but I can see the female in you, even under all that bravado. We're like animals, us men. Like horses that can smell fear from their rider, we can smell attraction. And I was right. You've melted just listening to me. We sniff you women out, whether you like it or not.'

'So you're a woman whisperer,' I joked.

'Perhaps that's it.' He stretched the neck of my jumper and pulled it deftly over my head. Thank God I was wearing yet another of my marvellous bras: a seamless, smooth cream satin which didn't show under the tight polo neck but which still lifted my breasts up to him like a snack. 'We rugged outdoor types have more instinct than the city types I daresay you come across in London. We're closer to the soil. We just go for it. We just listen to our loins, no argument or discussion, see the woman, PR executive or kitchen maid, and take her.'

'I don't know anything about city types,' I gasped, as he reached under me and easily unclipped the bra. I could almost hear my breasts sigh with relief as the constraints were lifted away from them. 'But you're as civilised as the next man, whether you like it or not. Just because you wear ripped jeans and drive a battered old truck . . .'

'Sure I'm civilised. And you're just a simple country girl, I suppose?'

I decided not to tell him too much. Let him think he was taking a posh city girl by storm, if he liked. I didn't want him to know how similar we were. He was gorgeous and already familiar, and that was enough. My foot hurt, I was tired, and the bed was soft, and the fire was kind of singing, and I didn't want to stop him. I suppose I should have put up some kind of token struggle, but I didn't. I was aching for it the moment he laid his hands on me. He didn't feel like he was a stranger. Sir Simeon could vouch for him, anyway, so it felt totally natural, but more than natural, it was still all new, because my whole body was kind of crackling and singing, like the fire, and we were in this strange bed.

Suddenly, he was a beautiful new man, delivered to me on a plate, or at least on a horse, with a mouth, hands and a cock, offering me all this pleasure, all this luscious pleasure was just radiating out of his fingertips. I sat up again, put my mouth on his, and started kissing him. It was possibly the first time in my life that I'd taken the initiative. But now I wanted it, wanted him, more than anything.

'I wanted to rip off your jeans the moment I saw you back there,' he muttered into the corner of my mouth. 'I knew there was a real woman under there, instead of a flat-chested boy, and –'

'Stop talking, Merlin. The ghosts might hear.'

I couldn't get enough of his lips. They were straight and firm, like a man's should be, and yet they had a softness in them, and I was making them wet with kissing. I could taste port, and coffee, and the outdoors.

I could have gone on kissing him all day, but when I felt the tip of his tongue, warm and slippery, all kinds of bells and whistles started up and down my body. The rest of me was opening and loosening until a deep sinking feeling started right between my legs. I was warm and slippery, like his tongue, and I wanted him inside me. Already I was aching for it, like he'd pressed the accelerator and it was too soon. I didn't know what to do with myself. I'd already forgotten how just licking someone's mouth could send all those ripples down inside you. I wasn't sure if I'd ever felt quite like this, not with the prince, not with anyone. I was afraid the sensation would drown me and I'd look stupid, so I kissed him harder, sucked on his tongue and his teeth, it was feeling so good. He lay me down again and pulled away. He was smiling, and his mouth was wet. He tugged my hair out of the net I'd put on for the hunting, and I tried to shovel it back in, it was always so messy, but he pulled it out around my head so that it was spread all over the pillow. It had grown long while I was living in the sun. When it was brushed out properly, it fell right down to my waist. I was planning to get it cut.

It was the first time for ages that I'd felt truly feminine. He was looking at my hair, tangling it in and out of his fingers, as if it was some kind of treasure, not just an annoying appendage that I never took any notice of other than to shove it out of sight. As he played with it, and the tugging of the roots on my scalp turned me on even more, I wondered why it was that, since I was a kid, I was often so determined to distort myself, hide myself, deny this womanhood. Chrissie was always chiding me for it.

The prince had unlocked something primeval and wild in me, but after a while I had realised I wasn't the only special woman. I was just part of his stable of women. It hadn't particularly mattered and, anyway, he was ancient history now. But this Merlin, after an hour or so since meeting him, was making me realise what I was put on this earth for and, for the moment, I was the only woman in it. So I let him lay me back down on the bed. He took my clothes off, just made me lie there and, all the time, we were silent in that fire-lit room. He unbuttoned my breeches, pulled off my damp knickers, then he sat and looked at his handiwork. His eyes kept returning to my breasts. His face lit up, lust burning in his eyes. I started glowing all over because I realised what he was seeing, and I was proud of it. He made me proud of my body. I knew I was fit and toned but, for the first time in months, I saw myself as sexy and beautiful as well, and I wanted to show him.

Then he opened his breeches and there were the tight black boxers again, outlining the contours of his cock. He was a god to look at, and even more so naked. He peeled his own clothes off slowly and, with every inch I saw of shoulder, chest, stomach, all tanned and smooth, with every inch that he showed me, I was gibbering with longing. I couldn't believe what I was seeing, he was so lovely, and we were all alone, and he was showing me his body. I was dizzy with longing way before he got down to his groin. He hooked his fingers in the boxers and slowly pulled them down. My heart was knocking somewhere in my throat. I crossed my legs to still the uncontrollable trembling and fidgeting. And there it was, hot and hard and pulsing with its own beat. I'd seen stallions worse hung. I longed to touch it. It was standing out, pointing at me, quivering and proud, and tanned dark like the rest of him. I wanted to cheer when it sprang out from his trousers to greet me. All I felt was greed, lust and a powerful longing when I saw it.

His fine mouth went on smiling as he leaned over me, pushed my hair out of my eyes, smoothed the same hand down over my face, down my throat, over my breasts, and paused. He took one breast in his hand and made it bounce heavily against my ribcage. He licked his lips and mouthed the words 'later, later' as he stroked my breasts and made my nipples perk up in surprise, and my excitement mounted at the thought of more of this, the whole day spent like this, lying with him, rolling with him on this huge bed, with the thrilling threat of Sir Simeon – where was he, anyway? – coming home any time and discovering us humping on his bed. My bruised foot was forgotten amongst all the other, deeper aches that were taking me over.

He played with my breasts for ages until I was arching and writhing beneath him, trying to sit up to push them into his face. I wanted him to fasten those firm lips round them; I'd never realised my nipples could burn so urgently, throbbing in their hard desire for him to lick and bite. But he kept his big hands on them and he was laughing softly, teasing me, but he was teasing himself as well, because I could see his cock quivering and jumping, feel it nudging and pushing against my thigh. I opened my legs to wrap them round him, feeling the ready wetness of my swollen sex lips slapping against his balls and the tiny sound was suddenly huge in that quiet room, and it was too much to resist any longer.

He let go of my breasts and raised himself further up on his strong arms, so that he was hanging right over me like some kind of big hound. There was too much air and space between our bodies. Through that space I could see the fire burning lower in the stone fireplace, and a feeble ray of winter sunshine arrowing briefly through the window, and then he was closing the gap. I could feel the warmth of his torso before it came to rest on me, his elbows shaking with the effort to be gentle, and I sank into the soft bed beneath him, raising my hips to meet his, feeling the tip of that beautiful cock introducing itself to me. He was cautious, edging the first couple of inches inside, stopping and starting gently, so that I started to wonder how experienced he really was, despite his cockiness. But my body enfolded his taut length easily because my lubricating juices were already trickling out of me on to the tapestry bed cover, welcoming him, making an easy slide for him.

My body melted effortlessly into his, literally melted so that I couldn't tell where my stomach and pussy and legs ended and his stomach and cock and legs began. He rested on his forearms, leaned down and started kissing me again, nudging my mouth wide open so that his tongue could imitate what his long hard cock was doing, reaching its destination deep inside me, filling me completely and stopping my cries.

What had I been wondering about his experience? This guy was stupendous. For a sizzling moment I wished I *had* been there for his first time.

As soon as his mouth slid sideways, my cries started up again, louder and higher. He thrust inside me and all the tiny muscles and surfaces of me held on to him, rubbed themselves against him to milk every last new exhilarating sensation out of him, driving on the wave of ecstasy that had been hovering in hidden places I couldn't describe. The wave started building and approaching. I opened my eyes and looked at him. My knees flopped sideways and my head was washed through with utter bliss, and then there was an explosion of colour and the sensation of millions of big flowers bursting open inside me. I was calling his name as his cock slid in and out of me, and we shuddered like our horses would after a long hard gallop. Just when I should have been expecting it, but wasn't, I came in a juicy flow all over Sir Simeon's brocade bedspread.

Leaving the gorgeous Merlin asleep on the bed was like Chinese torture, but the sun was setting and I had to return the car, and myself, to London. I looked at him for a moment or two, after-shocks of pleasure jabbing through me. I noticed that the silver earring was not in the shape of a dagger, as I'd at first thought, but was curved into the Roman nose of a horse.

'Like Cinderella,' I said, when he pulled at my arm to stop me leaving, his eyes still shut, 'I have to go.'

'Go then,' he muttered, flopping on to his back. 'It was only a bit of fun between stable hands.'

He was still half-cocked, his penis lifting a little from the nest of jet-black hair. For two pennies I would have lowered myself on to it. But his insolent air had returned, and I didn't want to hear how he might sum me up after our surprise coupling. Besides, Sir Simeon, Mimi and the club all beckoned, and he wouldn't like me to admit to that, either. Best to put on the London face, and be gone.

As if it had been watching me, my mobile phone trilled the moment I slid into the cracked leather seat of the MG. I had crept back through the house and walked gingerly over to my horse, but Merlin's tender care had done the trick. The frozen peas had prevented any bad bruising in my foot and brought down the swelling.

I had thought about his own swelling, his ample cock rising and hardening as I lay upstairs on Sir Simeon's bed. I had to close my eyes as the watery rush of remembered pleasure flowed through me again. But I had to put that sensational encounter down to the heat of the moment. It wasn't to be repeated. Sir Simeon would be livid if he knew what we'd been doing on his bed and, anyway, Merlin had just told me he was having a laugh at my expense.

I had gritted my teeth and got up on to the horse, urging her into a fast gallop back to the stables so that the breath was knocked out of me and I couldn't think about anything else. In the yard, a couple of stringy girls I hadn't seen earlier were mournfully raking dirty straw in to the back of Merlin's truck. They had taken the horse off me, eyeing me up and down suspiciously as if I'd stolen him, and I had dashed to the car. It was only as I settled into the seat and answered my mobile, that I realised my bra was hanging out of my jacket pocket as I'd been in such a hurry.

'You're rather breathless, Summers?'

It was Mimi.

'Yes. I've been riding.'

'Sir Simeon will be pleased.'

'Hope so.'

There was a pause.

'I'd like to see you tomorrow morning, at my place, if that's OK?' Mimi said. 'You're excused for tonight. I daresay you've earned your stripes dealing with the Greys. She's notoriously difficult...'

'Not really, I'm afraid. They went hunting without me. I hurt my foot. I've been well looked after, though.'

I couldn't wipe the smirk off my face. If Merlin wanted to see it as just a laugh, then I could, too. And now I was irritated that if I didn't need to report for duty at the club, I needn't have left that smooth brown body in such a rush after all.

'Oh? Who looked after you?'

I thought I'd better make light of my recent juicy encounter on Sir Simeon's bed. 'Just some arrogant little oik named after a wizard who seemed to know more about my new job than I did.'

There was a gasp, followed by a throaty laugh at the other end of the mobile. 'Miss Summers,' Mimi said at last, 'wash your mouth out with saddle soap.'

'I'm livid with him, if you want to know. The day hasn't turned out at all as I thought it would, and I think I've disappointed Sir Simeon. This chap wouldn't let me do anything. He wanted to take over everything, including the clients. Sorry, members. Why should I wash my mouth out?'

'Because, dear girl, that arrogant little oik is Merlin Symes. Sir Simeon's son.'

5

Chrissie would have cackled with disbelief if she'd seen the transformed me finally taking up my duties at the club. But I was determined not to tell her, for the time being, about the exact details of my new job.

Miss Breeze had told me to meet her at her tall white house in Kensington. When I pressed the doorbell and stared into the video entryphone, a buzzer sounded, and the heavy door clicked open electronically.

The interior of the house was all white, cream and blood red, hopelessly elegant. Even the lilies in their tall vases and the candles flickering on every surface were either white or red.

'Up here, Summers,' her throaty voice called from somewhere above my head, and I obeyed the direction, following her heavy scent up the curving stone staircase until it wafted out in almost visible clouds from the first white door I came to. I pushed it open and stepped inside. There was the sound of running water from the en-suite bathroom, and no sign of Miss Breeze. This had to be her bedroom, but I felt as if I'd wandered into Aladdin's cave. Draped over the bed, over the chairs, on the shelves, was a stunning array of sensational underwear. Creamy satin kickers, midnight-blue camisoles, burgundy bras with delicate straps, black basques, sheer pink stockings and see-through negligees, everything you could think of, were heaped in abundant piles around the room. A haughty mannequin posed in the window, dressed in a scarlet corset with suspenders and stockings to match, one plastic hand thrust brazenly between her legs and her chin tossed sideways.

'Well, underwear is your weakness, isn't it? Or your strength.'

Miss Breeze was beside me, draped very loosely in a white silk dressing gown embroidered with tiny red flowers. I looked at her, and was taken aback. In the dim light of the office at the club I had thought her face was white, but now I could see that she had simply been caked in make-up. The black kohl and spidery mascara had gone. She looked years younger, though I was still sure she was older than me. Her skin was the colour of light toffee, and there was a light dusting of freckles over her throat, leading into the dark shadow between her breasts.

'Won't you call me Suki?' I asked, as she took my coat off and threw it to one side.

'Perhaps, in time. But remember, for the moment, you work for me. But you can call me Mimi.'

'Do you ever invite the members to this lovely house?' I asked, as she sat me on a low window seat and thrust a cup of coffee at me. 'It's as beautiful as the club.'

'That's because I designed both of them, darling,' she said, disappearing into a small dressing room. 'And in answer to your question, no. On the whole, I feel it's best to separate business and pleasure. I say on the whole. I can always break my own rules. And frequently do.'

Mimi Breeze emerged with an armful of clothes which she dumped on the floor and came to sit beside me on the window seat. She started playing with my hair again, and my scalp tingled in anticipation of feeling her fingers and nails massaging me to light-headedness again. Thank goodness I'd brushed it that morning as I rushed out of my cheap bed and breakfast in the Earls Court

Road, hoping that I wouldn't bump into Chrissie or her new fiancé Jeremy on their way to work.

'Tell me more about what I have to do,' I said hesitantly, my eyes closing as she soothed me. 'That Merlin rather knocked me for six with his disdain for anything to do with the club.'

'Ignore him. He likes to play the bumpkin. His father and he are always at each other's throats. Too similar, if you ask me. Did you really not notice the eyes? Surely the eyes gave him away?'

'I wasn't looking at the eyes,' I said, and laughed. Mimi watched the flush rise up on my cheeks, perfectly aware of what I meant.

'Give him a wide berth, Suki,' she advised quietly. 'Sir Simeon would have a fit if he knew. And I'm not too happy about it, either . . .'

'I'm sorry, Mimi.'

'Right.' She was happy again, pressing her fingers firmly across the plates of my head. 'Now. The first thing we do this morning is to sort you out. It'll have to be a full makeover, I'm afraid. A shower first, my girl. The full works, in fact. I have a hairdresser coming in, and a manicurist.' She picked up my hands and held them close to her face so that I could feel her breath on them. 'What have you been doing with your hands in the last few years? They're rough, like a navvy's.'

I laughed, and tried to pull my hands away, but she held them fast.

'Miss Sugar obviously didn't show you the famous CV,' I said. I looked at Mimi's hands holding mine. 'I'm better with my hands. Brain work bores me.'

'You will need both in this game,' Mimi said, lowering my hands to my lap but still holding on to them. 'Though, to be fair, the brain only has to engage if there's a problem. You very quickly have to work out what to do if the member isn't happy with you or with the club. Dear, dear. The manicurist has her work cut out to soften these digits.'

'Do you see the job as a game, then?' I asked, letting her cluck over my nails.

Mimi waved her hand dismissively.

'Not at all. It has its serious side, like any other job, and of course we are all paid for it. But it's fun, as well, and totally unique.' She looked up at me through thick dark eyelashes, bit her lip as if choosing her words. 'Basically in this job you will often have to act like a wife. That's what they all want, deep down, you know – a wife.'

'But I thought that's what they were running away from?'

'That's what they *think*, darling, but they're mistaken. They just want a wife with knobs on, as it were.'

She lifted her hands and her eyebrows in theatrical amusement at her own joke, and I obliged by giving a disbelieving, filthy snort of laughter. 'What does a wife with a knob do?'

'She gives them everything that they want and more and demands nothing in return.' She paused, then peered at me down her nose like a schoolteacher. 'And what are the main things that a wife does?'

I was enjoying this conversation. Mimi had dropped the initial severe veneer. Perhaps it was because we weren't in the confines of the club. In her own home she was just being great company.

'Fuck husband and keep house?' I replied.

Mimi clapped her hands with more theatrical flourish, then tapped my cheeks triumphantly.

'Well, you didn't hear it from me, but I'd say that definition will do. Oh, Suki Summers, I'm thinking you're just made for Club Crème.'

'Hang on. I didn't mean I could do all that,' I protested. 'Look at me. I'm a scruff. They wouldn't look at me twice. I wouldn't have a clue where to start.'

'You don't need to start at all unless the situation crops up and then, believe me, you'll know what to do. It'll come to you when you're least expecting it,' she soothed as my voice rose in alarm. 'These guys don't know how lucky they are. Don't you realise your particular understated image is what will make you all the hotter? All the better? We can't employ knowing little minxes who will stroll about with all guns blazing, can we? We'd be out of business in no time. No. We need girls who are beautiful but subtle, so they don't know what's hitting them. We found you in the nick of time, didn't we? I knew you had this ... unquenched quality when I saw you, and you won't let me down.'

Mimi stroked my cheek again, and held up her finger. I looked out of the window at the smart street below. A man was hurrying towards the house, dressed in a trilby hat and a long dark overcoat. From up here I couldn't see his face at all, only the top of his head, but he was definitely limping.

'Who's that?' I asked, jabbing at the window to get her to stop looking at me.

'Sir Simeon probably, come to attend to some business or other,' Mimi said, without looking out. She frowned slightly, as if she didn't want to be distracted from our conversation. 'I recognise the sound of his walk.'

I felt a flush circling my throat. I still hadn't worked out whether it was alarm or interest every time Sir Simeon was mentioned. 'He looks smarter than he did yesterday.'

'Like all of us, a master of disguises.'

'Aren't you going to let him in?'

'He has his own key. He often pops in and out to check on the running of things. He doesn't always bother us if he's dealing with matters of accounts. Which is none of your concern, by the way, Summers,' she said. She sighed, a little impatiently, and pulled me away from the window towards the bathroom. 'And on the topic of Sir Simeon, I think we'd better keep your unguarded description of his son a secret between ourselves, don't you?'

'Yes, Mimi,' I said obediently. 'But just one more question: why was Sir Simeon riding his horse in such a state that he broke his leg like that?'

'It happened after his wife died. Merlin's mother. He was devastated. But in the end the accident knocked some sense into him. Now there's more life in the old dog than anyone I know.'

She seemed to switch off for a moment, and I had a chance to really study her. Mimi was like a duchess, or a queen. The queen bee, sitting in her hive, drawing her drones and workers towards her. I wondered if that was how the club members saw her. Sir Simeon obviously did. I couldn't take my eyes off her. Maybe it was because the attention she was lavishing on me was making up for the lack of something permanently male in my life, something which I had been reminded of yesterday with Merlin. It was certainly very pleasant being around Mimi, I thought drowsily, as she started to run the water and the steam hissed out of the cubicle. But it wasn't just a man I needed. It was the whole package, the whispering, the holding, the touching . . .

Shaking her head and tutting softly as if she was reading my mind, Mimi took my old sheepskin jacket off and dropped it on the floor, then pulled my sweater roughly over my head.

'No ill-fitting trouser suit today, then?' she asked. She laughed softly, flicking at my hair. 'Is all this – combat gear – your natural style?'

I hesitated, then pulled my T-shirt off in front of her, and threw that on to the floor. I was getting less shy every minute. After being fucked for England on Sir Simeon's bed yesterday, what was the point of being shy? I was wearing a camisole today which held my breasts in invisibly elastic cups. The heavy mounds were supported in the pale-green lace, which then hugged my torso to my waist like a vest. It looked better under T-shirts. In fact, it looked great on its own in the summer, with my favourite pair of low-slung Levis.

'This is how I'm most comfortable,' I answered, unbuckling my jeans and kicking them off. Mimi's eyes gleamed, and her hand went up to her throat and stroked the tender skin just above her breastbone.

'But see how good you look undressed,' she remarked, stepping close to me and circling my waist with her hands. 'These long legs; I didn't notice those at the interview that never was. And these breasts, which I *did* notice. These breasts could nail an unsuspecting victim all on their own!'

She was so elegant and actually half-naked herself in the dressing gown which was slipping dangerously off one shoulder, that I didn't mind undressing in front of her. In fact I was enjoying it because she looked me up and down with truly appreciative eyes, and I felt relaxed under her scrutiny.

'I haven't been as bare as this in front of a woman since my modelling days,' I remarked, trying to make light of the situation. 'And even then I was always part of a herd of models shoved about in a crowded, stuffy studio.'

Mimi didn't reply. It was as if she wasn't interested in

my past. Now I was sure she hadn't even looked at my CV, despite Miss Sugar's hanging on to it.

I stepped into the shower and stood there for ages, frothing up the soap over my skin, buffing the blood flow so that my whole body tingled and holding my face under the needles of harsh spray until I was totally invigorated. I turned the water off and groped about for a towel, and Mimi was there, rubbing me dry.

'I can't help it, Suki,' she said. She rested her wide mouth against my face, just beside my lips. I stood perfectly still, motionless with surprise. She puckered her lips and kissed me slowly, leaving a damp patch on the corner of my mouth. 'I just can't resist a challenge. If you haven't been touched by a woman before, I want to be the first one.'

Mimi's hands slid down my ribcage, over my hips and round to my buttocks, before rising up my body again. Suddenly, she whisked the towel away and the breath rasped in my throat as my breasts thumped softly into her waiting hands, the nipples shrinking instantly into points as the steamy air met them. My insides started swirling as Mimi moulded my breasts in her palms, pressing them together as each forefinger circled each raspberry nipple. I couldn't look at her face, but instead found myself staring at her own, almost exposed breasts beneath the open dressing gown.

My legs were shaking. To steady myself I went to grab Mimi's shoulder, but by accident, or not, my hand fell on the neck of her dressing gown. It slithered away like a shy animal, falling off her like a skin, and one brown breast was exposed, round and ripe, with an incredibly large, chocolate-coloured nipple sitting in the middle. She was casting a spell on me, I was sure of it. I had never had any interest in touching or being caressed by another woman before, despite what Chrissie used to think. Nothing like this. There were electrical charges sizzling through my belly, forbidden and intoxicating, seizing me with the violent, unthought-of urge to crush Mimi's red mouth with mine, but more violent than that, to lick at that chocolate nipple, knowing it would harden with the pleasure my own nipples would feel, knowing that it would elongate and spring against my teeth.

Mimi chuckled. I was sure she could read my thoughts. She was like some kind of beautiful witch. She released my eager breasts and glanced down at her own. Then she stepped behind me and pushed me back into the bedroom, where there was a huge Venetian mirror dominating one wall. Normally, I avoided my own reflection, but now I straightened, gazing at my curvaceous, clean body prickling with all this untried pleasure. All I could see of Mimi was her face smiling over my shoulder and her hands, smoothing up and down my sides, towards my tingling breasts and away again. My green eyes, set wide apart in my face, grew larger as I watched her brown fingers start to march down my stomach. I could feel her breath on my still-damp neck.

'I thought you asked me here to tart me up a bit,' I said, when I could form the words. 'I didn't realise you felt like this about me.'

'Oh, don't take this too seriously, Suki. I'm only doing this to wake you up a little,' she murmured, her fingers tickling my skin. 'Let's call it an initiation. My own sort of initiation, unlike Sir Simeon's ideas of initiation. My initiation doesn't involve horses, nor arrogant little oafs. You don't mind. I can tell. And I can't have you going into battle without being warmed up, can I?'

'Battle?' I asked.

'Taking up the cudgels at the club. It'll be a walk in the park, for you,' she soothed.

I shook my head, watching her fingers walking

towards the curls of my tawny bush, still dark with the shower water. My thighs parted a little, even though my legs were still shaking. Her fingers paused, then traced the hidden crack, sliding right down it until she reached the secret opening located there, then whisking up again. My reflected mouth was open as I gasped for breath. I wasn't even trying to look cool now. I pulled Mimi roughly round so that we were breast to breast. Our faces were so close that her dark eyes merged. I closed my own eyes and pushed my still open mouth on to hers. Her lips were like cushions, giving softly as I ground mine on to hers. Was I acting too much like a man? I didn't want to because I felt completely womanly, doubly womanly in a way, as there were two of us in the quiet room.

I flicked my tongue out and instantly it met Mimi's, which was tickling the corner of my mouth. I sucked hers in against my teeth, and felt it probing, like a penis, and then her fingers were doing the same to my pussy, creeping back down the crack and then plunging between the lips.

We had both started to writhe against each other, barely realising it. For the first time in my life, I felt compelled to make a grab for another woman's crotch. I felt aroused by her much as a man must feel, and began to be drawn towards her intimately and to play a little rough. I wanted to feel her cunt now, but she pressed up closer to me, still kissing me, and jammed her fingers further into me, while her other hand circled round one little spot. The sparks exploded in my head as she located my clitoris and delicately manipulated it with her thumb.

I gave up trying to reach into her crack and, as I was bending my knees slightly in an unconscious effort to open myself even more, I grabbed her buttocks and spread them open a little. I opened my eyes in surprise as my fingers slipped inside the warm crevice between her buttocks. As I explored this unknown place, I glanced sideways and saw our twin profile in the mirror: our breasts rubbing from side to side as we swayed so that the friction kept our nipples rock hard. The muscles in Mimi's arms were working, her hands invisible between my legs, while my arms were stretched round her, my hands reaching inside her butt cheeks.

The sight of us, the pale body and the brown body lit by the harsh winter light so that there was no mistaking what we were doing and how it looked, was too much for me. Tongues of ecstasy started lapping at my clit, as Mimi's fingers pumped rapidly in and out. Her fingers and thumb kept playing me while I pulled my mouth away to take in silent gulps of air. The waves started to radiate from Mimi's fingers and I moaned out loud as I felt the juices ooze between my trembling legs. My climax came, hot and quick, and shook me.

As I let go of Mimi and sank to the white carpet, my cunt still twitching and moist, I felt exhilarated. What with yesterday's encounter at Symes Hall, and this unexpectedly sexy sisterly groping, London was looking up. I hadn't bargained on two such horny experiences in two short days. I felt no embarrassment and no shame. Something had changed in me. Or perhaps it was just that London had changed when I wasn't looking. Either way I was eager for more where that came from.

I closed my eyes, still gasping, and heard Mimi moving around the room, humming under her breath.

'You'll be glad we did that, when you've got your head round it,' she remarked quietly. I looked up. She was picking through some of the piles of silk and lace underwear. She picked up some flimsy garments. Her brown feet padded across the carpet and stopped in front of me.

Her big toe came up under my jaw and lifted my chin so that I had to sit up straight.

Behind her, the mannequin's head had turned to look at us.

'You're ready now, Suki,' she said. She smiled, and dropped the garments in a silky shower on top of me. 'It's time to dress you up for work.'

Like I said, Chrissie would have cackled at the sight of me. She'd have walked up and down in front of me like a sergeant major, unable to believe her eyes. Not only did the designer chalk-striped jacket in purest wool fit me like a glove this time, its one large button deliberately under a little strain to cover my bosom, it was also lined with silk, which meant I didn't need to wear a blouse. There was nothing between my lace-sprinkled breasts and an unsuspecting world. Or in this case, an unsuspecting new member whom I was detailed to welcome to the club.

And instead of manly trousers, Mimi had zipped me firmly into a pencil skirt, stockings and killer-heeled court shoes. Earlier, the hairdresser had tamed the ferocious red of my hair, bringing it down to a kind of burgundy sheen, and ironed out all the curls. Mimi had twisted it tightly up behind my head and secured it with a silver clip. I had never worn my hair up before, except scrunched into a hair net, an occasional ponytail or a charlady's scarf. My face was unfamiliar: the cheekbones and chin all sharp angles, my eyes with their new, mascaraed lashes huge and unblinking under my white, bare forehead.

'Isn't it all too businesslike?' I complained, tugging at the skirt in front of the mirror in her hallway as Mimi gave me money for the taxi back to the club. 'I don't feel natural in this get-up.'

'Believe me, this is what they like to see when they first arrive. All the career girls in London dress like this. And now that we've sorted out your hair and your make-up, you look as if you were born to all this –'

She gave me that unnerving kiss again, just on the corner of my mouth.

'Do you kiss all your new girls like that?' I asked, emboldened by being dressed again, in my new sophisticated uniform.

To my relief Mimi grinned. 'What new girls? The club only opened a month ago. Miss Sugar deliberately misled you, making out it had been here for years,' she said.

'Sir Simeon's new toy,' I said. 'That's how Merlin described it.'

'Did he now? And did he approve?'

'No. He seemed to resent it, if anything,' I answered, shaking my head. 'But I digress. I want to know. Did you kiss Miss Sugar like that when she was new?'

Mimi tipped her head back and laughed from her chest, like a trooper, like she had on the mobile phone last evening. She opened a silver cigarette box and tapped a long, brown cigarette against its lid. She had slipped on the white dressing gown to see me off, but hadn't bothered to tie it up. Her body was a sliver of pale-brown skin and the hint of curves was visible between the white silk folds.

'Miss Sugar is not at all as she seems, Suki,' she said. 'Don't be fooled by that schoolmarm exterior. No. We had to initiate her in a very different way when she first came to work for us. Practically had to tie her down.' She laughed again, and pushed me through the front door. 'Now off you go.'

6

I punched the security buttons at the door and strode into the shimmering hallway of the club, lit this evening only by a net of tiny white fairy lights. The rest of the hallway was in darkness, but the white marble walls seemed to glow with their own light. I felt a surge of pride. My suggestion about the fairy lights had been taken up, a mere few hours after Mimi had asked me for my ideas.

I wondered why I felt as if I owned the joint. It must have been the clothes. They made me feel on top of the world. In charge of the world, in fact. And, as Mimi had told me just as I was leaving her house, that was, in fact, the case. I was on my own. Neither she nor Miss Sugar were working tonight.

For a second, despite the pinstripes, it all felt scary.

I hesitated in the silent atrium, breathing in Miss Sugar's scented pot pourri to calm myself. You could almost imagine the building was deserted, it was so quiet, but I knew, from my instructions, that there were several members in the club this evening, plus a guest. If you cocked an ear, you could hear soft music wafting through the door on the right of the hall and light filtered through the red, green and gold fragments of the stained-glass door, beckoning me in.

'Don't march in like the cavalry and announce yourself. Sometimes having the staff hovering about inhibits them,' Mimi had advised, spraying scent behind my ears. It was a heavy musk, not the sophisticated one she usually wore, but one that made you think of silk cushions scattered across a harem tent. 'Remember they won't know who you are yet. You could be another guest. Just blend into the background at first and keep an eye. Make sure they're enjoying themselves.'

'And if they are? Do I leave them alone?' I had asked.

'Play it by ear, darling,' she'd murmured, turning to look at herself in the mirror. I learned that that was her way of dismissing me. 'You'll soon cotton on to what they need.'

The bar room was done out like a comfortable library, with bottle-green book-lined walls, leather Chesterfield sofas and chairs and a roaring log fire which reminded me of the fire that had crackled in Sir Simeon's bedroom. I found a seat by the fire and crossed one unfamiliar, exposed leg over the other with a swish of stocking. A handful of men were sitting or standing around the bar.

Mimi had promised me that Mr Hall, the new member, would be easy to spot.

'He'll be the one looking unsure of himself, and he'll probably look a little younger than tonight's other members. They will all look ultra respectable, like judges or politicians. Most will have grey hair. I say respectable, but I daresay their wives would describe them as complete shits!'

I was sitting too close to the fire, and my skin was prickling up with the heat. I flapped the collar for a moment to cool my skin. The black lace of my camisole tickled the surface of my skin as I fanned myself, and was swallowed into my deep cleavage as I sighed. I glanced down at my leg and saw that my skirt had ridden up, exposing an inch or so of flesh at the stocking top. I was about to tug at my skirt when I thought better of it. The sight of my own thigh had stirred me. I liked seeing the firm white skin exposed there. The sizzling feeling in my stomach from Mimi's ministrations hadn't entirely gone away. It was as if I'd taken some kind of drug because I was in a horny mood, and had been ever since I'd left Mimi's house.

I left the stocking top showing. One or two of the men in the room had noticed me, and were now looking at my leg. My smile grew wider. I swung my foot gently, so that the sliver of flesh between skirt and stocking stretched and shrank with the movement.

A couple of men came in to the room. One of them hesitated at the doorway, looking around the room. Mr Hall, I reckoned. I sat up a little to take notice. I decided that if he hesitated for another count of ten I would go up to him and introduce myself.

But I was distracted by his companion, who marched straight up to the bar and sat down confidently on a bar stool. He was ice blond, stick thin and wearing a very tight white trouser suit. As the barman bent to take the order, I noticed with a thump of shock that he was a she. Was this the unexpected guest? And if so, whose guest was she? Mimi hadn't specified. She hadn't mentioned anything about a woman coming. Was she Mr Hall's wife? Or some other sort of guest?

Mr Hall had also come into the room and was shaking hands with someone who I couldn't see, someone sitting in a high-backed wing chair.

Meanwhile, the woman's eyes travelled round the room, resting for a moment on my leg. I swung it again, I thought to shock her but instead her eyes moved up to mine, and she tipped her head up in a kind of greeting. Something about her was familiar.

I could feel a dampness across my upper lip now. I really was too hot. I stood up, desperate to throw the jacket right off so that I could cool myself. I grasped the lapels, ready to do it. I had a mad urge to strip in front of them all, make those sombre mouths snap open at the sight of my bare breasts, invite them to touch me, do more to me if they chose. Why shouldn't we all be uninhibited? This was private property, after all. We were all members. We were all consenting adults.

It was also the first night of my new job, and I didn't need to get myself sacked.

I closed the lapels again, breathing hard, trying to ignore the nipples stiffening against the jacket lining. Don't be daft. Be discreet. I repeated this mantra. *Don't be daft, be discreet.* It seemed to sum up the two halves of my personality. Mostly as I crashed through life, dressed like a boy, I was daft, but as long as I was working for Club Crème, I had to be discreet.

A central switch suddenly dimmed the lighting, and some low, jazzy music came on. I had clean forgotten Mimi's instructions about how long to wait before letting on who I was. The barman seemed to be in charge of the ambience, if it was he who had dimmed the lighting. I realised I was at a real disadvantage. How could I exercise any kind of quiet authority if I didn't even know the barman's name?

Mr Hall was talking animatedly to the invisible man in the chair. Everyone was happy. I was the one who looked out of place, I realised. Apart from anything else, I didn't have a drink, which was pretty lame when I was sitting in a bar. I was hot, I was thirsty, I was a trifle nervous. I was damn well going to have a drink.

I walked up to the bar. The blonde was still there, still alone. She glanced at me and her eyes travelled down the front of my jacket. Then she glanced away, twiddling the stem of her glass. One foot swung idly, dangling a spiked stiletto. I drummed my fingers on the chrome, trying to attract the attention of the barman. I must have a quiet word, introduce myself to him.

The icy blonde looked at me again. Her pale, frosted lips parted, as if to speak.

'Allow me.'

Mr Hall pushed between us, and picked up her empty glass. I took a good look at him. He looked like a rugby player: handsome, but stocky, his body restless and uncomfortable, as if it wanted to burst out of his immaculate suit. The blonde and I continued staring at each other as Mr Hall presented us with two daquiris. He obviously thought I was a guest. She and I were the only two women in the place, and I suppose I did look as if I had come here to relax after a hard day at the office.

It was fun, no one knowing my identity, but I suspected the barman must know who I was, even if I didn't know *his* name. Mimi would have told him, but he seemed to be ignoring me. I got the same feeling I'd had that sweltering day when the prince took me to his hotel in Cairo for the first time. I was anonymous for the time being. I could do what I liked. Within reason, obviously. After all, I was working and, if anything went wrong, it would be reported back to Mimi and, presumably, Sir Simeon. But my brief for tonight was simple. I had been given free rein to watch and please the guests as I saw fit.

The alcohol started to take hold, heating up my veins. I decided to loosen up and enjoy myself.

'Thank you for the drink,' I murmured to Mr Hall, bending my elbow to rest it on the bar. The jacket slipped off my shoulder. I drew my hand slowly inside the collar and caressed my skin where the jacket lining had slipped silkily down. My fingertips brushed my breast. To my amazement this lightest of touches sent a bolt of excitement sizzling through me. I hadn't realised how horny the intimate, rarified atmosphere had made me. Still looking at the blonde woman, I took hold of my breast

73

and started to rub my already perky nipple. The blonde woman's eyes flashed directly at what my hand was doing. She started to mirror the action, except that her hand moved over the surface of her white jacket, tracing the small swell of her own breast.

'It's a pleasure. I gather it's the tradition here. For a new member to buy everyone a drink. Though mine's a rather small round tonight. Where's everyone going?' Mr Hall said and cleared his throat to call the barman.

I glanced round. I ought to have known the answer to that one. The few old gents who had been scattered round the bar were melting away, nodding at the barman as they headed for the door.

'Dinner is being served in the oak-panelled dining room next door, sir, and our older members always like to get there sharpish,' the barman explained, looking from Mr Hall to his companion and still ignoring me. 'It's an Italian menu tonight. Do you want to go through?'

'I don't think so,' the blonde woman answered for him. 'We're quite happy where we are, aren't we, Jez?'

The blonde and I pushed our empty glasses together so that they clinked and our hands touched, a few inches from Mr Hall's.

'Er, yes,' Mr Hall said, looking at me for the first time. 'I'm perfectly happy staying right here.'

That sorted my job out for this evening, I thought. I wondered if I should just beat a retreat. Everyone was happy without any help from me.

'In that case, we'll have champagne this time, and we can have some fun,' the blonde woman said. Her hand shot out and flipped undone the button on my jacket. 'Oops. I gather *that's* a tradition here, too. Having fun, I mean. And guests get special treatment. Isn't that right, brother, dear?'

'So my membership form tells me, sis,' Mr Hall answered, grinning, but he was still looking at me. 'But what it doesn't tell me is who our fellow guests are?'

Brother and sister, eh? I very much doubted it. Chalk and cheese, more like.

But before I could work out whether there really were any similarities between the two, the same shape nose, for instance, or similar colouring, I found myself grinning back at him. He was definitely the nicer one, whatever else was the truth of their peculiar relationship. My jacket had fallen open where she'd flipped the button undone. It was already halfway off my shoulders. My heart started to race. I realised they could see my hand, still lightly caressing my breast.

I sat up straighter and ran my tongue across my dry mouth. 'Perhaps I should introduce myself. I'm not actually a guest,' I started to explain.

'Does it really matter, now that we're all here?' said the blonde, rising from her stool and pushing past him. She pushed my jacket sleeves down so that my elbows were pinned to my sides. Now my breasts jutted out of their expensive lace. 'You're not exactly trying to stop me making free, are you? So you must have a pretty clear idea what's on our minds.'

She sat down again, calmly sipping her champagne and looking me up and down. Just at that moment the music track came to an end and there were a few beats of silence as she and Mr Hall stared at my breasts. The attention made them tingle.

'I guess you could say the membership is open to interpretation,' I said, out of the blue. 'And of course, the aim of the club is that everyone coming through those doors feels totally welcome.'

Mr Hall was standing behind his blonde 'sister' now, one hand in his trousers, and I could see the thick bulge of his erection straining at his zip. There were only the three of us present, and the barman, who was staring into space at the other end of the bar, polishing one wine glass over and over again as if he was hypnotised.

'Better and better,' the woman breathed. She turned to look at her brother. 'The people here are high quality, aren't they? I'm getting horny. Is it OK to talk like this, do you think, Jezzie? After all, you are the new boy.'

Mr Hall's eyes veered past me for a moment, as if he was casing the joint, or as if he was checking the score with an invisible umpire. A flicker of uncertainty went through me, and I fingered my lapel to pull it closed. I wondered if I should consult the barman, or check the club rules, if there were any. Then again, although I knew the woman had mischief up her sleeve, I didn't yet know what exactly she meant by 'fun'. So long as it didn't involve drugs or disaster, what was there to stop?

In any case I wasn't one to back out of something that looked intriguing, and these two had a plan. As if in answer to my thoughts, Mr Hall's grin stretched wider and he nodded again.

'Quite all right, sis. I've got the OK from on high. We're free to do whatever we like. It's why I joined this particular club.'

The woman's tongue poked between her white teeth as she stood up again and brushed very long, white fingers across the swell of my breasts. Her tongue slicked back and forth across her lips, her hard blue eyes sparking with excitement.

'Then those *on high* should think about changing the club's name to Liberty Hall,' she remarked very quietly, stretching her hand towards my tits. 'Because I intend to take every liberty going.'

'That would give it away, though, wouldn't it?' the barman observed from his end of the bar, and we all jumped. We'd forgotten he was there. The blonde woman snatched her hand away from where it had been about to caress my left nipple.

But she'd started something now. There was a devil hopping about inside me. And the weird thing was that the barman's sturdy presence, and his only comment, just excited me more, gave me the green light to carry on where the blonde had left off. I wasn't about to stop now unless someone marched in and arrested me.

'Oh, don't mind him. He's here to pour drinks,' I said, pulling my camisole aside and refusing to catch the barman's eye. I knew I was echoing the woman's imperious tone, and I liked it. 'Please feel free to continue.'

One nipple popped out. Still nobody moved, but all eyes were on me now. I took another risk. My other nipple tipped over the edge of lace. The blonde and Mr Hall leaned towards each other very slightly. I pinched my nipples out into red points, relishing the unveiled lust in their eyes. My nipples were still sore with rubbing against Mimi's earlier, but the soreness made everything all the more intoxicating. The barman carried on polishing his glass.

'You never told me the club was *this* good,' murmured the woman to her brother, half clinging to his sleeve, but straining at the leash as well. Then she turned to me. 'So, who are you?'

I inched my bar stool closer to hers and, as I did so, my groin rubbed against the seat, sending a shock of excitement through me. Tentatively, hoping that no one would see, I rubbed myself across the seat again while I decided what to tell her. There was the shock again, hotter this time, urging for more. My tight skirt rode further and further up until the suspenders and then my knickers were visible. The other woman tottered slightly on her high heels, and balanced herself on her own stool.

'I'm here to keep an eye on things,' I told her. My voice was thick with excitement. 'And to make guests and members all feel welcome.'

Still challenging her, in amazement at myself more than anything else, I started rubbing myself very slowly back and forth across the leather seat, locking the heels of my shoes on to the foot bars. This way I could raise myself slightly off the stool so that my pubes were only just making contact. This was private pleasure. This was something I could and did treat myself to whenever and wherever I wanted: on a plane, on a bus, in a cab, in a restaurant, in the library, wherever there were people close enough to see.

Usually no one could tell what I was doing – that was half the fun – but now I saw that the ice woman was watching the slow sliding of my fanny.

'Ah, so you belong here. You're a member of staff. An employee. A servant, even. In other words, you're paid to allow us carte blanche to do whatever we please,' she said. Her voice petered out in a little gasp as she grabbed the seat of her own stool, and started to copy me, pushing her bottom hard back across the seat, and forwards again. The tiny muscles in my pussy were really convulsing now. I wondered if in fact they'd ever stopped twitching since I had left Mimi's bedroom.

'A servant? I can be a servant if you want me to be,' I said, my voice sinking lower. My brain wasn't interested in engaging just now. Everything was focussing far, far lower down. 'But it's more accurate to say I'm certainly at your service. Night and day.'

Dampness started seeping through my knickers as the silk wrinkled away from my pussy. The blonde liked my answer. She nodded and bit her lip hard as she rubbed herself faster. I felt the cool leather meeting my sex lips and I nearly squealed out loud as they spread open, my little clit peeping out and retracting as it, too, made contact with the hard seat. I knew the blonde woman could tell what was happening. I wanted her to see my knickers in the shadow of my skirt, and she was gyrating her own hips on her seat, grinning at me, both of us in a private circle of excitement.

All at once she jerked upright. 'Oh, I'm so horny now, Jez. See what she's doing to me? Is she doing it to you?' she said.

Mr Hall, standing behind her and watching me, had stopped grinning. He was breathing heavily and I wanted to match my breathing with his, match it with the pulsating rhythm tantalising my cunt.

'Yeah,' is all he could manage to say. 'I'm ready.'

'Jez? Now's the time. Tell him. I need fucking.'

I thought she was talking to me. 'Jez. The lady needs fucking,' I yelped obediently. 'But Jez? So do I.'

Her precious Jez had been lusting after me, surely, not her. But he looked away from me, undid her white jacket and pulled it open. She was wearing nothing underneath, not even a bra, and her small breasts were like white apples, cute against her thin frame. He lifted her off the stool so that she was standing, and edged her trousers down her hips. His hands were round in front of her and, with two thick fingers, he parted her startling, completely shaved pubes so that her crack was a sudden red. One of his fingers disappeared inside her and I gasped, rubbing myself more frantically as droplets of desire moistened the stool.

'What are you doing, Jez?' shrieked his supposed sister as Mr Hall pulled the ice blonde woman round behind her stool and bent her over it. 'I meant *him*, not you!'

'Who are you talking about? There's just the three of us, so I shouldn't complain if I were you,' I murmured as she kept jabbing her finger in my direction. 'You're the lucky one. I'll just have to do this for myself.' I grabbed my crotch and thrust my fingers against my clit, desperate to bring myself off.

'OK, OK.' The blonde's voice was shivering as Mr Hall started mercilessly to finger-fuck her. 'Do whatever you want, Jez. But I want to see her getting it, too.'

My fingers, circling across my pleasure button, were an echo of what his were doing to her and were stirring up delicious tremors of excitement. I would frisk myself in front of them, I thought, pleasure myself while they went at it. That would be almost as exciting as getting myself properly seen to.

But there was someone else in the room with us after all. I thought she'd been hallucinating but now whoever she'd been pointing at was behind me, taking me and pulling me backwards by the waist, making me slide wetly off the seat. I was forced to tumble backwards. I couldn't see who was manhandling me. As I tried to grab on to something to get my balance, I looked up and down the bar. The barman had been the only other person in here. One clean glass and his cloth lay at the far end of the room, but the barman had vanished.

'Who is this?' I tried to ask, twisting about. I realised I didn't know the barman's name. 'It must be you, barman?'

There was no answer. The blonde didn't hear me. Mr Hall couldn't help. I was roughly pushed forwards. My sore nipples brushed the leather seat, then my breasts were squashed as someone bent me further over so that my bottom was tilted in the air, my skirt right round my waist. My silk knickers stuck unevenly to me, dark and soaking with my own juices.

'I'd say you're the lucky one, lady,' my new friend whispered to me as Mr Hall bent her over in the same way.

My face was up close to hers, close enough to kiss. Why am I the lucky one? I wondered. I looked at her mouth, her madly staring eyes. I didn't want to kiss her. Kissing Mimi, the first woman I'd ever kissed, had been too glorious to repeat so soon. But I still wanted to see what was going to happen to the blonde. The music seemed to be getting louder. All I could see were my two companions, the wooden bar and my stool. Mr Hall still had one hand rubbing at her pussy, but the other was unzipping his trousers. I couldn't wait for him to take his suit off. I wanted to see him naked, or at least in a pair of muddy shorts.

'Because you've got the jackpot, bitch,' she said, as a colossal cock came thumping out of Mr Hall's flies, already pumping and jumping. He grabbed it as if to quell it, and held it lovingly for a moment as he rubbed the round, purple knob over the ice woman's bottom. She moaned, biting her lips and stretching her throat.

As I gaped at the enormous cock about to plunge into her and wondered where this jackpot was coming from, my knickers were suddenly peeled aside and my own warm, throbbing sex-lips were pulled open. I felt a smooth long shaft nudging under my buttocks and edging towards my cunt. I gripped the stool as the unseen prick circled blindly round. It brushed over my clit, making me jerk backwards. I wasn't going to stop him. I was ready to take the milkman, the traffic warden, anyone.

'Promise not to tell,' I said over my shoulder, as the invisible cock nudged at me. 'I'm sorry if I insulted you earlier, but you *are* just here to pour the drinks. God knows what Mimi will have to say when she hears I've been screwed by the barman.'

He didn't reply, just shoved harder.

'The barman! Oh, that's good. That's very good,' the

other woman said and started to cackle, but then a hectic flush suffused her white cheeks as she was suddenly thrown forwards, her face brushing mine. Mr Hall slammed into her.

'And that's very good, too,' I said breathlessly, slowly gyrating my hips, the hidden cock following my movements, hovering just outside my crack. 'Talk about in your face. Brother and sister, didn't you say? Doing it, right here in the club ... Perhaps I should be putting a stop to all this. What do you think, barman? It's all getting pretty kinky.'

'And who started it, eh?' she breathed into my ear. 'Butter wouldn't melt a minute ago, would it? But now look at you. Who are you to put a stop to anything?'

And then she was pulled back as if sucked by a tide. I watched her bucking back and forth across the hard little stool, her small tits bunching and swinging over the edge of the seat. Her mouth was open and her eyes were blue and unblinking, fixed on mine. Mr Hall tensed his buttocks as he started to fuck her in earnest. Her face was eerily calm, but there were high, keening cries coming from her as he pumped her, his hands round her waist, his jacket, shirt and tie still tidy, though his neck bulged as if it wanted to burst out of his collar.

As he speeded up his rhythm, his sister suddenly looked up at the invisible man behind me and said at him, 'What are you waiting for? If I can't have you this time, *she* may as well enjoy it.'

I'd been so aroused by watching them rutting that I was only dimly aware of the shaft of male muscle edging its way carefully inside me, getting deeper and deeper. All at once the man behind me grabbed my hips and pulled me against his groin. The force of his action made me realise that my legs had become like jelly. I couldn't have resisted or got away even if I'd wanted to. My knickers, which kept sticking to various parts of me, were wrenched aside, and then a long hard cock was at me like a missile, pushing over my eager clitoris. Then, cruelly, he pulled back again, leaving spirals of hot desire in his wake. He circled his knob around me, teasing me, then plunged straight in, throwing me forwards.

'Gotta keep up,' gasped the ice blonde, as we rocked towards each other.

'Just watch me,' I flashed back.

The metal feet of my stool scraped across the floor as my legs were spread wider. My forehead knocked against her bare shoulder. I could hear her starting to groan as I raced to catch up with her. Wild, fierce lust climbed through me, jagged and sharp and violent, goading me onwards in this wild display. I heard myself crying out like she had done, my hands scrabbling to keep a hold of the madly rocking stool. Her cheek rubbed my cheek before she started to build towards her own climax right into my face. The sight of her must have spurred on my unseen lover, as it was only a couple of seconds before he reached his own, spurting climax.

The two men withdrew as if by a secret signal to pack their sated cocks back inside their suit trousers. The ice woman and I remained slumped on our elbows across our stools, close enough to kiss as the pleasure faded and our energy struggled to return. I closed my eyes eventually and let myself collapse for a moment, my legs splaying out like a colt's, my arms still imprisoned in my jacket.

'Bravo, lady.'

I stood up. The woman was sitting up on the stool again, her bare legs crossed and the champagne glass in her hand. She had the white jacket on, but not the trousers. Mr Hall was leaning his arms on the bar, his shoulders heaving as if he'd run a marathon.

'On the house,' I replied, rather pleased with my retort. I looked eagerly round. The barman was back, flicking cocktail glasses into a pyramid formation as if nothing had happened.

'Meet your fuck for the night,' the woman said in a brittle voice, waving her glass and looking past me. Mr Hall's head swung up, and he tapped her on the shoulder to hush her. I swivelled round. The man who had taken me from behind was not flicking cocktail glasses. He was fiddling with the knot of a red silk tie, and reaching for a champagne glass. He nodded slowly at me, his blue eyes like lasers. His face had no expression, neither approval or disapproval.

Bang goes my job, I thought. Blown it on my first night. A trickle of juice tickled my inner thigh. My knees were threatening to buckle completely beneath me. I clutched the stool for support.

'Er, good evening, Sir Simeon,' I mumbled, falling backwards on to the seat and yanking my skirt back over my legs. How silly. He'd just shot his load inside me. What was the point of trying to hide my legs? I racked my brain to remember Mimi's instructions, but there was nothing there about shagging. Shagging anyone. Shagging club members. Shagging the staff. Shagging the boss . . .

I scrabbled for my shoes. I thought I'd better make my exit before I was thrown out. Sir Simeon leaned towards me. I thought he was going to bawl me out.

'Please, finish your drink,' he said in my ear. I wanted to die with gratitude.

The ice blonde woman wasn't smiling at me any more. She tipped the rest of her champagne in a pale shower straight down her throat and tapped her glass on the bar for more. You could cut the atmosphere with a knife. The barman looked from one to the other of us hopefully, no doubt expecting fireworks and, on an unseen signal, he popped the cork of another champagne bottle.

'I didn't have her down as your type, Simeon,' the woman remarked sharply, as Sir Simeon took the champagne from the barman and started to recharge our glasses with another bottle. 'I didn't know you liked them red haired and busty? Exhibitionist hussies, who don't even look round to see who's doing them?'

I flushed then, my cheeks burning.

'I'm not like that at all,' I started to say, buttoning up my jacket. 'I've never done anything like this before.'

'You could have fooled me, encouraging us like that, showing us your wares,' she snapped. 'You looked like a pro.'

'You wanted me to go on,' I retorted, because it was true. 'You can't deny the lust in your eyes when you saw me. I thought you and I – I thought we were in it together. You told him to fuck me.'

There was a nasty silence. She couldn't deny it, surely?

'And anyway,' I ploughed on, 'what does it matter what part I played? You got your brother. I would have thought that was enough for anyone! So we all got something out of it.'

She tossed her head and bit her lip for a moment as she glared at me. 'I don't think you should speak back to your clients, sorry, your members, like that, do you?' she asked.

'Avril, you can cool it now,' Sir Simeon said. His voice was calm but deadly. The effect of a gunshot. 'Everything Miss Summers does in my presence is with my approval. I gave your ... Mr Hall the nod earlier, too. As Miss Summers says, surely everyone is happy? A little flabbergasted by events, perhaps, but happy?'

My heart lurched as the penny dropped. Avril ... the

woman at the meet. She was a member, or at least the wife of a member. Mrs Grey. The special guest. But what was she doing here without her husband? Mimi had said nothing about this.

'I'm sorry, Simeon. I was just carried away. It's the atmosphere of your marvellous club, you see. It's magical.' Avril was starting to grovel. She took out a silver compact and widened her eyes into the mirror. She glanced at me over the top of it. 'And you were carried away, too, Simeon. You were supposed to ignore my command. I thought special guests got special privileges? And *you* were the special privilege I had in mind.'

'I had other plans, I'm afraid,' Sir Simeon replied, tapping me very lightly on the cheek. 'This one was ready for her own initiation, you see. I understand that someone prevented her from carrying out her duties properly yesterday at Symes Hall. How is your foot, by the way, Miss Summers?'

'It's fine, thank you,' I started to tell him. 'The frozen peas did the trick. I can put weight on it and everything.'

'You were supposed to resist the temptation to stick your cock up her fanny until you'd seen to me!' Avril screeched like the wicked fairy, furious that we were ignoring her. I continued to waggle my foot vaguely in Sir Simeon's direction and he bent politely to inspect it.

'It really doesn't suit you, Avril,' he replied, his voice harsh with warning. He straightened slowly. 'And it doesn't suit the *mores* of my club, either.'

'What doesn't suit me?'

'All this sewer language.'

Avril stuck her hand out, and jabbed me in the chest. 'I was only using the language our hostess here might understand.'

I took a step towards her, fighting to keep my fists from coming up.

Sir Simeon was beside me. He looked at me for a moment, staring me down until I felt the anger subside. I could see a pulse going in his neck as his eyes grazed my throat and instantly I wanted to lie down and wave my legs in the air. Literally. I remembered what I'd said to his son, Merlin, about his instincts around women. Both Sir Simeon and Merlin were woman whisperers.

'I think you'd better leave, Avril,' Sir Simeon said. The quieter his voice became, the more everyone listened. 'By insulting my new right-hand woman you are insulting me. I think she's survived her first evening in exemplary fashion. Her job is to oversee everyone's contentment while they are guests or residents here. Not only did she do that, but she took an active part, as well.'

I couldn't stop the smile spreading across my face. He was the one with the active part, I thought, my pussy smarting from the memory. He didn't need to defend me like that. But now I felt six feet taller.

'Perhaps there is something we could salvage from all this,' Avril said, standing up and very slowly pulling on her skin-tight white trousers.

'An apology might do it,' Mr Hall butted in, finding his voice at last. 'After all, some people might have thrown us out after what we just did.'

'I'm sorry, Simeon.'

'Not just to Simeon, stupid,' her brother exclaimed. 'To Miss Summers.'

I was feeling so grand just then that I rewarded him with a smile, and was amused to see him pull nervously at his tie. As well he might. I thought I'd lived a pretty wild life out in the desert but compared to what this guy had just done with his sister ... I decided to ask Sir Simeon, or Mimi, to go over the club rules with a fine-tooth comb. If there *were* any rules. Because obviously indulging in incestuous relations in front of two equally randy members of staff, even if your sister was pretty churlish about it afterwards, was fine by the management.

'I'm sorry, Miss Summers,' Avril said curtly. 'Actually, I'd like to make it up to you, if that's all right with Sir Simeon?'

Everyone waited to hear what she would say next.

'That depends on what you have in mind for Miss Summers, Avril,' warned Sir Simeon. 'So long as it doesn't compromise her position here at the club.'

'Quite the opposite. I want to remove her from the club. At least temporarily. You were right, Miss Summers,' Avril said, turning to me. 'We were in it together. Read each other's minds. I had the advantage because I knew all the players. You were totally new to it. New to the club, new to the kind of reprobates like me who occasionally come here and stir things up. New to the kind of hold this place has over people who come up that alley and through that front door. Because once you are inside the club, something happens to you. Haven't you noticed?'

'I think I had noticed. But please explain it to me,' I urged her sweetly. I glanced up at Sir Simeon and could see a crease down one side of his mouth that might or might not suggest amusement.

'Well, it's pretty obvious after what's happened here tonight!' Avril exclaimed, flicking her fingers at the four of us. 'Everyone becomes ridiculously turned on.'

'Which is why we normally keep the really voracious women out, Avril,' Sir Simeon said as he stepped forwards and took her elbow, ready to steer her towards the door. 'Although I am just wondering whether I should employ you to write a glowing brochure for us, singing our praises?'

'I want Miss Summers to come home with me,' Avril

said and pointed at me again. 'Tonight has been too good to waste. We can carry on, the three of us. You could be our playmate. You look game. What do you say?'

I waited for Sir Simeon to answer for me, but he wasn't going to help me with this one. Not that I needed help. It was an easy decision.

I drained my champagne glass to give me time to think, then buttoned up my jacket. 'I'm sorry, Mrs Grey. My job here has only just started. I don't think I can favour one member over the others. And I've got other club members to see to.' I glanced over at Sir Simeon. The smile had materialised, pulling up the corner of his mouth. The eyes were still boring in to me. The jacket was done up, the trousers zipped. You would never have guessed that ten minutes ago he was bent over me, slipping his length right inside . . .

Now I knew the true meaning of 'pillar of society'.

'See to? In what way?' Avril demanded.

I cleared my throat. 'In any way that they, or I, deem necessary, of course. But I can only act on the precise instructions I've been given by my boss. So you'll have to excuse me.'

'You've got her well trained, Simeon,' Avril sniffed. She opened the glass door. The white light streamed in from the hallway, rousing us all from the cocooned atmosphere of the bar room. 'But I'll see you again, Miss Summers. Here or somewhere else. Be sure of that.'

When they'd gone I waited for Sir Simeon to stop me leaving the room, perhaps invite me to 'see to' him, but he simply gave me a little bow, his face rearranged into its customary sombre lines.

'Rick, the barman, is ready to go off duty,' he said. 'Perhaps you'd help him clear up? He doubles as our bouncer, so he'll lock up once you've gone.'

So the barman/bouncer had a name. He also had black

eyes and night-time stubble to match. As I scuttled about with trays of dirty glasses, feeling well and truly like a skivvy, those eyes were fixed on me, but he said never a word. That suited me just fine. I couldn't look him in the eye. I stayed until about one and then Rick turned the lights out and disappeared.

Outside, the night was fresh, with the usual drizzle. I took a deep breath as I started to walk towards Piccadilly to find a cab to take me to my dingy bed and breakfast. So that was how it would be, working at Club Crème. On the one hand, wicked, forbidden pleasure conducted in a safe, enclosed room, planets apart from anything I'd ever experienced, even with Mimi. On the other hand, the constant reminder that I was, in the end, the hired hand.

The rain began to pour as I walked towards Hyde Park Corner. I couldn't tell if I'd succeeded or failed. I dreaded facing Mimi tomorrow. I had a feeling she had a claim on Sir Simeon. What would she say about my being bent double by him over a bar stool and fucked in front of the brother-and-sister act?

I took my shoes off. I wanted to run, but my foot was still tender. I was happiest when I was running. I walked fast instead, to keep the blood pumping round and to try to empty my mind. I had no idea what tonight's kinky activities had meant. The beginning or the end?

It doesn't have to be permanent, I told myself, as I hurried past the opulent windows of Harrods. I thought of all the tatty scraps of newspaper on the table in my room, advertising flights to every tempting corner of the globe. I'm only doing this until I have enough money. And then I'll be off.

7

Late autumn had turned to winter overnight. I turned the scraps of newspaper over on my table: Australia, India, Egypt – the hotter the climate, the better. A bitter draught whistled through the metal frame of the ill-fitting window. I hadn't slept well. It would be a relief to get out of this dismal room this morning, even though it meant reporting to Mimi on the fruits of my first dubious evening's work.

This time she opened the front door herself. She was dressed in black leather trousers, a black skinny polo-neck jumper that emphasised and clung to every curvy inch of her and gold hoop earrings. Her black hair was plaited into a thick rope that fell over one broad shoulder.

'You were supposed to meet me at the office, not here,' Mimi snapped. 'Now I'm just dashing out.' She turned her back on me and picked up her silver fur coat. 'Something has cropped up.'

'Nothing to do with last night, I hope? Nothing I did?' I ventured. She didn't appear to hear me, but opened a drawer in the hall table and took out a set of keys, which she counted before handing them to me.

'The keys to every door at the club,' she said, glancing at the big clock and almost shoving me back towards the door. 'There's a change of plan. You are going to be acting mistress of the place.'

'About last night –'

Mimi sighed, and I got a delicious draught of her musky scent.

'Summers, I'm in a hurry. I am going to be in and out of town for the next few weeks. Just take charge, will you?'

I took the keys. 'Thank you for having such faith in me, Mimi,' I said.

'Don't thank me, Summers. Taking charge is part of your job. Now, I'll see you in a couple of days. I'll send some more clothes round to that hovel you live in. I can't have my girls looking like ...' Her eyebrows were thin arcs of disdain as she looked me up and down. 'You look like a drug dealer in that hooded effort.'

'Did I make a mistake last night? I'm worried that I might have got it wrong. It didn't go according to plan. I barely even spoke to Mr Hall, who, after all, was the member I was supposed to be looking after.'

'Everyone's taste and desire was catered for. That's what they come to the club for. That's why we keep it so exclusive. Can't have any Tom, Dick or Harriet wandering in and seeing what members do in their free time. Whatever happens there is for their eyes only.'

We were out on the doorstep now. Gone was the sensuous warmth of yesterday's encounter. There was no sign of that big scarlet smile. She was displeased with me for some reason. That was obvious. But I couldn't press the point. Mimi double-secured all the locks and was looking up and down the street almost furtively, as if she was worried about someone spotting her.

'But Mimi –' I tried again. She wheeled round.

'Miss Breeze, today,' she said, scowling. She leaped down the steps towards a silver Mercedes coupé. 'And I don't have time to discuss the minutiae of your job. You can find it out for yourself.'

'I thought I was supposed to report back to you,' I offered.

I froze on the pavement, the keys jabbing into my

hand. She got in to the smart car, started the ignition, then closed her eyes impatiently for a moment. The electric window whizzed down.

'I've had a full report, thank you. You're off the hook for today. Just enjoy a bit of time out, Suki,' she said, the edge in her voice smoothed out. I looked into her eyes and felt a tiny bit reassured.

'Time out?' I asked, stepping across to the car and bending down to look straight into her face. 'But I've only just started working. You've only just given me these keys.'

'Every day is different. Today I'm busy and you're not. I'll see you in a couple of days.'

The window whirred up, nearly snapping off my nose, and she was halfway down the street before I could blink.

I stood watching the exhaust of her car hanging in the still, cold air, and saw the day stretching ahead of me. All very well to have some free time, but I was uneasy about not being given another shift at the club and, to make matters worse, she hadn't paid me for last night. I was stupid for not asking about the money. I still didn't know if I'd blown it by letting Sir Simeon, of all people, do what he did last night. Then again, perhaps she didn't know that particular detail?

Now I had the keys to the most exclusive club in London, and virtually no money. It was a bizarre situation to say the least. I walked back down Earls Court Road to the bed and breakfast, and paced about in my room. But I couldn't relax. I decided to get some exercise. Maybe I'd try the health suite in the basement of the club. The keys jangled happily in my pocket. Why the hell not? I thought.

On my way to the tube I stopped at the entrance to Chrissie's building, but there was no answer when I pressed the bell. Of course not. It was a weekday morning. Jeremy would be counting someone else's money somewhere in the City, and Chrissie would be in her smart domain, spraying perfume over some heavily rouged ladies in the already suffocating air. I was the one with all the time in the world. I could wander into the store and speak to her. Except they probably wouldn't let me through the revolving door. A drug dealer, indeed!

The health suite was approached through a completely different entrance under the Club Crème building, and was open to a wider circle of 'day' members as well as the members of the residential club upstairs. The reception area was modern, full of green plants and minimalist prints. I was afraid the muscular blond guy sitting behind the desk wearing a tiny vest and shorts wouldn't believe who I was and would try to turn me away, but then I noticed a couple of people jogging in off the street and straight through a big red door to the side. They were wearing 'hooded efforts' like mine, trainers and cycling shorts, and carrying little bottles of water. I didn't look out of place at all.

'Excuse me,' I said as I approached his desk, jangling the keys casually. 'My name is Suki Summers. I work upstairs.'

He nodded as if he knew who I was, reached behind him, and gave me an entry card.

'Swimming pool, sauna, jacuzzi, health spa – help yourself,' he said with a wide, white grin.

I pushed through the red door and was instantly enveloped in the hot, steamy atmosphere of the health club. It was another world. Amongst the vast palms and colourful mosaics, people drifted about like half-naked ghosts in the tropical mist, stepping out of the sauna's pine cupboard and plunging into the ice pool. Others ploughed up and down the swimming pool, heads held stiffly above the water. At the far end of the pool, a spiral staircase led up to a café, one vast wall of which was painted with a mural depicting a long sandy beach and sapphire sea.

'Fancy a massage before your swim or after?'

The muscular man was right in front of me, climbing out of the pool and shaking the excess water off his head with a casual flick, as a champion surfer might. Slanted blue eyes peered through his towel, expecting an answer, and I shook my head.

'I have to swim,' I mumbled, staring longingly at the water. 'Then I have to –'

'After your swim, then. All part of the personal service here.'

In the communal changing room I scrabbled through my rucksack. All I had to swim in was a dark-green leotard, a faded remnant from my modelling days. It would have to do. In seconds I was diving in and striking through the water, not looking to right or left until I'd done thirty lengths. The blood was racing through me. My body felt cleansed of the London grime and my head felt clear at last. I'd forgotten how good it felt to expel my nervous energy. Stretching my body to its limits, testing my lungs, eyes stinging with the chlorine, the cold winter world kept at bay by a layer of plate glass.

I lay down on a lounger, panting for breath, my pulse hammering in my ears. Two beautiful blonde girls in matching white bathing suits approached me.

'A massage, madam?' one of them asked in a thick Nordic accent. 'You are new here, yes? It's all –'

' "Part of the service", yes, I know. This is my call, girls, thank you.'

The blond man was back, still in his trunks, but dry. I kept my eyes firmly shut but the goose pimples rising all over my skin told me that he was still there. I felt the energy draining out of me. Let him try to persuade me. After all, I had all day to be pampered, didn't I?

'I don't qualify for the service,' I remarked dryly. 'Don't you have to be blonde to be a member here?'

I heaved myself into a sitting position. He sat down casually on the end of my lounger. He looked like someone who preferred to run or swim every day, like I did, just in order to function. He obviously kept fit, probably fanatically so. But who wouldn't, working in a place like this, surrounded by pampered and toned bodies to keep up with? Although he was a bit too cocksure for my liking, I had to admire his unrelenting eyes, the flared Slavic nostrils, the sculpted body, the thick muscles lying like ropes beneath the taut skin. It was almost impossible to avoid glancing down to see what he had packed away in his multi-coloured Speedos. Instead, I kept my eyes on his pecs.

'You're our first redhead,' he said and laughed. 'And what a glorious change it makes. Anyway, most of the blond hair you see in here comes out of a bottle. Apart from mine of course.'

He combed the said blond hair back over his head and winked at me. My flesh was beginning to heat up again, the cooling effect of my swim evaporating as the steam swirled around us.

'But you won't be able to take up full membership of the health suite until you've had Mikhail's massage,' he said.

'Whose massage?'

'Mine. You are in desperate need. I watched you preparing to dive in. Your face is too pale, your shoulders too tense,' he said. He trailed his thick fingers over me, sketching my features. 'You have a fantastic body. You obviously like to run. But you also look as if you have come out from under a stone.'

'Charming,' I spluttered, folding my arms round my knees. 'I've just come back from Egypt, actually.'

'So why on earth did you leave such an exciting place?'

I hugged my knees closer towards me. He pulled a spotless white T-shirt over his bulging chest and started dragging my towel out from under me.

'My man turned out to be married,' I told him. 'With six wives.'

'Henry the Eighth, was he?' he chuckled.

My laughter shook the towel right off me.

'Oh, that's the best therapy of all,' I said. We laughed again. I tried to be serious. I stared out of the window at the grey sky. 'But he really did have all those wives. Some of them were girls I was mates with. All nationalities. None of us knew about the others.'

'A regular harem. Nice!' Mikhail smacked his lips.

'Yeah. It sounds sexy, doesn't it, and exciting? But when you've been told you're the special one, and then you find you're next in the queue, it stops being quite so funny. Anyway, it was time to move on. I always have to move, in the end. I thought I'd be happy to come home.'

'And you're not?' he asked. He was folding the towel in half, lengthways.

'It's only temporary, but it isn't working out too well. It's too cold. I've got no money. English men all seem so bland ... You're not English, are you?'

'Well, don't tell anyone, but I give myself this Eastern European name to match my Aryan looks and to please the ladies. I am English, yes. I come from Bristol. And I can assure you we Englishmen are not at all bland.'

'Well, the jury's still out on that one, though you're proving a remarkable exception,' I said. I'd discovered one or two other exceptions recently, I reminded myself.

You didn't get much more English than Sir Simeon, although you couldn't say the same of Merlin.

'Go on,' said Mikhail, busy with oils and body buffs. There was something slightly camp in the way his great big hands flew about. 'Part of our therapy is to listen.'

I did some stretches on my legs. 'It's not just the weather and the men,' I went on slowly. It was good to be able to bounce my thoughts off him. 'I think I've already cocked up my new job. And I don't know what to make of my new boss. Or his mistress, who is also my boss. Or his son.'

'Maybe they don't know what to make of you, either. Now, you need a massage,' Mikhail stated. 'Life doesn't have to be complicated. You should be like me. Just do the next thing that comes your way.'

I laughed again and, taking advantage of my distraction, he stood up, holding the towel ready. Then, he flipped me like a pancake on to it and started pumping a concealed foot pedal under the lounger, which raised it to hip height.

'No one leaves any part of this building until they are relaxed and pampered,' he said. 'Now, I'm just going to wheel the massage bed behind this palm, for a little more privacy.'

'Why do we need privacy?' I asked sleepily, face down in the towel.

'Because –' and he had my leotard rolled down to my waist as quickly as peeling a banana.

I struggled to stop him, but his hands were on my shoulder blades, pressing me hard down on to my front. It felt as if he was going to press me right through the bed, and my resistance evaporated. He squirted some oil on to my back, and started to rotate the heel, the palm, the knuckles of his hands. My cheekbones dug into the towel, my body rocking, and I bit my lip as the surface of my skin started to tingle in places he hadn't even reached yet. The oil slicked up and down my arms, back to my shoulder blades and along the knobs of my spine. The blood started to drum again in my ears. It sounded like the hoof beats of that chestnut horse, galloping across the frost-hard fields around Symes Hall.

'Too tense. So tense,' Mikhail tutted, pushing me down hard again. 'You are going to be a tough nut to crack, I can tell.'

'Not tense,' I said. 'Just remembering something. Someone.'

'If you are remembering something, then forget it. Please just concentrate on the pleasure I'm about to give you.'

His hands continued over my back, over my hips and down the backs of my legs. I did as I was told, but my sexuality wouldn't let me forget it. Every so often, my lower parts twitched, as if I was still gripping Merlin's penis.

My whole body had become ridiculously sensitive. When Mikhail touched the crease behind my knee my foot jerked up. I expected to meet thin air, but I met the solid muscle of Mikhail's back or buttocks. He had climbed on top of me, light as a cat, and was kneeling astride me. He deliberately tickled the back of my knee until I kicked him again and, this time, I could tell I was kicking at his buttocks.

'Not much control, have you?' he remarked, as if making notes. 'Like a race horse at the starting gate.'

He bent himself so that he was lying on top of me, but still almost weightlessly. I enjoyed the feeling that I was like a pinned butterfly. He could have squashed the life out of me just then, if he'd chosen.

His hands were still working. He had edged them under me, so that they were round the front of my hips, and I felt him arrange himself across me so that, when he stopped moving, I could feel, resting between the cheeks of my bottom, a long, hard shape. His hip bone? I wondered frantically, wriggling myself around it. Or the bottle of oil?

All around us were the distant sounds of people diving and splashing in the pool. With nothing but a few fronds of palm separating us from the other drifting bodies, this guy was arousing me. He'd got me halfway into a trance, and I had no strength to move away from him. And what was more, I didn't want to. I didn't know what kind of massage this was. He was massaging me into a jelly. A jelly with no arms or legs but who was being steadily aroused as he massaged my spine and his groin rubbed very carefully up and down the crack of my butt.

Automatically, I arched my back, raising my bum to meet his burgeoning cock, pressing its hardness into the soft crevice. He blew sharply on my neck, raising the hairs into tiny prickles of growing desire. Then his weight was off me: cock, thighs, hands, everything.

I stifled a groan of frustration and opened my eyes.

'Thank you,' I croaked. 'That was great.'

'Now your front. We have to do you all over.'

Once again he flipped me over and now I was lying on my greased back. He sat astride me and this time I had a good look. I examined his crotch. His cock was trying to get vertical, tenting his tight trunks like a schoolboy getting a hard-on at his first topless beach. I didn't know whether to laugh or reach up and grab it. My whole body was fizzing with a mixture of arousal and anticipation about what he would do next. He calmly balanced himself astride me. I could see how strong his legs were as they supported him a few inches above my stomach. Too late I realised that the leotard was halfway down my legs and I was totally naked, but instead of alarm I felt a sharp surge of excitement. This guy was as clinical as a doctor. His friendly face had closed in with concentration. I couldn't tell if I had imagined the cock-rubbing moment, imagined his tangible excitement. My bare breasts appeared no more interesting to him than a pair of water wings. That should have quashed any remaining lust in me, but his impassive face only fired me up more. My nipples stiffened as his hands began to massage the area just above them.

'Just as I thought,' he murmured, squirting a spunk-like jet of different cream on to my chest and rubbing it slowly in circles over the plump flesh, but avoiding my nipples, which were standing out like acorns. 'Carefully concealed, these were. Most people would never have thought, seeing you coming in here dressed like a skateboarder.'

'Thought what?'

'Thought that you had the body of a goddess under those baggy clothes and that dreadful hat. But it was your eyes that gave you away.'

'Go on,' I urged him, shifting restlessly under him. 'Make me feel like a goddess, then.'

My pussy brushed the thick bulge in his trunks, and the contact made me realise how damp my crotch was. I couldn't believe myself. Aroused by some cheap masseur with a line in chat up as old as the hills? I'd come across endless people like him in Egypt, when the prince's back was turned, and I'd never been interested. But there was no denying it – Mikhail was good at this. Maybe I wanted him to go on just *because* he was an anonymous masseur, not a 'client' or a secretive member of the club, or a past love. I strained myself upwards again and, instead of moving away, he pressed down so that once again the thick shape in his trunks was lying along the crack of my sex, nudging the lips apart. Once again he started to move his hips back and forth, but so gently you would barely notice.

He stared at his own hands as they circled my breasts. 'Your eyes. They're green and they flash, like a witch's,' he said calmly, rotating his hands. 'You might look like Huckleberry Finn, but it's your witch's eyes that give you away.'

He walked his fingers past my breasts, suddenly businesslike, and seemed to be counting my ribs. Instantly, I felt my neck and head loosening. I hadn't even known how tense they were. I was ready for more of this. But then he jumped off me, shaking out his legs and arms as if he'd just been lifting weights. He hitched up his trunks, and then I saw why. The two blonde girls had appeared and were standing beside the palm tree, tapping their bare feet, and jerking their heads towards the clock. God knows how long they'd been there.

'That should make you feel like a new woman. Now, if you'll excuse me. I have an engagement upstairs,' Mikhail said. He pulled my leotard up briskly and pumped my lounger back down so fast that I almost lost my balance trying to get my arms through the straps.

'Well, thank you anyway. I feel a whole lot better now,' I said, standing up. It was true, though my legs were shaking. 'I think I'll have another swim.'

As I stood at my little window that evening and watched the lights come up over the city, there was a knock on the door. Miss Sugar was there, wearing a floor-length grey raincoat and holding out a couple of carrier bags.

'Your clothes,' she sniffed, thrusting them at me. 'There are various outfits in there to tide you over for the next few days. I'm to take your others away for burning.'

'No chance,' I said, folding my arms over my T-shirt.

'Won't you come in, Sugar? It's getting dark. I've not even turned the lights on yet. I'm a bit lonely up here in my ivory tower.'

She looked tempted for a moment, then shook her head, her pale-grey eyes sliding away from me behind the glasses.

'No. I've not been instructed to stay.'

'Who cares? It's after hours now.'

She poked her head through the door and could barely conceal her disdain at the poky studio room.

'I had a flat a bit like this when I first came to work at the club,' she said. 'Now I've been given a room there with a fascinating view over Shepherd Market. It's high up, like this, but instead of the tube station, I can look straight across the rooftops into the windows of the flat opposite.'

'Isn't that a bit like being a prisoner?' I asked. 'Living above the shop like that?'

'It's just the way Sir Simeon and Mimi operate. And don't get me wrong. I love living there. You just get used to their whims. The perks are worth it, if you play your cards right.' She allowed herself a private smile, which faded just as quickly. 'Now, if you won't give me your clothes, you'll have to bring them to the club. That wasn't a joke, about burning them. They like us to throw everything away which connects us with our past lives.'

'They can whistle,' I snorted, tossing my new glossy hair. 'They don't own us.'

'For as long as we work for them, they do. Which brings me to my second reason for bothering you. As long as you work for Club Crème, you can expect to have your spare time invaded as well. You're required to work this evening, after all. One of the members is holding a private party there and they want you to go. He's a pretty flamboyant character and they want you to keep an eye. Mimi's even left a note about what you're to wear. And don't say they can whistle!' she added quickly, as I opened my mouth to protest. 'This isn't negotiable.'

'I still have a job, then?' I said, reluctantly taking the designer bags off her.

'Of course. Why else would they have rewarded you with a brief like this?'

Despite her brave words I thought I saw her glance enviously past me at the sunset glowing through my window. Then she turned to go back down the stairs. She was hardly best mate material, but I could have done with the company, I thought, pausing in my doorway.

'Don't you feel a little imprisoned living there, Sugar?' I asked, stopping her in her tracks. 'Doesn't it feel like a kind of demotion? A punishment for something?'

'Quite the reverse, Miss Summers. Believe me. Moving right in to Club Crème was very much a promotion. But, sure, they like to test our loyalty from time to time,' she said, the inscrutable smile reappearing briefly. 'And they knew that I would always be loyal to the club, no matter where I live. Have an interesting evening.'

I shut my door and walked slowly over to the tarnished mirror in the bathroom. I studied myself. My clothes were awful; they were right about that. And one of the reasons the clothes looked awful was that my face didn't fit them any more. I wrenched the T-shirt off and looked again. That was better. Now my face was floating above pale shoulders and breasts. I could imagine Mimi standing beside me, grinning with approval, snaking her hands up to cradle my breasts, and I felt a twinge deep inside.

Although I'd been swimming, my hair seemed to recognise the new shape Mimi's hairdresser had given it because instead of springing away from my scalp in horror, it coiled gracefully in two very slightly wavy sheets on either side of my face. The witch's eyes were big in the dying light. I switched on a lamp and the pupils shrank in the glare so that they were wicked points, the green irises gleaming in the mirror. My normally pale cheeks had a flush of colour in them, and my lips were parted as if I'd been running.

I recognised the look. I used to see it in the early days, when the prince first installed me in the flat near his palace. I used to see something like it when he had been to see me, and my thighs were still bruised and sticky from our exertions. I was ready to rock. I would put all my energies into doing exactly what Club Crème required of me, blowing life into the lust that Mimi had coaxed from me, the recklessness that I had uncovered in the bar last night, the restlessness that had seeped through my leotard beside the pool. Anything to welcome the new horny me.

I looked through the bags that Miss Sugar had deposited and read Mimi's bossy note. She wanted me to wear the sort of dress that two days ago I would never have considered buying. It was a diaphanous black sheath, with tiny spaghetti straps, ankle-length but slashed to the navel both front and back and covered in sequins. I tore off my combat trousers and left them in a heap, and slipped the dress on. I held my new obedient hair off my face and wished someone – Mimi, Chrissie, even Sir Simeon – was there to admire me. Perhaps I would seek out Miss Sugar in her humble little room when I got to work. I could show her my new image.

8

So far I hadn't ventured upstairs at the club. The stairs curved enticingly up from the hallway, lit by gas torches flaming up in front of gothic, arched mirrors. At intervals, the stairs paused, tipping the visitor through an archway leading on to an unexplored landing studded with closed doors. I imagined that the higher you got, the quieter everything would be, but tonight, when I reached the topmost penthouse landing, I could hear loud music.

As I looked up and down the landing, there was a sudden burst of giggling. I half expected to see Miss Sugar scuttling to her humble little cell. But she wouldn't giggle like that. To my astonishment, the two blonde girls I'd seen at the swimming pool emerged from what looked like a set of lift doors at the far end of the landing. The health suite obviously had its own entrance to the upper levels of the club. They didn't see me, but jostled each other excitedly as they knocked at one of the closed doors. They were dressed identically in sleeveless black dresses, so tight and short it was a wonder they could breathe, and what looked like pointed witches' hats. Under the hats, they both wore dark glasses. The door opened, coughing out a blast of rock music, and they were drawn inside.

I hesitated, still with one foot on the stairs. Surely this wasn't the party Miss Sugar had directed me to? I'd been expecting a sedate sherry party, perhaps some ballroom dancing. I caught sight of myself in one of the arched mirrors. My reflection flickered spookily in the torchlight. The smoky eye make-up and blood-red lipstick Mimi had also supplied made me look as if I was exploring Blue Beard's castle. I stuck my tongue out and gave myself a kick up the arse. I had a job to do. I tottered after the two blondes and knocked at the door.

A man dressed as Dracula opened the door. He wore white tie and tails, a black cloak, mirrored sunglasses and had fake blood dripping down his chin. He smiled, revealing a fat cigar clamped between vampire fangs.

'I hoped you'd come. Welcome to the lion's den!' he yelled above the noise. The lighting in the room was bright, almost dazzling. 'But you'll need to wear these,' he added, handing me a pair of Jackie Onassis-type sunglasses but, before I put them on, I suddenly recognised him. It was Mikhail, the masseur from the health club.

'How did you know I would be here?' I yelled back, flying after him as he pulled me through the black-and-white crowd. 'And why is everyone dressed up?'

'It's Halloween or hadn't you noticed?' he said as he handed me a tall glass of vicious-tasting punch. 'These are the rules. We all have to be in some sort of disguise. There will be a terrible penalty for anyone who removes their shades. I see this evening you're disguised as a beautiful classy woman with no name. Unlike your rapper's persona this morning.'

It was a fair enough comment. If I didn't recognise myself when I looked in the mirror just now, all dolled up in my finery, why should anyone else recognise me? And the last time he'd seen me, he'd been dripping oil on my boobs.

He slipped away to talk to a man who was leaning against the huge attic window of the penthouse and staring out over the rooftops. This man was dressed as a matador, with a cape, a sombrero and high-waisted trousers with a scarlet stripe down the sides. Beneath his sombrero, his eyes were concealed, like everyone else's, by dark glasses. I wondered if this was the host of the party.

I put my own sunglasses on and realised why the lights were on so bright. It took a while to adjust to the weirdness of wearing dark lenses indoors.

'Hello, again.' The two blondes were on either side of me. 'What are you doing here?'

'Oh,' I said, casting about for something to tell them. Instinct told me not to reveal that I worked here. At least not yet. 'I get around, you know.'

It seemed the right answer. The two blondes pulled me out into the sitting room. I brushed past the matador's cape and a sharp, pine scent stung my nostrils.

'Who is that?' I asked the girl on my left, pointing at him.

'No idea,' she said shrugging. 'But Mikhail can throw a good party, can't he?'

The two girls giggled and pushed me down into a leather chair which looked as if it should be on the deck of the *Titanic*. They knelt on the floor on either side of me, fingering my dress, their fingers brushing my legs.

'Mikhail is throwing this party?' I asked, astonished. 'Is there no end to his talents?'

'Got your eye on him, then?' they twittered. 'He's quite a catch.'

'Not at all,' I said. I laughed and sipped my punch. The alcohol zoomed straight to my head. 'He's just a lifeguard, for goodness sake.'

The two girls laughed again, and a few people, including the matador, turned to see what the commotion was.

'He's not a lifeguard,' one girl shrieked, her Scandinavian accent noticeably slipping into Estuary English.

'He's a founder member of this club. And he owns the entire building! He's the richest man we know, and the most powerful. You want to make friends with Mikhail, you know.'

I was looking at Mikhail with new eyes, ashamed of what a snob I'd sounded.

'I take it all back,' I said. 'He is pretty gorgeous, isn't he, in a Mr Universe sort of way?'

The two girls nudged each other, and one of them got up and went over to Mikhail and the matador. She started to whisper in Mikhail's ear, while the matador's head swivelled in my direction. I couldn't tell for sure if he was looking at me or not, but I decided I was going to make him take notice. My brief was to keep an eye on things without looking obvious, so the logical tactic was to get busy chatting up one of the guests. I hadn't seen him smile yet. I would put a smile on his face. Might even put an erection in his trousers . . .

I straightened my back, relishing the cool leather of the chair caressing my spine. If I was to keep an eye on the proceedings without standing out like a sore thumb, I might as well join in. I uncrossed my legs and rose up on my high silver heels, ran my tongue across my teeth, took another glug of punch and held my hand out to the blonde girl. I meant for her to help me up from the low chair so I could sashay over to the matador, but before I could stop her she led me towards the dance floor, and the other girl joined us.

The music was heavy and sexy, and the three of us started gyrating suggestively round the dance floor. The girls obviously knew how to dance. They were moving like lap dancers. We cranked up the rhythm and grinned at each other, aware of how good we looked shimmying up and down each other's bodies, thrusting our pelvises forwards, beckoning to the other guests, who had crowded round to watch. The matador had sat down in my leather deckchair. He was holding my glass, his face like stone.

Suddenly, Mikhail leapt in amongst us, his cape swirling. He started doing a Russian Cossack dance, keeping his arms folded in front of him, lowering himself right down to the floor, kicking his legs out, and springing upright again. We all clapped and stamped around him. Everyone's faces were flushed and hectic, surreally grinning beneath the blind sunglasses. I felt alive and wild and, what was more, I was in the thick of the attention. It was something I was used to avoiding, but the new me relished it and, as a member of staff, surely it was my duty to take part.

'He's totally different when he's not running his property empire. He's so much fun,' one of the girls shouted in my ear, and I reckoned that she wanted Mikhail. I decided to leave her to it. I would approach the matador and see if I could crack a smile out of him, but then the music suddenly dropped tempo. Now a tango started sliding through the air, and various couples stalked on to the dance floor and took up their positions. I started to back off the dance floor, but Mikhail grabbed me in his arms.

'Did you know this was designed as a human mating dance?' he cried, spreading his hand just above my buttocks and tipping my groin into his. 'It was invented in the brothels of South America. I believe the punters used to dance with each other while they were waiting for a whore.'

'That must be why it's such a rigid dance. Why you hold each other so far apart. But I daresay it turned them on,' I replied, and he grinned.

'Men on men. Not my thing. Now, redhead on redhead, that would be more like it.'

His other hand took mine, and held it stiffly out to the side. He knew what he was doing and it was magical. I had tried the tango long ago, when I was in Brazil. I tripped after him for a few steps, then started to follow his lead, flowing round the floor, our heads turned haughtily sideways on our necks. When we changed direction, snapping our heads the other way, I noticed that a lot of the watching guests had melted away to the sides of the room, leaving us to take the floor.

A thickset man dressed in a silver spacesuit had joined the two girls and started dancing oddly between them, his arms and legs sticking out, straight and stiff like a robot.

Before I could get a good look at who was dancing with the blondes, the music slowed and the lights went very dim. With the sunglasses on, it was virtually impossible to see anything at all. Mikhail still held me, but now he dropped my arm so that both his hands were cupped round my buttocks, pulling me tightly in against him. The music was totally seductive. I held on to his shoulders loosely, my head spinning.

He tipped me backwards over his leg, and slid one hand right up the deep slit cut into my dress. At first it was part of the dance, but then his fingers reached my sensitive parts before I even considered stopping him. For once in my life, I wasn't wearing any underwear. I owned nothing that would fit under this clinging dress. He paused, then brought his other hand up so that all his fingers were fanned out over the tight curls of my pubes.

'What a bonus!' he shouted. 'No knickers!'

I had to grip his shoulders more tightly to avoid falling backwards, so I couldn't slap his hands away even if I'd wanted to. His breath was hot in my ear.

'This would have been very unprofessional if I'd tried

it on downstairs wouldn't it?' he chuckled. 'But up here in Club Crème I can do what I like.'

'They told me you were flamboyant,' I shot back. 'So what *do* you like?'

My legs were shaking with the effort of staying upright. Barely aware of what I was doing, I slid my feet apart so that my legs opened and some of his fingers slipped automatically round to the tender tops of my thighs. We moved slowly in one more circle, his fingers gripping me there, and then he backed me off the dance floor. I couldn't see where I was going. I raised the sunglasses off my nose and had time to see that the matador was still there. I was pleased. If I couldn't get to talk to him, I wanted him to watch me. I just had time to see the two girls with their arms round each other's waists, bearing down on him. He turned his face to speak to them, and then my hand was smartly slapped and the sunglasses clunked back over my eyes.

'I warned you not to take the glasses off,' growled Mikhail. 'Now you suffer the penalty.'

I started to laugh, but Mikhail wasn't joking. He spun me round several times, making me dizzy, and I stumbled on my high heels and then toppled onto something soft – a sofa or some cushions – at the side of the enormous room. It was even darker over here. He must have kept the lights low. I had no hope of seeing anyone or anything. All I could do was feel, and I thought I was feeling Mikhail, but he had somehow got to the sofa first. I put my hands out as I landed. He was lying there already and he was half naked. I groped about to suss him out. At least, he had taken his trousers off. He still had his top on. I expected to feel a stiff-fronted shirt, with studs not buttons, like a dinner shirt. But this shirt felt almost as if it was made of plastic. Like body armour, rather than clothing. I moved my hand up to the neck, to feel for the bow tie, but there was a kind of solid collar there instead.

Someone was changing the music. It was faster again, more heavy rock, but when I struggled to get up off the sofa to see if the lights had been turned up again, I was toppled from behind. Now I was totally confused. I couldn't tell how many people were on this sofa with me. The man beneath me couldn't possibly have pushed me from behind. And now there were definitely two pairs of hands. One pair heaved me into position so that I was straddling the hips of the man beneath me, and it must have been the man underneath who was wrinkling my dress up towards my waist, fingers crawling over my bare skin. The other hands were still on my back, keeping me where I was.

'See what I mean?' Mikhail's voice tickled my ear as he fought the loud music. 'Now me and my friend here are going to put you right in your place.'

I thought I could see shadows flitting around us, some of them bending as if to see what was going on, then flitting off again. The virtual darkness and the heavy music filled my head and, as the fingers inched higher up my dress, circled my waist and came back down again, I tried feebly to knock them away, but they were simply joined by the other fingers probing from behind.

'Just do as Mikhail says,' a girl's voice shouted in my ear. I reckoned it was one of the blondes. 'Everyone else does.'

I decided to stop the struggle and give in to what I really wanted. Because I wanted the fingers to go on feeling me. Without any real use of my eyes and with my ears deafened, I was in a surreal world now where all my other senses were on red alert.

And the most alert sense was my sense of touch. Except I didn't have to do anything. I was the one being touched, and I started to relish the experience. But who was I sitting on top of, if it wasn't Mikhail? They hadn't totally removed my dress, and it felt like a second skin as I shifted on the hips of the man beneath me. I thought the sequins would scratch him. He obviously took my shifting about as a sign that I was ready for something because his hands gripped my hips and lifted me right off him.

'Who is it this time?' I yelled, leaning my head right down towards his face. 'Perhaps it really is you, Ricky the barman?'

He must have been incredibly strong because, without answering, I was hoisted up and away. For a moment I was hovering in the blackened air, my weight supported only by his hands, my own fingertips scrabbling for support on his bare torso. Then I felt something jabbing at me. I'd lost count of the number of fingers that were exploring me, probing inside me, over my buttocks, inside my buttocks, separating my pussy lips, exploring some more, but this wasn't a finger. A little scream bunched up in my throat, but it was a scream of excitement, not fear or surprise. Why was I screaming? I was being groped by two determined men, in the pitch dark and, so far, I hadn't offered one jot of resistance.

It wasn't a finger. It was an incredibly thick, rock-hard penis. I must have been sitting on it or perhaps its owner had brought it to life on his own. I was enjoying the silent permission just to sit here and be slowly and surely touched up and then fucked and, as the filthy thoughts flashed up in neon across the inside of my eyelids, I laughed at myself. My laughter must have made my whole body shake because the hands steadied me for a moment, then started to ease me downwards, forcing my sex lips open to engulf the waiting penis. I tilted forwards a little and the penis slid rapidly inside. I could feel the tiny muscles up and down working to hold it in place.

'Call this a penalty?' I shrieked triumphantly as I was slowly impaled. 'I'd love to know what you think is a reward!'

But it was impossible to hear any reply against the music. I decided to relax, let Mikhail and his henchman do the dirty work. He started to push his penis in further, his movements getting rougher, and that tilted me forwards even further over him so that my hands balanced me on either side of his shoulders. Now my butt was raised higher in the air. My body automatically started its own sensual rhythm, trying to slide up and down the cock, but he didn't move, and I stopped moving, just feeling the cock standing still and erect inside me. Exercising this kind of control was exhilarating, but I couldn't stop my body instinctively gripping and nor, it seemed, could he stop his cock jolting every time I squeezed.

I was holding my breath and, just as I wondered if we were going to sit like this forever, my buttock cheeks were eased apart, tipping me forwards yet again, and the warmth of another torso pressed up against my back. The music was suddenly turned down.

'You don't mind two men going at you like this, do you?' It was Mikhail again, his voice difficult to pin down. I recognised the macho scent of his cigar and his ridiculous politeness. 'You are my guest, after all. You have only to say.'

'Far too late for that,' I croaked. 'I broke the rule of the party, didn't I? And remember, you are actually *my* guest. You're all my guests, here at the club.'

'In that case,' he purred into my ear, his deep voice vibrating through the music, 'turn the volume up, and let the game really begin.'

I let myself fall, or rather be pulled, first forwards, and

then towards Mikhail, who had his erection wedged up between my cheeks. He was sliding it up and down the warm crack, sliding right under me to reach the tender spot where the other man's dick was splicing me open, parting my sex lips still further so that as well as having a big dick stuck inside me, Mikhail's dick was rubbing my clitoris. Someone turned the volume up. I started to rock, wanting to dance in time to the throbbing bass, up and down the pole inside me. The knot of desire which had been tightening behind my navel started to loosen. I wanted to dance, to fling myself wildly about between my two seducers, exercise my new loss of inhibition.

But both men took hold of me and made me stop dead still. Stopping was as titillating as moving, both mentally and physically, because the rest of me still quivered rebelliously and I knew that the men wouldn't be able to hold back for long. The man beneath me took my arms and kept me suspended above him and I flung my head back, willing the hovering orgasm to recede. Then Mikhail brought his stiff cock up to my butt and, instead of sweeping it down through the crack, he started to push it towards my buttonhole. I could feel the virginal, never-touched hole tightening like a clam against the impending intrusion but, at the same time, there was an insistent pulse beating just the other side of the delicate barrier separating the two orifices.

The man beneath me must have felt the new pulsating because his fingers dug into my legs and he started to move his hips. My insides were melting. The other little hole loosened to let Mikhail in. His thick knob pushed in a fraction. I felt myself trying to push him out again. Then the tight muscles slackened to accommodate him, not only to accommodate him but to welcome the alien length of male hardness, so that inch by inch it slid up my backside. I had two thick cocks wedged inside me, impaling me. I was a machine to milk them for all the hot spunky pleasure they had to offer.

I was the Smithson sandwich. The image was as stark as if it had been projected on to the wall in front of me. I could see my mate Chrissie, wedged up against the brick wall, buffeted between the enormous Smithson brothers.

Mikhail was deep inside me now. To think I'd thought he was a trifle camp when he was massaging me in the health suite now seemed ridiculous. His thighs propped me up from behind, and he started to rock back and forth, his breath hot on my neck, one big hand fanned out over my stomach to support us both in that position. I let the rocking move me, carefully at first, amazed at how the complicated design of my body could accommodate two cocks at once. I relaxed and it was like I had two entirely new bodies, front and back, both with conflicting zones of exquisite pleasure, heightened by the novelty of this undiscovered ability and by not being able to see who was doing this to me.

I fell first forwards on to the rigid cock inside my cunt, then back on to the one inside my arse and, as I moved off one, the other penetrated me, so that the storm of orgasm gathered at both places, sluicing up both orifices. My mouth was open and I must have been groaning out loud, though nobody could hear me through the deafening music. We were all three rocking frantically, both men ramming their cocks up so that I was burning down on to them at the same time until the man beneath me could hold his spunk back no longer and the tide came spurting out of him, met by my own convulsive orgasm, and then Mikhail, bringing up the rear literally as his spunk rocketed up inside. I heard him yell out loud with his final thrust just as someone turned the music off.

'Bravo, again!' someone called out, and a leisurely handclap started up all around the room.

I toppled sideways, still gripping one man inside and still with Mikhail wedged up my backside. We lay in a muddled heap for a moment and the clapping got louder and faster. This time I didn't care about disobeying instructions. I flung my sunglasses off, blinking against the blinding glare of light.

The other party guests had gathered round for a good look. Not one of them had sunglasses on. What kind of sucker was I, obeying the rules? This wasn't like the scene in the club bar where the old guys had buggered off to feed their appetites leaving the four of us, and Rick the silent barman, to discover our own devices. Tonight's sex session had been a deliberate, planned, public display. I stared round wildly, unable at first to recognise anybody, but standing inches away from where we had all been writhing about, icy eyes wide with her version of delight and wearing the same white trouser suit, was Avril.

And stretched out beneath me in his spaceman's top, his thick cock subsiding and beginning to slip out of me, was her burly brother: Mr Hall.

'Oh, you're too good at this,' Avril cackled, putting one thin hand out and stroking my face. I crashed off the sofa onto the floor, tugging my dress down over my wet bush. 'It's like pick 'n' mix, isn't it? Club Crème is a veritable treasure trove!'

'I didn't know it was your brother down there,' I protested, still searching the faces of the guests crowding round us. I was searching for the matador. I'd wanted him to watch me. Now I wanted to know what he thought of what I'd done. Was he turned on or shocked? But I couldn't see him. Avril squatted down and turned my face to look at her. She was grinning.

'Well, I knew it was him. I put him there. You've done wonders for me, as I tried to tell you last night,' she said. 'I'm going to have to poach you from this club.'

'It didn't look as if you and Mr Hall needed wonders working,' I replied caustically. 'Though I am a little anxious about what your husband would say. He is, after all, a member of our club as well. He's bound to hear about this.'

Avril put her hand behind her ear. 'Can't hear you with all this noise,' she cried. Then she turned to the others. 'This girl is a natural. Sex on legs. Any man who goes near her can't keep his prick in his trousers, no matter how well brought up he thinks he is. You should have seen her corrupting her aristocratic boss last night.'

'Hang on a minute,' I protested. 'He was corrupting *me*.' But no one was interested in listening to me.

'And she's unleashed a whole new kinky side of me, too. She wasn't to know I'd be hanging around yet again to see what was going on. Now I've discovered the voyeur in me. I wouldn't mind a piece of her myself. This girl is quite irresistible. Isn't she, Jez?'

She got up, and went to sit beside her still-silent brother. He was lying where I'd left him, unable to move in the rigid silver plastic top. Avril started to fondle his softening prick.

'But what about us?' one of the blonde girls piped up, kneeling down and putting her arm round me. She was addressing Mikhail, who was fiddling with his cape behind me. 'How do you think we feel about you screwing the most beautiful girl here?'

'I didn't know you cared,' Mikhail teased.

'Not you, idiot. We want *her*,' the two blondes chorused, pointing at me.

They all started squabbling, and I switched off and let them get on with it. The matador was sitting on the window sill. He was the only person still wearing his sunglasses. As my eyes adjusted to the light I noticed that he was wearing a silver earring. I wanted to get out of the tangle I was in and speak to him. But when he saw me he sprang to the floor.

'Hey, you can't go yet,' Mikhail said when he saw the matador about to leave. 'You haven't told us what you thought of the floor show. Or what you think of the club's luscious new housekeeper.'

'Delightful. The club chose well. She looks good enough to eat. Perhaps next time.'

Everyone laughed and clapped again. Mikhail and I were encircled, like gladiators trapped in the ring. I stood up. I tried to push through the guests to get a closer look at the matador. But they were all crowding round me, stroking my hair, fingering my dress, and the two blondes were acting like bodyguards, each holding one of my arms.

The matador was making for the door now, pushing the sombrero impatiently to the back of his head. And then I saw his hair, smooth, dark, glossy like oil, and the earring, glittering against his dark stubble. He turned his head towards me again. I could see the pinprick of my wide-eyed reflection in his black glasses. I could see my mouth opening, trying to explain myself.

Then Merlin was gone. I went and stood where he had been standing, and looked out of the window. The landscape of rooftops made a different world out there. It was tempting to climb out into the cold air and walk among the chimney pots above the streets. There was bound to be a door leading out from the penthouse on to some kind of roof terrace. But as I felt along the glass for some kind of catch, something outside caught my eye and I saw what Merlin had been looking at so intently.

Directly opposite, separated from this building by a

narrow gulf, were the big windows of a similar pent-house flat. And through the window I could see Sir Simeon. He was naked apart from a towel round his middle and he was doing a series of press-ups on a huge fur rug in front of an open fire. His body was super fit. His skin had the same olive glow as Merlin's, and his arms and legs were long and sinewy. I was impressed. He was in very good shape. But then I knew that, didn't I? At least, I knew that one part of him was in very good shape indeed, even though I'd only felt it sliding up inside me. I'd never set eyes on it.

Mikhail snaked one arm round my waist and lifted me off my feet. He jerked his chin towards the view of Sir Simeon.

'My business partner likes to keep fit,' he chuckled, edging his fingers up under my dress again. 'And just look at who likes to help him.'

As Mikhail bore me away, I just had time to catch sight of Mimi walking over to Sir Simeon's prone body, kicking it over so that he was on his back and lowering herself, very slowly, on to his face.

9

'I've changed my mind. You can take them. Burn them. Whatever. It's time for a change.' I dropped the bag full of my old clothes down in front of Miss Sugar's desk and flung my new camel-hair coat over the back of the spare chair. She continued tapping at her laptop.

'I said –'

'Yes, I heard you,' she snapped, her head jerking up at last. She whipped off her glasses and I wondered how much of a barrier they were intended to be. Her eyes widened and I noticed how long her eyelashes were. She tucked a wisp of hair behind her ear and her small mouth opened a fraction as she took in my new image.

'What do you think? Cool leather trousers, aren't they?' I asked and gave her a twirl. 'Just like Mimi's, in fact. And they fit me like a glove.'

'They certainly do,' she agreed, nodding slowly. She picked up a silver pen and rubbed it across her lips. I saw the tip of her pink tongue licking the end of it. 'And that crisp white shirt suits you perfectly. Tight, but fitting. You look ... totally different. I doubt your best friend would recognise you.'

'That's the idea,' I said laughing, and paced about the office, pretending to look for some papers. 'Miss Breeze here?'

'No. She's gone abroad on business. She told you she was going.'

'But I thought I saw her in Sir Simeon's flat the other night.'

Miss Sugar sighed and shook her head as if I was a thick pupil. 'It was me who summoned you to come here this morning. Not Miss Breeze.'

'You're not going to give me the sack, are you?' I asked. I twisted a strand of hair round one finger, still unused to its new soft sheen and lack of frizz. 'Only I thought I'd displeased Mimi – Miss Breeze – in some way.'

Miss Sugar opened up a pale-blue file from the tidy pile on her desk and read some typed notes stapled inside. The silver pen slipped in and out between her teeth and her thin cheeks hollowed slightly as she sucked the tip of it.

'Much to my surprise, you've had a glowing report,' she remarked, dropping the pen on top of the notes so that a tiny slick of saliva smeared the paper. 'This is the Grey file. It seems that you hit the jackpot with Mrs Grey at the Mikhail party. And he's cross-referenced this report to the Mikhail file, too.'

'So what's the verdict?' I asked, gripping the back of the chair in front of her desk and tapping my new, shiny high-heeled boot impatiently.

Miss Sugar picked up a bright red file and studied it for a moment. Again she tucked an imaginary strand of hair behind her ear. 'Don't get too high and mighty, but Mikhail and Mrs Grey both seem to have taken a shine to you. A good thing too. He's extremely well connected. Just our sort of person.'

She closed both files and took them across to the filing cabinet. She was wearing a severe black suit today. The long jacket was tailored so that it avoided revealing any hint of breast or hip. The skirt skimmed her ankles, which were encased in a pair of pointed ankle boots.

'I like him,' I enthused. 'He's just my sort of person, too.'

'But I'm not so sure about Avril Grey,' Miss Sugar

continued. 'I hope you haven't become too intimate with her. I'm not comfortable with her coming here twice in one week. After all, she's only a guest.'

'Did you know Merlin was at the party too?'

'Merlin? How do you know Merlin?' she asked, her voice high with alarm.

'I met him at Symes Hall.'

'There's no way he was at that party. Sir Simeon would never allow it,' she stated and slammed the filing cabinet shut.

'I'm telling you, he was there.'

'And I'm telling you, he's persona non grata,' Miss Sugar interrupted me sharply. 'But plenty of other people were there. Did you know our Rick the barman was there, for instance? Dressed as a little devil, I daresay. I must admit, Summers, that I have been proved wrong. I never expected you to be such a success quite so soon.'

'So did I get a report from the matador. I mean, Merlin?' I asked eagerly, swinging my leg over the chair as if I was mounting a horse. 'You're a hopeless liar, Sugar. You know he was there.'

'Sir Simeon would kill me, you, everyone, if his son had been allowed to attend that party,' she replied sternly, tucking the cabinet key inside the top drawer of her desk. She lowered herself on to her chair. 'And I'm not at liberty to tell you the details of these reports, anyway. It wouldn't do to give our employees ideas, good or bad, with too much detail.'

She bit her lip and left a small dent.

'Come on, Miss Sugar. You can tell me the truth,' I said softly, leaning forwards a little. I had sprayed on some of Mimi's musky scent which I had found in one of the designer bags, and it wafted off my skin whenever I moved. 'I'm part of the family now, after all.'

She was so bloodless that it took a while for the dent

to fill out again. I stared at her mouth and then realised with a start that her eyes were fixed on mine. I stopped swinging my leg and rested one hand over the other on the edge of her desk in exactly the same way as she had folded hers.

Miss Sugar leaned towards me, as if I was hypnotising her. Her eyes flickered over my face, which must have looked positively radiant compared with her ghostly complexion, and down towards the man's frilled white shirt which I had left unbuttoned as far as the divide of my cleavage so that a suggestion of frothy white lace could be seen curling over my breasts.

'This is strictly confidential,' she whispered, and we both glanced round the empty office. I could smell peppermint on her breath. She was still staring at my cleavage, her nostrils quivering as she breathed in my scent. 'But Sir Simeon and his son Merlin are sworn enemies. They've disagreed over practically everything, from whether or not to sell Symes Hall to whether or not to start the club, which Merlin has always claimed was his idea originally.'

'You told me it was Sir Simeon's brainchild.'

'They both think it was their brainchild,' Miss Sugar said and looked down at her nervous fingers. 'Merlin wanted to fill the club with his brash young friends, but I much prefer the more select, more mature crowd Sir Simeon has targeted since we opened.'

'Hmm,' I mused. 'I had Merlin down as the country bumpkin rather than the man about town, actually. Until I saw him dressed as a matador, that is!'

She didn't share my amusement. 'How well do you know him, for heaven's sake?' she asked.

I shrugged and flicked a paper clip across her desk. 'Enough to fancy him, even though he acts like a mud-spattered Lord Fauntleroy.'

'Well, getting in between those two is like playing with fire,' Miss Sugar said. She picked up the paper clip and started to unravel it. 'To top everything else, they've been fighting over Miss Breeze for years.'

Now she had my attention.

'And if you want my opinion,' she went on, 'they both need to pack it in. It's taking its toll on Sir Simeon and it's a stale old feud. Miss Breeze will probably up and leave them both before long anyway. She's a gypsy at heart.'

Miss Sugar put her hand on her mouth and widened her eyes as if seeing me for the first time.

'You hope!' I remarked cheekily, widening my eyes as well. 'Don't you secretly rather worship Sir Simeon?'

Miss Sugar laughed, a sound that so surprised me that I wasn't sure I'd heard right at first. It was a kind of fishwife's cackle, low and dirty.

'Sir Simeon?' she gasped, swallowing the cackle to silence it. 'It's a long story, Summers, but the short answer is no. I admire and respect him, but I don't want him. Not in the way you mean.' The cackle was allowed out for another brief burst. 'But enough about me. What Sir Simeon and that brat Merlin need is something new to squabble over. New blood. That could be you. That's why you have to do well here.'

It was the first time she'd used my name and, for some reason, I blushed. I sat up abruptly. Two red spots appeared across her cheekbones and she sat up as well.

'Don't you worry about a thing. This job ... those two ... it'll be a piece of cake,' I said and then lowered my voice. 'But I would do a whole lot better if someone paid me.'

Instead of reprimanding my tone, Miss Sugar nodded and opened another drawer in her desk and drew out a cheque. It was for five thousand pounds and it was made out to me.

'Two nights at two and a half grand each,' she said, pushing the cheque across the desk. 'That's how good you are.'

'Sydney, hear I come,' I said under my breath, taking the cheque and holding it up in front of my nose.

'What?'

'Nothing,' I said hurriedly, folding it into my pocket and trying to look as if I got cheques like that every day.

'Who's Sydney?'

I started to laugh. It was a genuine, delighted laugh and it forced a tight smile out of her, too. She had no idea what I meant. She had no idea how important this money was to me. Just in case everything here in London went pear-shaped. It represented a round-the-world ticket, not a man called Sydney. I was halfway to my dream already.

'Talk about easy money,' I chuckled, trying to calm myself down. 'Honestly. A few more group sessions like those and I'll be able to do this job standing on my head.'

'It's not all about sex sessions, Summers. You've been lucky, if you like that sort of thing. But each scenario you find yourself develops differently. You might be playing dominos tonight.'

I pretended to yawn, but she was serious.

'You've only just started. Don't get too complacent,' Miss Sugar said sharply. Her half-smile vanished and she put her glasses back on. I recognised the sign of dismissal. 'OK, you can go now.'

She got up and came round the desk, kicking aside the plastic bag bulging with my old travelling gear. She glared at it as if it had just jumped up and bitten her.

'Don't you wish you were out on the job, Sugar,

instead of stuck in this poky place?' I asked, shrugging on my expensive coat. I couldn't resist stroking the soft camel wool as I buttoned it up, and nor could Miss Sugar. She walked round me, tweaking the back panels of the coat so that it fell easily to my ankles.

'Oh, don't you worry about me. I am still picked by one or two of the members to keep them company on occasion,' she replied, pulling my hair over the coat collar then retreating quickly to the safety of her desk. 'My time will come again. You can be sure of that. Now go. I'm shutting up shop for the day.'

I went out in to the hall and turned. Miss Sugar was still standing by the desk, nudging disdainfully at my old clothes with her foot. She looked like a cross between a nun and an undertaker.

'Ever thought about wearing scarlet, Miss Sugar?' I tossed the remark over my shoulder and escaped into the kitchen to discuss my new idea for a school dinners' menu.

10

Miss Sugar was right. I spent the next few evenings playing an extremely ferocious version of Racing Demon in the pale-yellow drawing room with three gentleman farmers, a gay interior designer and two earnest fly-fishermen. Not one of them suggested a strip-Racing Demon, or anything more wicked than a round of Irish coffee, but I had to admit that the card games were fun nevertheless.

Each night Rick the barman brought in a tray of drinks before locking-up time. The Irish coffee soon gave way, at my persuasion, to fiery shots of tequila which sent rapid flushes into everyone's cheeks and evil glints into their eyes. Rick the barman just looked at me and gave a little nod. He never uttered a word about what he'd seen in the club bar. My days with the accounts ledger and my evenings with the card players were so tame that I began to wonder if my first few days working at Club Crème had been a wet dream.

Either that, or someone was deliberately keeping me out of the loop.

On my next day off, I left my crummy flat to go for a run. If I wasn't going to get my kicks from any more antics at the club, I would at least keep myself in shape. I decided to treat myself to a Mikhail massage later, too. Perhaps see what else Mikhail had to offer.

But first I had to get the blood pumping. Once I'd got into my stride I ran north as far as Kensington Gardens, where I decided to have a mini picnic. I sat down on a bench by the Round Pond, munching a cream cheese and smoked salmon bagel. It was too cold for a picnic, or any other outdoor activity, but I had to have sustenance before I made the run back home to get ready for work.

I stared at the people going by, all leaning against the icy wind as they picked their way carefully over the slimy droppings left round the edge of the pond by the hungry birds. Suddenly, a thin wiry woman with white-blonde hair cropped very short jogged past me. She'd already been past me once, I realised, and I also realised with a jolt who she was. Her cheeks were pink with exertion and she had a portable CD player clipped to her waistband. She was wearing a lilac sweat top, minute lilac shorts and fingerless gloves, but it was Avril Grey all right.

I pulled my hood up quickly and she didn't recognise me. She glanced briefly at my own trainers and old jogging pants before dodging off the path across the scraggy grass in the direction of the bandstand. I tossed some crumbs to my gaggle of ducks and stood up. I couldn't sit still any longer. I shook my legs, keeping my ankles loose, and glanced round the pond once more. Hardly anyone was daft enough to hang around on a freezing day like this. A couple of black guys were holding hands and skating up and down the wide walk-way known as the Broad Walk, a young family was trying to launch a fleet of model yachts onto the glassy water and a bloke dressed in multicoloured lycra and a helmet was hunched on the ground, trying to fix the chain back on to his upturned bike.

I jogged after Avril. Perhaps I would try to make friends with her. She was prickly and competitive, not to mention decidedly kinky, but she could be a helpful ally if I wanted to have some fun. The last few nights had been dull, but not even a spate of sedate card games could dull my appetite now that it had been whetted. Perhaps I could invite her to the club tonight, liven things up a little. Perhaps the two of us could attract Sir Simeon's attention. Avril wanted Sir Simeon. But so did I. Even without Miss Sugar's encouragement, I wanted to dig underneath that cool exterior. Get face to face with him, this time.

Avril was over by the bandstand now, one leg resting on the edge while she did some stretching exercises. She had unzipped her lilac top and wore a cropped white vest underneath and, as she leaned back, I could see her stomach, ridged with muscle. Then she bent herself forwards until she was lying along her own extended leg, and the ridiculously tiny lilac shorts slipped right into the crack between her tight buttocks, showing quite clearly the dark curve leading towards her pussy. The crease where the cheeks met the top of her legs parted and closed as she stretched. The shorts were struggling to keep her covered. It was just possible to catch a glimpse of her pubes separated by the dividing cotton crotch, the pale lips parting with the movement of her leg to reveal a delicate magenta sliver of flesh before vanishing again.

I jogged a little nearer, unable to resist a closer look. It must be deliberate, I thought, her wearing tiny shorts like that on a cold day but, apart from me, no one else was near enough to notice.

I veered off onto another path, speeding up my stride, taking lungfuls of air while London hummed in the distance, losing myself in the growing power of my limbs. What was I thinking, trying to get close to a woman like that?

I heard a muffled shriek behind me. I spun round in time to see the lilac jogger slipping on some bird mess and crashing to the ground right in front of my abandoned bench. I jogged up and down on the spot for a moment, wondering whether to go over and help, but the cycling man was already there. He had propped his bike up against the bench and was helping her to her feet. I could see she was swearing, holding one leg out and hopping about, and I could also see that he was trying to calm her down, patting the bench.

There was obvious confusion before he realised that she couldn't hear him. He reached up and took the earphones off her ears and repeated what he had been saying. She blinked at him, and bowed her head, perhaps apologising for her language. He seemed to have tamed her. She sat down obediently on the bench and he sat down beside her.

As he did so, something glittered against his cheek. I squinted, but I couldn't see that far. Then I remembered I had brought my tiny camera with me, sentimentally thinking I'd take some wintry pictures of London. I fixed the zoom lens on the pair. The cyclist was wearing a silver earring. My heart started thumping. I wanted Sir Simeon, sure. But I wanted his son, too.

On impulse, I decided to take some photographs. I fired off a couple of shots, then kept the zoom fixed on the pair as they started talking. He lifted her ankle and prodded it, just like he had touched my bruised foot when we were sitting in the kitchen at Symes Hall. She tipped her head back, grimacing in exaggerated pain. Then she leaned forwards, gripping the bench behind his neck, and kicked her foot playfully into his chest.

These two knew each other. This was no chance encounter. They had planned to meet. So much for Merlin fighting his corner for Miss Breeze. He obviously had a taste for the butch, crop-haired type as well as curvaceous red-heads and dusky older women. What a hound.

I kept the camera fixed on Merlin and Avril the jogger, using the zoom lens as binoculars, and felt a weird raw heat of jealousy spreading through me. I wanted him to touch me like that. Seeing him again made me hungry. I had been permanently hungry since he'd fucked me on his father's bed.

Their faces were very close, but it looked as if they were just talking. I raced over to a tree that was closer to the bench to get a better angle. This way she wouldn't see me, but Merlin would if he looked up. I wanted him to see me. But what would he see if he did look up? I wasn't tarted up in a sequinned sheath dress today like I'd been at Mikhail's party. I was wearing an ancient long-sleeved Breton shirt and navy jogging pants and my hair was scrunched up in a ponytail. Meanwhile, his new companion had a barely there vest (and barely there tits too, I thought cattily) and tiny shorts. Where would he prefer to look?

I squatted down in the longer wet grass beside the tree, lifted the camera again to look and bit my lip until I tasted blood.

He had let go of her foot and she had allowed it to slide down, but her knee was still hooked over his and she swung her leg so that they both rocked slightly with the momentum. From here I could see that his full-length cycling gear was skintight, like a wetsuit, black over most of his torso and thighs, then flaring into flame colours down the arms and legs. I could see his rangy, lean frame, which the cycling kit hugged possessively. It would be hugging his crotch possessively, too. That bold young cock would be lying in wait, waiting to be coaxed into life. And she was going to be the lucky one to do it, if I didn't stop them.

A few people were still strolling or skating up and down the wide walkway, but the family of model-boat sailors had gone, and the afternoon was drawing in. A cold breeze came off the pond, ruffling Avril's short hair, and I shivered, but the two of them were warm enough. He was sealed inside his cycling outfit and she was still panting and flushed from her run.

I zoomed the camera in closer. She was fingering his neck now, her hand coming off the back of the bench and sliding under his tight collar. He started to take off his helmet but she stopped him, patting it playfully back on to his head. From here it looked as if he was maintaining the good Samaritan approach, while she was evidently out to play. Watch and learn, I told myself. This woman knew how to get a man to scratch her itch.

She was already at work. I knew how a brisk run in the cold air could get the juices flowing. Her blood would be singing. She would still be out of breath. Her veins and muscles would be fired up with exercise and with fury at falling over in front of him. But now she had his attention. I realised he was going to do nothing to encourage her. She was going to do it all.

She shifted herself on the bench, waving her other arm about as she obviously started to tell him something about herself, and crossed her legs into the lotus position. Merlin glanced down at her crotch, which was now open and inviting. He allowed one finger to trail up her shin. Soon she wouldn't be able to help herself. I clicked the camera. I wriggled on my haunches, itching to know where his finger would go next, my breath catching as the sensitive skin inside my own fanny started to fidget.

Merlin fiddled with the catch of his helmet, doing it up again as if he was preparing to leave, and the woman grabbed his wrist and pulled his hand down, pressing it on to her thigh. She started to rub the inside of both her thighs then, rising closer and closer to her shorts which were straining across her crotch, and then suddenly she jammed her thumb up under the hem of her shorts, yanking the material aside. She tweaked her finger between her sex lips and flipped them open. Her pubes were still completely shaved, and I could not stifle my own gasp at the sudden intimate redness revealed there. She held the material away from herself, inviting, demanding, that he look at her.

His face was impassive. She would like that. This was a woman used to a fight, I could tell. But I wanted to be where she was. I wanted to be sitting in front of him with my legs open, seeing his haughty blue eyes sizing me up again. He'd not been impassive with me. His reactions, once I was stripped bare and lying beneath him, had been written clearly all over his face.

I picked up the camera and clicked again. I realised I could zoom the powerful lens in closer still, and now I could see that there was a definite bulge in his groin. I felt a mixture of horror and fascination. There was no denying his male reaction to Avril's brazen mating display, even though he was still giving nothing else away. And she had noticed his growing hard-on, for sure, because, while she started to slide one finger up and down her exposed red slit, she put her hand on his groin, stroking the outline of the erection she could see there. She was talking to him again. He kept his hand on her leg, didn't try to move hers away from his crotch, and I burned again with envy as I stood up to focus my camera more closely.

Avril started fingering herself urgently while her determined other hand slid up and down the length of his bulging groin. He bit his lip, but still didn't move to help her or touch her. I chuckled to myself. She would have a hard time finding her way inside his all-in-one suit. There wasn't even a visible zip. But she knew better. Her hand disappeared for a moment and then I saw her easing the tight top over his stomach and pulling at the waistband of the trousers. They may have been tight, but they obviously had to stretch while he was cycling and, using both hands now, she was able to get them down over his hips. He wiped one hand under his helmet and she, like me, took that as the first sign of weakening. She got his trousers halfway down, so that the tip of his penis showed, and then she let go of him for a moment so that she could quickly wriggle out of her own shorts and toss them onto the ground.

They both glanced about to check if anyone could see them and that was when Merlin caught sight of me. I couldn't see the expression in his eyes because I quickly lowered the camera and he was too far away, but he kept looking in my direction. I stiffened, wondering whether to run away, pretend that I hadn't seen what they were doing or keep spying.

Avril murmured something to him, unaware of me, then spread her legs wider and holding her sex lips open with one hand, started to frisk herself, sliding several fingers in and out of the hairless crack, lifting her bum off the seat as the obvious excitement started to take her over. Then she grabbed his hand, the one that was still resting on her thigh, and forced it towards her so that she could start rubbing herself up and down the palm of his hand, then across his fingers, swivelling and twisting her hips as she opened and closed her legs over his hand.

For a moment longer, Merlin kept his eyes on me and it was only when I lifted the camera that he turned to see what she was doing.

My legs were shaking, both from a horrible jealousy at watching the pair of them and from my own unwelcome, violent arousal. With every seductive wriggle that she gave on her naked butt, with every flex of her arm as her fingers drove up inside her, my own snatch wept sympathetic juices until I could bear it no longer. I squatted down again, sitting squarely on my heel so that my clit was pressed against my ankle bone and I felt dampness seeping through the soft cloth of my jogging pants.

Suddenly, Avril sprang like a cat onto the seat of the bench so that now she was spread over him, balancing just above his legs. She held on to the bench with one hand and with the other felt for the tip of his cock and slowly drew it up, out of his trousers. His hand, the one that had been resting on her thigh, gripped the bench an inch or two from hers, but didn't touch it. I smirked to myself. He didn't really fancy her, I was sure. I didn't know what he was up to, but surely this wasn't a meeting of long-time lovers. More likely he was doing this to spite Sir Simeon. And now he'd seen me, he would be spiting me as well.

Avril wouldn't know it. But I knew it. How angry she would be if she knew. The delight at this possibility coiled up inside me, dragging my sexual excitement with it. She must be getting a trifle irritated by his lack of response.

As if she could hear me, she yanked his trousers right down and under him, so that his flat stomach, the sudden, shocking mat of dark curling hair and the long, straight cock were all revealed in the open air of the park. I shut my eyes for a moment. Did I really want to catch all this on camera?

Yes, I did. I gritted my teeth and focussed the camera right in on his groin, but I was nearly knocked off balance as his handsome coffee-coloured cock reared out of his trousers. It quivered slightly, as if it was greeting me. I whimpered out loud, grinding my wet cunt on to the hard bone of my heel.

Avril was obviously stunned at the sight as well

because at first she didn't touch it. I held my breath, shocked at my own reaction, and I willed her to leave it, leave it alone. This one's mine.

When I turned back she had regained the upper hand. She pulled his cock right out of his trousers, stretching it to its full splendid length. She rubbed her thumb over the plum end, then curled her hand into a fist and moved it up and down the hard shaft. I didn't want to look at his face just then; I didn't know how much lust, if any, it would register. But my clit was bleeping, burning for attention, yearning for that cock to be pleasuring me.

But she was rising up over it now, kneeling up so that his face was against her chest. Now she seemed keen to get his cycling helmet off, but it was his turn to shake his head. Again I felt a hot coiling of nasty delight inside my chest. There was pure, physical lust going on over there. There was no affection. He wouldn't touch her intimately. He wouldn't take his helmet off, even to fuck her. That pleased me. It was different from the way he'd been with me, even though he'd pretended to be indifferent afterwards. I longed to tell Avril Grey she was second best.

But then again, how could I complain after what I'd been up to in the last few days? Just one flick of the clit and it seemed that I was anybody's, so how could I object to Merlin letting this rampant jogger wriggle all over him?

Once more I lifted the camera, checking first how many frames I had left. She was lowering herself slowly on to the tip of his dick and, without any pubic hair obscuring the details, it was clear as day what was happening. I watched in fascination as her fleshy, naked lips nibbled at his cock, then slowly engulfed the first inch, then the first half of it. His hand on the bench tightened, the knuckles white.

I gave myself a break and looked round the park. Dusk had nearly fallen. There was no one else in this part of the gardens, only a few people making for the gates and, at the Bayswater end of the Broad Walk, a pair of bright headlights switched on. Merlin and Avril noticed, too. She grinned broadly and thumped right down on his lap, swallowing his penis whole. She wrapped her strong legs round his hips and started to buck against him.

The light was failing. The only way for me to catch this ultimate moment was to get closer and risk being seen. Under the cover of the gathering dusk, I slipped out from behind the tree and dodged to the next one. Even Merlin had not noticed me this time. He was supporting his weight by leaning backwards a little on the seat of the bench while she tilted herself wildly, grinding herself against him, flinging her head right back and pumping against him so that he was shoved across the seat with each of her determined thrusts. I ran silently like an invading soldier across the wet grass to the next bench, and the trusty camera clicked silently, catching the pair of them, arching away from each other more like dancers in a modern ballet than ecstatic lovers, arms and heads flung apart, their bodies joined at the groin.

The headlights were swinging slightly as the park warden's vehicle got closer to the pond. Merlin and Avril were up against it if they didn't want to be caught. I had one last exposure. The red light on the camera showed me that it was using its automatic flash, it clicked silently one more time and caught the woman as she rose up on her muscled thighs, straightened her spine, flung her arms out sideways and let out a ragged howl of triumph.

The creaking engine of the vehicle had reached the pond now. The headlights swept briefly over the scene as it started its circuit of the pond. I couldn't hear whether Merlin called out in the height of his own pleasure. I couldn't tell if he had climaxed or not. His torso was still angled away from Avril, even though she was trying to wrap her arms around his shoulders and pull him towards her for a kiss.

He pointed towards the headlights, which any moment would sweep over this side of the pond and catch, not only Merlin and Madam Jogger, but me as well. I ran across the grass to the set of trees that led towards the Kensington exit and waited. He would have to come this way and I wanted to get his attention.

By the time I looked back, they were both standing. The headlights had fixed on them and they were shielding their eyes against the glare. I felt a bubble of laughter rising in my chest. What stories this park warden must have to tell. Before he had a chance to get out of his cart, Avril, after some sort of argument, started to run away from the scene. Merlin stood and watched her go, then swung his leg over his bike. He paused and looked around. I stepped out from my hiding place and waved, but he didn't see me and, before I could make a move towards him, he pushed his bike off in the opposite direction and disappeared into the darkness.

11

He'd slipped through my fingers twice now. Once dressed as a matador; once masquerading as a cyclist. Once watching; once being watched. Yet I had to go after Merlin and taste him again. I risked enraging Miss Breeze, but I had the excuse that Miss Sugar was virtually ordering me to do it.

The weekend was already upon us. I hadn't returned the MG to Sir Simeon. I would hold it hostage for the time being; it might provide a handy excuse for getting under his skin when the time was right.

The listless-looking girls I'd seen last time were just trotting out of the stable yard when I arrived at Symes Hall. Two teenage lads were forking up piles of dung and straw from the stables. But there was no sign of Merlin or his dilapidated truck, and the boys didn't know where he was. In any case, they said, they were leaving now, too.

I debated for a moment whether to turn round and go back to London. But that was stupid. An empty Saturday stretched in front of me. I was dressed in my older riding breeches today and, when I saw that the chestnut horse was here, I decided to take her out for a ride anyway.

I wandered into the tack room to find her saddle. I remembered the sight of Merlin's cute butt bending over in his tight boxers when he was in here getting changed. What I hadn't noticed before was a big western saddle strapped to its own frame in the darkest corner, big as an armchair. I jumped up and sat astride it for a moment, my legs spread wide to get comfortable on the wide seat. No wonder cowboys had bandy legs. My cunt quivered faintly with the rocking motion as I pretended to be riding along. The leather felt warm, as if it had only just been lifted off a sweating mount, and creaked as if it was speaking.

Outside, the wind rattled the stable doors and knocked over a bucket, but there was no one else here. There was only the image of Merlin's bottom offered to me as he got changed, and later his dark, sardonic (or was that satanic?) face gazing and his muscular torso arching as he held himself above me and fucked me on his father's bed. My body had grown hot with longing just thinking about it.

On impulse, I peeled my breeches off and climbed back onto the big saddle, wriggling my red satin knickers down in to it and smiling at the creaking sound it made. I grasped the high rounded pommel at the front with one hand and the back panel of the saddle with the other and slid myself back and forth until the leather heated up with the friction and I felt my private parts vibrating with the heat. The satin slid easily across the leather, the knickers quickly growing damp with exertion and secret excitement. The smell of the leather grew stronger, mingled with my own sweet aroma.

I closed my eyes, raising myself off the seat as far as the long stirrups would allow me so that the chilly air could get to my bare pussy. Then I banged myself down on to the seat, rubbing frantically up and down the saddle, tilting myself so as to feel the heat in every crevice, spreading my legs wider so as to press my clit down on the leather surface and start rubbing some more. I started to quiver with excitement. I couldn't stop myself. I was still holding on to the saddle to support myself, fingering the high, rounded phallic pommel itself. Now I was eager to get something big and hard inside me. I clambered to my knees and lowered myself on to it. It was too big to get inside me, but the shape of it was perfect for my private game and, before long, I was squealing with growing pleasure as I gyrated round it.

'Did you know,' came a deep voice into the dusty silence, 'that pommel means "little apple"?'

I half groaned, half laughed at the interruption, but I wasn't going to let him stop me now I was in full flow. I raised one hand in the air as if I was about to throw a lasso, grasped the pommel hard with the other hand and bucked myself wildly until the rapid climax streaked through me and I felt truly dirty and wanton.

Now I had to face the music, or, rather, the Merlin. I panted for breath and lifted my chin. 'Well, there's nothing little about you from what I can remember,' I jested.

'Been watching me a lot lately, haven't you? Got some good photographs?' he said with a smirk, as if I was some kind of peeping Tom. Then he walked in front of me and lifted a saddle and bridle from off their hooks. 'Don't they give you enough to do at that club?'

'Plenty,' I retorted, swinging my leg over as if I was sitting side-saddle, still wearing the knickers. I crossed my legs demurely. 'But you already know that.'

'It hardly looked like hard work from where I was standing. What could be so difficult about entertaining Mikhail and his friends?'

'I was there to keep an eye on them.'

He shook his head as if my bleating excuses were simply not good enough. 'Whatever you say. But if you're so busy, what are you doing here?' he said.

I didn't want him to think I was just hanging around to get a glimpse of him, although that was pretty close to the truth. 'I'm allowed to come down here to ride the horses on a weekend, aren't I?'

'Did you ask Sir Simeon? Strictly speaking they're his horses, not mine,' Merlin said. He sauntered back towards the door and kicked it open. The air whistling in from the yard was bitterly cold, and I jumped down from the saddle to get my breeches.

'Oh, he won't mind,' I lied airily, thinking fast. 'As far as he's concerned I can do what I like with his belongings. Got quite a soft spot for me, your father has.'

If I was hoping to get a rise from Merlin, I was failing. My opinion of him was starting to revert to square one. An arrogant little oik, no matter who his father was. I scrabbled into my breeches, pulled up my boots and stumped out after him.

He was already saddling up the grey horse and, without another word to me, he swung himself up on to her back and started to walk her through an archway towards the parkland.

'Wait for me,' I called, but he ignored me. Right, I thought. I'm not leaving here empty handed.

A few moments later, I squeezed the chestnut mare's sides with my ankles and we cantered out across the parkland. Merlin's horse was still walking slowly, almost thoughtfully but, when he heard me coming up behind him, Merlin clicked his tongue and spurred his horse into a gallop. Soon we were racing each other across the frost-hard fields with Sir Simeon's house crouching in the distance. Merlin kept in front of me, riding like a jockey with his bum raised off the saddle, his buttocks round and hard in his white jodhpurs, his long black hair streaming out behind him.

His long brown fingers were curled on the reins, controlling his horse as we raced. The blood was pounding through me, beating in time to the drum of hooves. I was determined to catch him, but he was keeping his distance. I was beginning to tire of gripping for dear life to my racing steed when suddenly Merlin swerved into a nearby coppice and disappeared. With one last effort I urged my horse and chased after him.

The coppice was dense, with overhanging branches and tree roots just waiting to trip us up. I could just see Merlin's horse flickering through the stark winter shadows up ahead, obviously knowing perfectly well which way to go. For a few seconds, they disappeared from view, and then I burst into a small clearing enclosed by tall oak trees and knee deep in fallen leaves.

He had stopped dead. He was already off the horse, feeding her some sugar lumps. Without a word he stepped forwards and pulled me off my horse, practically hurling me against a tree trunk. My legs were shaking from the gallop, my breath coming in ragged gasps. Before I could inhale any air into my lungs, Merlin's mouth was hot and wet, crushing down on mine. I twisted my face away, purely because I couldn't breathe. A dark look of uncertainty flickered across his face, but he knew damn well that I wasn't going anywhere. I got my breath then pulled his chin and mouth towards me again. I nibbled greedily on his lips like the horse nibbled its sugar lumps, sucking in his breath as he kissed me. Then he made me screech with pain and delight, making the horses look up and shake their heads, as he started to lift my shirt and my bare flesh scraped over the cold rough bark of the tree.

'Is this what you came chasing down here for?' he demanded. He grabbed my breasts so roughly that it hurt. 'A good seeing to in the open air with a real man?'

'Like you and Avril, you mean, out there on a park

bench? I'm not the only one who's ventured out of her natural habitat. What were you doing in London? You wanted me, didn't you?'

I enjoyed the flash in his eyes when he saw the scarlet bra under my scarlet shirt. He had no idea how horny it made me, having my shirt yanked aside, seeing the scarlet-clad tits poking upwards to greet him. Last time, he'd murmured 'later, later'. Well, now the time had come. I wanted to silence any remarks from that sardonic mouth, feel it wrapping round my erect nipples instead. I wanted to see him weakened by lust for my body, see if I could capture more of him. I wanted, with Miss Sugar's words ringing in my ears, to see if I could make him forget all about the charms of Mimi Breeze.

'Maybe I wanted to see if riding horses was your favourite thrill,' he said. He pulled the scarlet lace off one swelling breast and we both looked down at the dark red nipple springing up hard against the cold air.

'I'm happy so long as I've got something big and strong and red-blooded pounding between my legs,' I said. I was scrabbling about for something nonchalant to say, but it wasn't working. I could hear a moan of desire already gathering in my throat.

'But you'd rather be mounted by a well-hung man, wouldn't you, Miss Summers? Or do you fancy going bestial, trying a little stallion action?'

He bent his head and swiped his tongue across my tits, teasing me, circling the flesh, nipping, biting, keeping a few millimetres from the burning points. He let his tongue flicker out, just tickling the flesh that was puckering up with anticipation. Then he went in for the kill and I nearly screamed with gratitude. He took one taut nipple in his teeth and worried at it, causing actual, delirious pain.

'Is that what you reckon you are?' I taunted, pretty weakly. 'The stallion action?'

My breasts throbbed with the cold as well as the pleasure. They were desperate for more. The thrill of being outside, and the risk of being caught, was intoxicating, but so was the way the bitter cold whipped up the blood beneath my skin.

'Ask all the grateful wenches around here.'

His teeth were really sharp on me now, nipping and biting, and sending a livid desire zigzagging through me. It was weird. We had been more gentle, almost affectionate, with each other last time, even though we had been strangers. This time we were still strangers, exchanging insults, but he was the aggressor today, and I was only too happy to submit.

'What is it about you rough tough country types? Think you're God's gift to womankind.'

'That's because we are. You know bloody well how good I am,' he panted. 'But seeing that you've come all this way, I'll show you. Or rather, I'll remind you.'

He hoisted me higher up against the tree, holding me up with his hands and the strength of his thighs. I kicked my jodhpurs and knickers right off so that he could spread my legs open and I could grip round his body. The tensing of all my muscles only made me more horny, more impatient to get him inside me, but I could only grip him hard with my legs and ankles and wait for him to find his way in.

I couldn't even grab at his cock, but now he was scrabbling at his flies, getting his own jodhpurs unzipped enough to get his beautiful fat penis out ready to ram straight up me. He pulled me down on to it, still supporting me with his hands and thighs, and impaled me on his stiff length. We kissed until we were dizzy with lack of oxygen, and we humped against the tree, grunting like animals, the cold air trying to creep into every exposed orifice and under every flap of clothing.

'Bestial enough out here, you filthy mare?' he whispered into my ear. 'Or would you prefer to get on all fours back there in the stable? I'm sure me and the lads could easily arrange it. Give you a proper rogering.'

The horses stamped their feet disapprovingly and jingled their bridles as if they understood him. The idea was appalling, but still the thought of being at the mercy of several rough stable lads' cocks was intoxicating. His shocking words drove us on, gasping and grunting, my thighs locked tight around his waist while he ground up me and up me, until I felt his dick contract and, with a final violent thrust, he spurted his hot liquid into me.

'Don't you dare. I'm not done with you,' I groaned. I wriggled myself frantically down his length, tighter onto him, and caught up with him, squeezing the breath out of him with my legs until we slithered down, skin and clothes scratching and scraping, onto the mossy, muddy roots of the tree.

I looked past Merlin's black hair where he rested against my shoulder and blinked up at the white sky. The bony fingers of the bare branches were totally still in the windless afternoon. The silence was tangible. How different from London, where there was never silence, even high up in a penthouse.

I couldn't work out where I felt more at home. All my life I had felt at one with the earth and the sky, as I did just now, but perhaps that was because I had a gorgeous man lying on top of me, his warm cock still fitted inside. There was a part of me that was itching to get back to London, too. I wanted to know what else, or who else, might be waiting for me at Club Crème.

'Come back to London with me,' I said, sitting up and realising just how cold it was. 'We could have so much fun.'

'I know. I've seen what sort of fun you're into,' he replied, jumping to his feet and pulling up his breeches. 'Remember? I was at Mikhail's party.'

'And I've seen what you got up to in the park with Avril Grey,' I retorted. 'So if there's fun to be had up in the city, why do you skulk about down here all the time? Are you really a country bumpkin or do you stay away from the city because you and your father have fallen out?'

'Neither, as it happens,' he snapped. His response shocked me. 'I skulk down here, as you put it, because I run this country estate. I don't know if that makes me a bumpkin. As for what goes on between my father and me – that's none of your business. You are an employee, if I remember rightly. A housekeeper. And as far as I'm concerned you're just a roll in the hay.'

It was like a slap in the face. I grabbed his arm as he walked over to his horse and turned him to face me.

'I was right the first time!' I shouted, still heated from our lustful encounter. 'You *are* an arrogant oik! Your father is worth ten of you!'

'So they keep telling me.'

'Who keeps telling you? Mimi, perhaps?'

'Oh, very good. You really do have your snout in our business, don't you?' he said. His face was twisted with anger where a few minutes ago it had been close up against mine, loosening with desire and rapid satisfaction. Something told me to ease up on him.

I backed off. In any case, I realised I must look crazy trying to have a go at him when I was naked from the waist down, still dripping with our mingled juices and starting to shiver. I yanked up my knickers and trousers and buttoned up my jacket. But still I couldn't stop shivering.

Instead of galloping off and leaving me, he watched me silently, tightening the buckle on his girth unnecessarily and absently patting his horse.

'I'm sorry, Merlin,' I said, when I was dressed. I stumbled over the leaves to get to my horse, but my legs still felt weak and I was extremely cold now. 'That was out of order. You're right, I am just an employee. But I'm not *your* employee, remember. I work for Sir Simeon. And I was told these things about you. I wasn't prying. In fact, I only mentioned you because I saw you at Mikhail's party, and it was pretty obvious from Miss Sugar's attitude that you weren't supposed to be there.'

He nodded, and pulled me towards him. His body was warm, despite the dropping temperatures around us, and I huddled into his chest.

'I know. It doesn't take a rocket scientist to work out that I'm persona non grata at the club. The invisible man. The oik. Take your pick. But I was at that party because Mikhail is my friend, not my father's. Just as Mimi was my friend, before she was his ... it's a very sore point.'

'Tell me.'

'No. It doesn't feel right talking about her, when I've just fucked you.'

'Charmingly put. Now tell me.'

He sighed, but he still held on to me. 'I met Mimi Breeze in Paris. I was an art student, she was the nude model for our life drawing class. Nothing like as grand as she is now, but every bit as sensational. You can imagine it, can't you? Reproduced by the students' sweaty hands on canvasses throughout the land, as Venus, as the Madonna, as a thousand different women. Anyway, I persuaded her to come back to England with me. Like a fool I introduced her to my father. I was mad about her. Who wouldn't be? You've seen how she operates.'

I nodded, remembering her hands on me, on my hair, her fingers thrusting up me, our bodies reflected in her Venetian mirror.

'And so he came under her spell, too. She took him over. Club Crème was her idea. His flat in London was her idea. Becoming his lover was her idea . . .'

'Now that I don't believe,' I sputtered, trying not to laugh. 'Are you sure it wasn't the other way round? Your father's perfectly capable of deciding his lovers for himself.'

'Whatever. They're the same as each other. That's why he and I don't get on, because we're simply not the same. He wields his power like a big stick and everyone dances,' he said. His grip tightened around me. 'You dance to his tune, don't you?'

I flushed scarlet. I couldn't look at Merlin. I'd danced on the end of his father's prick, to be precise. He'd taken me from behind, cool as a cucumber, hardly mopped his brow afterwards. In the space of a week I'd been up close and personal with both Merlin's enemies, if only he knew it. The thought of Mimi and Sir Simeon, either as a pair or separate, made me hot and cold. And I wanted Merlin, too. I wanted them all.

Now it was my turn to fiddle with my horse's bridle.

'We'd better get going,' I announced. 'I'm freezing my tits off here.'

'But he's not as clever as he thinks he is,' Merlin went on, letting me go. 'Because she'll come crawling down here again to see me when he starts to show his age. I'm sure of it.'

I stuck my foot in the stirrup and hoisted myself up on to the chestnut horse.

'I wouldn't be so sure,' I warned him. 'Your father will never slow down. And Mimi doesn't crawl anywhere.'

'Not jealous of her, are you?' he mocked as we walked our horses out of the coppice. It was getting dark now, and I was yearning for a hot bath.

'Jealous? *Moi*? Not my place to be jealous,' I said. I leaned over my horse's neck, ready to take flight. I was lying. I *was* jealous. I didn't want to think about Miss Breeze sitting on Sir Simeon's face. I didn't want to think of her up against a tree, wrapped like a limpet around Merlin. But I couldn't tell him that, could I? 'I'm just the housekeeper, remember?'

'Not *my* housekeeper. Which means –'

'That we can do what we like. No one belongs to anyone else. We're all free spirits, after all,' I cut in, galloping away from him. I wasn't ready for what he might say next.

But I wasn't making sense. Because actually, I wasn't sure just how free I was any more.

12

The London Eye was deserted. Not surprisingly, as I'd agreed to be there at crack of dawn. No self-respecting tourist would try to queue up and sightsee at this hour and in this kind of suffocating fog.

In fact the whole area was eerie. The Thames slid silently between the two banks and even the rumble of cars and buses crossing the bridges was muffled. I shivered inside my camel coat, glad of the creamy pashmina I'd wrapped round my throat, and waited.

When I'd returned to London I'd dropped by the club, something I felt compelled to do all the time now. Miss Sugar had shoved the telephone at me the moment she saw me hovering in the doorway of the office, and I barely had time to ask who it was when Mr Grey, Avril's husband, started ranting into my ear.

'You saw them in the park, didn't you? Don't be embarrassed. She told me you saw them,' he had said.

'Well, yes, I did. I was running, and so was she, and then she bumped into Merlin.'

'They arranged it. She's insatiable. She'll fuck anything with a pulse if it'll get her to Simeon. She thinks all her antics will get his attention.'

'And I suspect Merlin did it to annoy Sir Simeon, too. He knows that messing with his club members, or at least their wives, is guaranteed to get Sir Simeon's back up.'

'Hah! Some wife.'

There had been a crackling silence as he breathed heavily.

'Why do you want to speak to me, Mr Grey?' I had asked.

'I want the photographs,' he had spat back. 'Don't be embarrassed. She told me you took photographs.'

'She calmly told you that? Wow. She doesn't give a shit, does she?' I had said and laughed with disbelief.

Miss Sugar had frowned at me and shook her head. Evidently we were not allowed to use bad language with members like that. But then again, we were allowed to copulate in front of them if the mood took us, so where was the harm?

'I want to see the photographs,' he had repeated miserably.

'I can get them developed this evening, no problem. They'll be here for you to collect in the morning, if that's what you really want.'

'I'm not meeting you there,' he had yelped. 'I'm not setting foot in that damn club ever again.'

And now he was ten minutes late for our rendezvous. The fog seemed to be getting thicker. I would give it another ten and then scarper.

'This is like a spy movie, isn't it?'

I turned. A man in a long tweed coat and spectacles was striding quickly towards me. I'd barely noticed him that first morning at Symes Hall, getting up on his borrowed horse to go hunting. I'd been too busy disliking Avril and having my foot stamped on. Now, as I shook Mr Grey's hand, I tried in vain to link him with Avril. The cheating wife who liked to shag her own brother. The tough, super-fit jogger with her washboard stomach and tiny lilac shorts. Where her white-blonde hair was obviously expensively and expertly coloured and trimmed every three weeks or so, his thick reddish hair was a trifle too long and kept dipping over his eyes. All in all, he looked as if he would be more at home in a lecture hall than a gym.

I felt sorry for him. But then my stomach plummeted at the image of his wife exposing and fingering her shaven red slit, crawling across the bench, firmly mounting Merlin as if he was her private stud, stuffing his hard, quiet cock up into her hungry snatch, wrapping her muscular legs round him, bucking against him as the dusk fell. Yesterday's visit to Symes Hall had done nothing to push the image out of my mind or to make me mind less. If anything, it had made things worse because now the image of him with Avril in the park, not to mention unseen images of him with Mimi Breeze, kept getting in the way of my triumph.

After my telephone conversation with Mr Grey, the sight of Merlin and Avril had kept me awake most of the night: the graphic image of her bits spread open like that. My mind had tried to veer away from the part Merlin had played in all this. In the night, I had managed to focus briefly on the silver earring glittering against his dark cheek, and the deep scratches on my back made by the rough bark of the tree, but then my mind's eye kept hauling me down to his groin, to that quivering penis being handled not by me but by her, used by her like a sex toy ...

'We have the place to ourselves,' her husband was saying. 'I arranged it. So we could conduct this meeting inside the pod, if you like? Give it a surreal air. Take the edge off this whole ghastly business.'

I stared blankly at him. He was over by the Eye, resting his hand against one of the spaceship modules that dangled off the big wheel.

'Yes. Sure. Why not? Anything to clear my head.'

He stood aside for me to enter, and we were sealed

inside. At least it was warm in there. I walked over to the far side of the pod, ready to rise over the river. The white air and fog seemed to rush at our glass prison and block everything out.

'We won't be able to see much today, I'm afraid,' Geoffrey said. 'But we're not here for a jaunt, are we?'

I shook my head and drew out the sealed packet of photographs. I turned my back to let him look at them in private and leaned my forehead and hands against the cool glass. We were barely moving but already we were suspended above the ground. The other pods dangled emptily round us.

Behind me there was a strangled cough and the flapping of paper as he dropped the photographs on the floor.

'Mr Grey?'

'I never realised how ghastly it would look in technicolour ... the bitch! And what kind of cold bastard is he?' he said. His hand was over his eyes and his shoulders were shaking. 'Just give me a moment, will you?'

I bent to pick up the photographs, meaning to put them straight back into the envelope, but curiosity overcame me. The first one I picked up was of their two profiles, talking, just after she had shown him that her ankle was actually fine. There was his earring again, very clearly outlined against his bristled jaw. But that was an innocent picture. The fleshy colours of the other pictures drew me and I stared at them, one by one, my breath rough in my ears with a mixture of horror and a wicked, growing arousal as the park action repeated itself in my hands, the shocking nakedness of her thighs and bottom when she had ripped her shorts off, the sliver of his stomach between his top and his cycling trousers as her greedy hand dived down to drag out his stiff cock.

'Mrs Grey in all her glory,' croaked her husband, coming up beside me. He wiped his hand across his nose and pulled his shoulders back. 'I know she's constantly hot for it, but in the middle of Kensington Gardens?'

I was starting to wish that I could open an escape hatch and eject from here. 'She fell over, you see, and he helped her up. He looked at her ankle but there was no injury,' I explained.

'Don't even think of trying to excuse her,' he said. He snatched the photographs out of my hand and picked through them again, more slowly this time. Neither of us could help devouring the shocking, ugly excitement contained in the pictures. 'Your Club Crème has a lot to answer for.'

'I'm not going to apologise for this, Mr Grey, though I am sorry you're so upset,' I said calmly. 'You are a fully paid-up member of our club, after all. I'm only here because you asked me to help you and that's what I'm paid to do.'

'I know, I know. You're right. You're very kind. I must get a grip. Let's tackle it head on.'

He held out one picture and we both looked at it for a long time. It was the moment of impact, you might say, when Avril had risen on her knees, poised above her target. She was fiddling with her hairless fanny, showing that brief red slash, shockingly bright in the wintry light. She was lowering herself so that the two bare lips could close over Merlin's knob and, little by little, nibble their way down its length. Her hand gripped the back of the wooden bench for balance, a few inches from where Merlin also gripped the bench.

'They didn't touch or show any real affection,' I told her husband. I realised we were standing very close. I could feel the tension in his body. The photograph in his fingers was shaking and I took it from him and put it back. 'It was only sex.'

He looked at me for the first time and I saw myself and the white sky surrounding us reflected in his glasses.

'Good sex, though, wasn't it? I mean, those pictures. Rampant, raw, urgent. You must have been turned on, watching it?' he wondered, stroking his chin and staring at me. 'I can tell from the way you've focussed the camera on them.'

'I . . . I don't know why I did that. I was only using the camera to see more clearly, but I wish I hadn't.'

'And how much further would your job extend, if I asked you? Are you in the business of restoring damaged egos?'

'I'm not sure what you mean,' I said. I twisted my head sideways to look out. We were much higher now, and I could see over the buildings towards St Paul's and the City. 'My job is to make sure our club members are happy.'

'So you keep saying. And I'm extremely unhappy at the moment,' he said. He took my cold face in his hands and turned me to look at him. His fingers were very warm. He wore a cream fisherman's sweater under the tweed coat and I could see tawny bristles pushing through his chin.

'I can see that. And if it helps, I didn't sleep much last night,' I said. His eyes behind the glasses were direct and unwavering. 'Nor did you, judging by that stubble.'

He grimaced and rubbed his chin. I took the opportunity to step away from him and take my coat off. We were in for a long ride. It was getting warmer in the pod and I felt flushed. I unwound the pashmina from round my neck. The silk of the ruffled red shirt I'd put on this morning was cool where it lay across my skin. The leather trousers clung to my legs and my new boots clicked across the floor. Despite feeling rattled by the photographs, I knew I looked good. Mimi would approve. I looked outside again. We were floating in the sky now. I would have preferred to be alone up here, but despite his anxiety Geoffrey Grey was quite easy company. I allowed my thoughts to drift out over the spires and rooftops of London.

'I wonder why you didn't sleep last night,' he said. His voice nudged open the easy silence. 'Were you jealous?'

I spun round. He had taken his coat off as well and was sitting on the long bench in the centre of the pod with one suede brogue resting up on the seat. He wore very worn blue Levis, and looked totally relaxed now.

'Jealous?' How could he possibly know my secret thoughts about Merlin?

'Of all that sexy action. Seeing a man and a woman copulating, out in the open air, unable to join in, skulking behind trees to train your camera on them, catching them on celluloid, humping like rabbits . . .'

'I couldn't say, Mr Grey,' I muttered, suspecting there was little weight in my words. 'It was all very quick, anyway. Not sexy at all.'

He patted the bench next to him. My feet were aching, unaccustomed to standing about on high heels, and I sat down obediently.

'I have a feeling it would all be much more sensuous and stimulating if it was you and me.'

He held up the final picture, of Merlin and this guy's wife arching away from each other. Merlin's face, I now saw, was twisted away from her and away from the camera's eye. Hardly true love, or even passion. Her arms were flung out sideways and her face was distorted with the power of her climax as she ground herself down on to him.

Mr Grey slid the picture back into the packet and put it carefully in his coat pocket.

'So how did the encounter go, exactly?' he murmured, sliding his hands up my silky sleeves so that the skin on my arms tingled in response. 'It might help me to hear it. Who made the move on whom?'

My breath must have been caught as I looked at the picture because now it came rushing out, whistling in my ears as I released the tension. The ruffles at my throat and down the front of my shirt shivered, and he looked down to where the shirt was buttoned tightly over my breasts. He stroked the silky ruffles and waited for me to stop him. But I couldn't move. I was just staring at his finger, moving so close to my breasts. They were heaving as I struggled for breath. We could both see them beneath the silk, the rounded, full shape of them cupped and lifted inside my bra with only the fabric separating them from an eager world. He flicked the first button almost hesitantly, and I bit my lip as it came undone and the shirt fell open over the lace of my matching red bra.

'Tell me,' he ordered.

'She made the move,' I said, my voice ragged. 'She was gagging for it. She took her shorts off and showed him her pussy. It was easy. She was barely wearing them.'

'Not like you. Classy and mysterious. You're wearing too many clothes for my liking, although they are beautiful and I can see that this underwear is the very best. La Perla?'

I nodded and blushed red, unable to reply. I looked down as he undid another button, and then another, until the shirt slipped down my shoulders, tickling my skin so that my eyelids fluttered shut.

I tilted my head back and felt his fingers treading

inside the warmth of my cleavage, and then both his hands were on my breasts, caressing them through the lace until my nipples started to harden. His thumb flipped across, catching the two sharp points, and then he stopped. Of course, I thought. He's not used to big tits, is he? Perhaps he can't remember what to do with them. There was a fidgety warmth starting up inside my fanny. It kept tightening and my knickers were getting damp. There was no need to think about what I was doing. I reached round and unhooked my bra, slipping it expertly off while leaving the shirt on. I still had my eyes shut, but I heard him gasp. I leaned towards him to encourage him. There was a pause.

'Did he suck her tits?' he demanded.

'Do we have to talk?' I groaned, distracted.

'I can only do this if you tell me how it was.'

'Then no, he didn't. He didn't even see them. She doesn't have big juicy tits, does she? Your wife leads with her cunt. It's like a Venus fly-trap, snapping up its prey,' I said. My voice was hoarse with excitement, and with something else. Spite. We could both spite Mrs Grey by doing this, taking our own fierce, illicit pleasure up here in the sky.

He gave a muffled groan and squeezed my tits until they hurt, the pain radiating into darts of pleasure zigzagging through me. He grabbed the bare breasts, pulling my body towards him so that slowly he could slide his face inside the warm cleavage. I held myself very still and opened my eyes. All I could see through the glass ceiling was white sky, the straight trail of an aeroplane shafting through the clouds. We were at the top of the wheel's ascent now.

'But you have breasts, don't you?' he said suddenly, pinching one nipple hard, and I squealed. 'Gorgeous, juicy, look at that, the way the little bud goes hard, how have I lived without tits for so long? You'll let me suck it, won't you? I can't resist sucking it.'

He pinched it again, and then took the other aching nipple between his teeth and bit it, and I squealed louder, enjoying the sound of my voice in our own concealed space and feeling wild and reckless. This was extra-curricular. We were outside the confines and rules of the club. Or were we? Where was the rule about clandestine meetings with club members without anyone else knowing? Neither Sir Simeon nor Mimi had told me what to do. I was my own boss. I could do what I liked. I could simply take this guy as I found him and give him the luscious body he had already taken a fancy to, make him forget his rampant wife, make me forget my own confusion, do this for the sake of relieving ourselves, do this because our mutual anguish had made us fucking horny.

'You can suck as much as you like, honey,' I crooned, stroking his hair and pulling his face hard into me, my own voice and his desperation turning me on. 'Suck, and nibble, and tease, and suck. Go on, as much as you like.'

He sucked at my breast and I wriggled up to get comfortable, straddling his lap. He didn't stop, and I went further. I pushed my breasts into his face, pushing my torso against him, so that he had to fall backwards onto his coat folded on the bench and I was bent over him, my shirt forming a red tent around us. I sat up abruptly, smiling at the sight of saliva on his lips, and started to undo his jeans.

'Did she undo his trousers like this?' he asked, starting to lose the thread of his questioning and suddenly looking vulnerable. 'Or did he do it for her?'

'What does it matter? They didn't have half as much fun as we're going to have,' I promised him, emboldened by the fierce throbbing in my breasts, throwing care to the winds. 'We can just forget all about them and their shoddy little encounter in the park.'

He grinned. 'I was right about you restoring damaged egos, wasn't I? It seems to be your speciality. Do you always take control like this?'

'Yes,' I lied.

'Don't talk, then. Just do it.'

I jumped up, shaking with excitement. I unzipped my boots and pulled my trousers off, taking the red silk knickers with them. We were still poised at the top of the wheel and, with a thrill of fear, I imagined our pod coming loose from its moorings and plunging to the ground.

'Amazing view,' I cried loudly, running to the edge and waving my arm at the world outside. I could feel my breasts bouncing as I twirled round.

'You can say that again,' he said, lifting his hips and wrenching his jeans down. 'Now, was young Merlin as well hung as this?'

I glanced down and gasped out loud. Mr Grey had the most enormous cock I'd ever seen, lying quite still, stretching up his stomach as far as the hem of his sweater. Who would have thought that a thumping great love machine like this was hidden under that slightly shambolic exterior?

'What the hell is that woman doing,' I breathed, creeping over to him, 'playing away from *this*?'

I swung my leg over him, pushing him down onto his back and hovered on all fours, gazing at his amazing member. A manic smile stretched across my face.

'What's so amusing?' he asked, reaching up to pull me down on top of him.

'Not amusing. Amazing. This,' I gabbled, spreading my legs further apart as I lowered myself just close enough to brush my bush back and forth over his waiting cock. 'Your wife hovered over his cock, just like this, in the park. She pulled it out of his trousers, and she got up on her knees, like this. There was a moment, like this, just before she took it in . . .'

'Go on. Don't stop,' he gasped.

'Well, she held herself over it like it was a sex toy, and the tip of it was just waiting at the entrance.'

Meanwhile *my* entrance felt as if it was trying to home in on a magnet. I reached down between my legs and took hold of what was lying there. It was vast. It seemed to go on forever. The smooth, taut surface was already trailed with moisture where I had brushed against it, and that sent stronger thrills of excitement through me. I took it in both hands, hitched myself back on his thighs for a moment to lift it and gawp at its incredible, swollen, stiff length. As I held it and looked at it, running my hands up and down it, it leapt up, the bulbous end winking already with a droplet of pre-come.

'Then I guess she couldn't help herself,' I finished breathlessly. 'She had to have it inside her. She couldn't wait any longer.'

I raised myself up again and placed the rounded tip against my moist pussy. Instantly, the tip made contact with the burning nub of my clitoris and I allowed myself another loud groan. It sounded filthy in my ears.

'Listen to this, Mr Grey,' I hissed, easing his cock slowly inside. 'Listen to that juicy wetness.'

My sex-lips closed greedily round the smooth length. I had to pause every so often to spread my thighs and to luxuriate in the huge, warm, animal mass filling me, pushing inside me, its rigid dimensions fitting inside me, feeling myself impaled on a great rod almost as if I could lift my legs away and balance myself, cunt on cock, even spin round on it.

He lay on the hard bench, hands still squeezing my breasts and pulling them so that he could suck and bite each one in turn while the other bounced and brushed against his face.

'So easy,' he murmured, stopping for a moment to watch my cunt swallowing him whole, tightening his grip as I slithered down to the base of his cock and we both waited for the new delicious movement to begin. 'You've made this so easy for me.'

His cock continued to swell inside me and I had no choice but to move, to start easing myself up and down the long shaft before it penetrated right through me. Once I started I couldn't stop because, as I raised myself off it, every inch of it rubbed against every screaming inch of me so that I could only go so far before slamming back down on him, groin on groin. When I did that, I could feel the end of his knob stretching me deep inside, testing me to the limits, showing us both what I was capable of taking.

'You can fuck me now,' I ordered.

His hips echoed the rhythm of mine. He drew himself back as I rose off him, then slammed up inside as I came back down. I could hear my voice rising in a crescendo of desire, whimpering with the powerful sensation of being impaled on this lovely pole, giving me more pleasure, more pleasure, rising to the peak, getting harder, getting wetter, tongues of fire streaking up inside me.

'Watch me,' I shouted out. 'This is what she was doing.'

His eyes watched behind the glasses and I could see my breasts reflected there, bouncing frantically as I rode him. Suddenly, he plunged in as deep as he could go. His mouth parted but no sound came out. His eyes closed briefly, and then he flopped back against the bench, pumping his spunk into me so that I was thrown upwards with the force of it, and I was crying out each time it lifted me, my own cries and his thrusting finally giving way to a wild, shattering climax that had me arching right away and then collapsing onto him, my thighs spread on either side of him, my bare torso and red silk shirt smothering him.

'I'm not sure I care any more what she was doing,' he said, the silk shirt lifting with his breath. 'It's you I want to fuck, Miss Summers. Again and again.'

The wheel was still turning, carrying us slowly in our descent. I sat up, still panting, and Mr Grey raised himself on his elbows, blinking as if he had just woken up. I pulled the shirt across my bosom and casually fastened one button, in an effort to appear modest. We both glanced up at the pod coming down immediately above us, and both started. There was someone inside. A long navy coat, a trilby hat and a face shrouded in shadow.

'Our turn to be watched,' said Mr Grey, pulling on his jeans and reaching for his coat. 'I can't see who it is. Do you think that man has a camera?'

'It's Sir Simeon,' I said, getting up slowly, standing for a moment, pussy and legs totally naked, letting Sir Simeon see my upturned face through the glass roof. 'How did he know we were here?'

'All seeing, I guess, with or without a camera.' Mr Grey chuckled. The tense, angry man of earlier had totally vanished. He looked positively cocky. 'Perhaps he likes to keep a special eye on his favourite member of staff?'

'Oh, I don't know about that.' I shrugged coyly, but I did just wonder. But then again, no phone call to the club would go unlogged, I was sure of that. They might all be recorded. Or Miss Sugar told Sir Simeon what I was up to.

'You can tell them you've added a new skill to your job description. And you performed it to perfection,' Mr Grey said happily when we reached the ground. He shuffled the photographs like a pack of cards as he waited for me to come out of the pod. I came and stood in front of him and he gave me a white envelope. 'I want to pay you.'

'I couldn't. It's all part of the –'

'You deserve every penny of this. Sod the club. This was your doing and yours alone. And after I've taught Mrs Grey a lesson or two, she'll come crawling back. She won't be screwing Mr Hall – don't worry, I knew all about that – or your Merlin, again.'

'Should I feel sorry for her?' I asked.

'She can take it. She likes punishment. And in a way, I should be rewarding her. Because if she hadn't kept cheating, I wouldn't have been driven to meeting up with you, and then we wouldn't have had our time today. So all's fair.'

'I have to know one thing,' I said, cocking my head. 'Why did she cop off with her brother of all people? I mean, how pervy is that? And how mad is that, when she's got a nice, not to mention hugely well-endowed, husband of her own?'

He pushed his glasses up his nose, once again the bashful lecturer.

'Shocking people is like a drug to Avril,' he explained, still shuffling the photographs. 'I've always known it. I admit I get a high from being married to it, even though it's painful. Her and Merlin? Par for the course. But her and Jez? That was different. Although he's not her blood brother, they were both adopted, I still can't get my head round it. It only came out into the open when he got engaged recently. Avril went ballistic with jealousy and spilled the whole story to anyone who'd listen. He's always been like her puppy dog, you see. Anyway, the fiancée understandably banned Avril from their lives, and I thought it was over, but who was I kidding?'

'It wasn't over when they came to the club the other night,' I told him. 'Or Mikhail's party.'

'I guess she thought she could just brazen it out, and the more publicly the better. With Jez, with Merlin, with her ultimate goal, Sir Simeon. Who seems to have vanished, by the way.'

The London Eye was indeed empty.

'Anyway,' Geoffrey Grey concluded, shaking my hand rather formally. 'Suffice to say now that the worm has turned.'

'You're not a worm,' I said.

'Not any more. Thanks to you, Miss Summers.'

He gave a curious farewell bow. There was more than a pang of regret as he walked away. I liked him. I thought of that amazing cock, filling me to the brim. I wanted to do it again, in some other wacky place. I wanted to spread my wings a little further. I was sure he would think of somewhere. The British Library, for example. Or the Reptile House at Regent's Park Zoo.

I wriggled with amusement inside my coat. Mr Grey and I weren't related, after all. So what was stopping us? Now he'd got the taste for extra-curricular sex, Mr Grey didn't have to be a one-off, did he? He was a club member. There was always his file. Like all the other members, his details were at my fingertips. Literally.

I walked along the Embankment for a while, my stomach rumbling with hunger now that the morning was underway. I watched the commuters scurrying to work, heads down, eyes fixed on the pavement, faces white and drawn.

I pitied them. As for me, I was beginning to forget the meaning of the word 'work'. Club Crème didn't feel like my office. It felt more like my playground. I'd done the big wheel. You could say I'd done some swinging; most definitely some sliding. That left the see-saw and the carousel.

13

I couldn't wait to see what was in the suitcase they had given me for this trip.

'I won't lie to you,' Miss Sugar sniffed that morning, opening and slamming drawers in her desk. 'I am livid.'

'Were you hoping he'd invite you to go?' I asked, trying not to lick my lips as I saw her count out some more cash for me.

'Of course I was. I've been here for much longer than you. And I'm way overdue a decent perk. You've just strolled in here and taken all the plum jobs. I'm sick and tired of this bloody office!' She slumped back into her chair and glared at the paperwork.

'Sugar ... this isn't like you!' I exclaimed, genuinely shocked. I came round the desk and put my arm round her thin shoulders. She tensed up, but I kept it there, squeezed her hard against me until I thought her bones might break, then released her. Her hand came up and rubbed the shoulder which had been pressing against my breast. 'I had no idea you felt like this. But what can I do about it? What can either of us do, if Sir Simeon has decreed it?'

'Nothing,' she said. She looked up, hooking one strand of hair behind her ear. A couple of hairgrips were about to drop out. 'It's not your fault. Just go, will you, and enjoy yourself. It's New Year's Eve, after all.'

'It's still work, Sugar, remember. It will simply be an extension of working here at the club. And I'm just obeying orders. I'm not supposed to enjoy it,' I said, but my words lacked conviction.

She snorted. 'It's a vocation for you, Summers. All this – *entertaining*. You've taken to it like a duck to water. I've never heard such effusive praise from a club member as we got from Geoffrey Grey about you. Not to mention all the other rave reviews since then. Quite sickening, in fact,' she said.

'I don't know *what* you mean, I'm sure,' I responded. I raised my eyebrows and picked up the suitcase. 'I was doing the poor guy a favour, that's all.'

Was that little dent in her cheek the merest hint of a smile? 'Yes, but off the premises, Summers. It's not part of the deal. We are only supposed to commune with our members here, at the Club Crème,' she said.

'Oh, sod that,' I scoffed. 'I didn't come back to the big bad city just to be cooped up here all the time! Anyway, we're all leaving the premises to go a-communing at Symes Hall, tonight, aren't we? From one commune to another, in fact.'

'Symes Hall counts as club premises, I suppose, although hiring it out for conferences, even if it's for a club member, is something totally new to me.'

'It's not fair, leaving you here while we all go off and have fun. But someone has to hold the fort,' I said. I leaned across her and flipped the pages of her ledger. 'I see that there's almost a full house here tonight. That'll be clients, sorry, members, escaping the horrors of Christmas and New Year at home, I daresay. So while the cats are away, Miss Sugar, the mouse can play!'

The dent in Miss Sugar's cheek deepened.

'Not a party, Summers. It's work. Oh, and just before you go. Car keys, please.'

'What?' I asked, getting ready to sulk.

'The MG. Miss Breeze needs it. It *is* her car, you know.'

'No. I didn't know. I thought it was Sir Simeon's. I thought he'd lent it to me specially –'

'Sir Simeon drives a vintage Rolls. Surely you didn't think he'd potter about in an MG?'

Sugar handed me a railway ticket. I decided not to let the removal of my little car get me down.

'Let's you and me have some fun when I get back to London, Sugar,' I suggested. 'You could do with it.'

It was already evening when the taxi dropped me off at the Hall. I couldn't see much of the countryside flashing past the train as the sky grew dark. I looked out at the passing silhouettes of trees and houses, remembering what it felt like to travel on foreign soil. It wouldn't be long now before I had enough money to go round the world, twice over if I wanted to.

But the job at Club Crème had long ago ceased to be solely about the money. A big part of me was reluctant to stop what I was doing. After all, I had discovered a closed world of intrigue and secrecy behind the veneer of respectability and, what was even better, I was virtually left to my own devices to set the scenes as I chose and conduct any liaisons as I wanted. I hadn't seen Mimi for nearly a month now, and Sir Simeon had stopped showing up to watch over me.

In the taxi I lifted my feet to examine the pointed toes of yet another beautiful pair of boots, this time knee-length ones in soft mulberry leather which matched my low-necked, long-sleeved mulberry T-shirt. I crossed my legs, relishing the swish of silk stocking, so different from my erstwhile uniform of sweatpants and jeans. I was just starting to doze, for some reason thinking about Chrissie and how I still hadn't returned the borrowed pinstriped suit, when the car started to throw up pellets of gravel and crunched to a halt.

Symes Hall looked beautiful at night, its yellow façade illuminated by arc lights. In the windows, oil lamps burned, as if we'd stepped back in time. I started to feel nervous, something I hadn't felt for weeks. The wind whistled and flapped my coat against me as the taxi driver dumped my case on the drive and drove away.

'Step this way, Miss Summers,' a voice said. The butler, who I'd seen briefly at the meet handing round the drinks, had materialised by my side and he led me into the house. I expected my inexplicable nerves to dissipate and to feel rather smug as I entered. After all, I'd been here before, remember, with the son of the house. But it looked totally different in the dark and there was no one I knew, let alone Merlin, to be seen. The place was shadowy, lit only by flames burning in the same braziers or holders as we had on the stairs at the club. My high heels clicked anxiously along the upstairs corridor.

Up ahead were the double doors of Sir Simeon's room, but the butler left me alone in another huge chamber with very little furniture except a vast cherry-wood bed all low slung and curved like a boat and piled high with snowy white pillows, a matching, brooding wardrobe with mirrored doors, which virtually covered one wall, and a couple of hard-backed tapestry chairs, the sort that you could only sit up in and beg.

I crossed to the French windows and stepped out onto the balcony. All I could see was the scudding clouds and a full white moon. There was a fire jumping in the grate, just as it had in Sir Simeon's bedroom. If I turned quickly enough I might catch Merlin creeping up behind me, ready to lift me bodily and sling me onto the bed, peel away my new, smart persona until all that was left to show him was my trembling white skin rising in goose-bumps ... Except this time he wouldn't know me. I wasn't a boyish stable hand any more with messy hair scrunched up in a net and mud in her fingernails. I considered myself a woman of the world now, an expert seducer of men, dressed in designer clothes and with a wallet full of hard-earned cash.

An owl hooted from somewhere close by and I backed hurriedly into the room, and straight into a pair of soft, waiting arms.

'Everything all right, Summers?' Mimi said and caught me close against her for a moment as if measuring me. Then she pushed me away. The candles and lamps dotted around the walls threw virtually no light at all and we had to peer to see each other. 'You seem jumpy. After all the training, all the free rein we've given you in the last few weeks, I expected you to have acquired a little more poise by now.'

'Training?' I retorted, finding my voice. 'What training? I've been left entirely to my own devices.'

'I know that's how it seems, but believe me, Summers, you haven't made one move without our knowledge.'

I fiddled with one of my earrings. 'Well, if it's poise you're worried about, I've acquired that in spades. I'm a very quick learner.'

I lifted my chin and walked deliberately slowly across to the bed. I wanted her to see that I could move like a catwalk model if I chose. Miss Sugar had spent enough time drilling me after all, marching me up and down in the office to get rid of my student slouch. Mimi watched me silently, and I sat down, flung my coat off and calmly crossed my stockinged legs. She looked me up and down, unable to hide her approval. She saw the clinging top, the elegant boots and the tailored skirt in honey tweed, shot through with a burgundy thread.

'Quite the beautiful swan now, aren't you, Suki?' she breathed, coming towards me. 'My instincts about a person are always right.'

She was dressed in a strapless ball-gown which flared out like a flamenco dress at the knees. It was made of a shot-silk fabric, which threw out varying shades of gold and red. Diamonds glittered at her throat, in her ears, on her fingers and, in this dim light, her lips looked blood red. Her hair was tied loosely at the nape of her neck. She came and sat beside me on the bed. The ancient springs dipped and squeaked alarmingly under our joint weight, making us both break into laughter. The ice was broken.

'I've got you to thank for all this. I mean, all these lovely clothes, all these adventures,' I said, and I meant it. It was lovely to see her again. Despite my new-found confidence I was still groping to find my way in comparison to her endless finesse. Mimi was like a beautiful ship, sailed back into harbour, and I was one of the tug boats bobbing about in her wake.

'I should give you more credit, I suppose. You can thank me for discovering you, if you like, but you've done all the rest,' she replied, stroking my face. 'I have had detailed progress reports from our Miss Sugar, not to mention all these grateful members, panting for more of you.'

A red-hot blush spread up my face.

'If I'm not careful,' she went on, turning my shoulders so that I was facing her. 'Someone will poach you away and I'll lose my best housekeeper yet. And I'm warning you, Summers. I won't allow it.'

'I'm not going anywhere,' I assured her. 'Yet.'

She narrowed her eyes at me. I wanted her to know that I was no servant. I would stay, or go, when I was good and ready. I looked steadily back at her, enjoying our physical closeness.

'So. This conference,' she said, suddenly brisk again. 'Allow me to lord it over you tonight and decide your look, would you? You have to be as beautiful and anonymous as possible.'

She quickly painted my eyes and mouth and patted my face with powder until I sneezed. She handed me a long velvet gown in the darkest sea-green and some matching dark green mules. Then she lit a cigarette. 'Get dressed, Summers,' she ordered. 'They are waiting for us downstairs. We are posing as guests this evening. It's a perfume convention. Mr Hall has organised it, as a gift, or should I say apology, to his fiancée.'

'Strange gift?'

'She's mad about her work, I believe, and he's in the doghouse after his antics with his ghastly sister Avril Grey, so he organised this venue to impress her clients and earn himself some brownie points.'

'Will she swallow it and forgive him, I wonder?'

'I don't know if she swallows.'

I spluttered with laughter.

'She's watching him like a hawk, but her clients, and some of her superiors, who have come here from the stores in London and Paris, seem overawed by the place, which will reflect well on her. He doesn't want her to know who we are, and certainly not that we're from Club Crème, or even that this place is connected to the Club Crème. She doesn't even know he's a member. He wants her to think this is all his own doing.'

'And we're all to be on our best behaviour?' I said, pulling a face.

'Yes. But who could resist committing wickedness in a place like this? Miles from home, buckets of champagne, a myriad of rooms to hide in . . .'

'All kinds of things could happen at Symes Hall. What with the randy lord of the manor and his hunky young son,' I agreed dreamily, looking round the shadowy room. Then I realised what I'd said. 'It's all right, Mimi. I know all about you and Merlin.'

'I very much doubt that. And it's dangerous ground, Summers. Merlin isn't invited this evening, if that's what you're getting at,' Mimi said in a voice tight with warning. She was stern again, staring at me hard.

'I'm glad he's not coming,' I replied coolly. 'He's trouble, that one. So it's good that you've chosen his father.'

I took the dress over to the corner of the room and started to wriggle out of my clothes. I could see her eyes glittering behind me in the tarnished mirror. My own reflection was unrecognisable. She had ringed my eyes with smoky shadow and kohl pencil so that my eyes were elongated like a cat's. She had painted my lips in the same blood red that she was wearing, which leeched my face of colour like a mask. I liked it.

'You've come on a lot in the last couple of months, Summers,' Mimi said. 'Changed beyond recognition, I'd say. Even when you wandered into our office on that first day wearing that ridiculous suit with that beret, I thought of you as someone who would learn to enjoy using her own body.'

'And now you're annoyed that you were proved right?' I queried, acutely aware of her watching me undress, and sucking my stomach in. I hoped that the underwear I had chosen to go seamlessly under the tight top would do. It was a strapless magenta corset, which clung light as a feather to my ribs while at the same time lifting my breasts in a cradle of subtle wire. I let the dress slither over my head, the velvet kissing my cold skin as it dropped to the floor. The green velvet brought out the same colour in my eyes, which flashed in the dim light. The neckline rested on the tip of each shoulder, then swooped in an elegant line to a row of delicate buttons just below the divide of my cleavage. The basque was perfect.

'No. I'm delighted that I was proved right,' Mimi answered. She blew out a plume of cigarette smoke and stood up. 'I'm just saying that you mustn't go hard around the edges. Stick to what you're good at, and remember your place. You mustn't start to meddle.'

She was annoyed with me, but she couldn't keep away from me. Quickly she coiled my hair into a knot at the base of my skull and fastened it with a couple of pins. I still couldn't get used to the way it stayed where it was put rather than falling straight down in a mess of curls and tangles. I could feel her breath on my skin as she fixed a tiny velvet cap to the crown of my head and unfurled a delicate, gauzy veil to obscure half my face. Her musky perfume filled the air.

'It's the clothes,' I murmured, surprised at how breathless I was. 'They make me into the person I am.'

'Don't blame your tools, Suki Summers,' Mimi replied softly, pressing her big lips against the bone at the base of my neck. Now there would be an imprint of her lipstick there. 'You've discovered the real thing and there's nothing like it, is there?'

We swept down the stairs and crossed the hall to arrive at double doors leading into what could only be described as a salon, except that it was as big as a ballroom. A vast fireplace crackled at one end and huge sofas and chairs were grouped comfortably around the room, which was mainly lit by massive, twisted church candles. Tall French windows ran along both sides of the room and were swathed in thick, brocade curtains. The room was so high that you could hardly make out where the curtains ended and the ceiling began.

Mimi held my arm to keep me standing in the doorway. She adjusted the little velvet cap and veil that went with the dress, tweaking the lace cobweb over my eyes. She knew that after a couple of heartbeats the people in the room would turn to see us latecomers.

'A devastating duo, aren't we?' I murmured, sliding my arm round her waist. She nodded, and didn't pull away from me. The crowd parted, and a man and woman both dressed in black walked down the room to greet us. The man was thickset, like a rugby player. Jez Hall. But things took a distinct dip for the worse. The woman clutching on to his arm and gazing up at him was . . .

'I can't do this, Mimi,' I hissed desperately, turning my back as they paused briefly to speak to a couple of other guests. 'I know her. She's Chrissie, my oldest friend!'

'And Mr Hall is her naughty fiancé,' Mimi hissed back, spinning me round and leading me towards them. 'Jeremy. How lovely of you to ask us here tonight. And what a divine setting.'

I shook Mr Hall's hand as if I'd never met him before, and he almost wept with gratitude.

'Meet my lovely fiancée, Chrissie,' he gushed. 'This is her baby, really. She might look like a pussy cat, but she's worked like a beaver today, and pulled in some big business, I believe. Now it's time to celebrate.'

'Thanks to you, Jeremy, for organising these posh surroundings,' Chrissie simpered, and then, as she remembered her manners and turned to shake hands, she let out a screech.

'Suki! What the fuck are you doing here?'

I thought fast. 'Lord Whatsit,' I said.

'What?'

'You know. Lord Whatsit, who I used to muck out stables for? This is his place. He rents it out. I kept in touch after I left. You know . . . the only job I wasn't sacked from.'

'Oh, yes,' Chrissie squealed obediently, 'Lord Whatsit'. I could have kissed her. My excuse for being there had been as clear as mud. She peered at Mimi, who was still holding Jeremy's hand. 'And you are?'

Mimi stepped in possessively as I waved my hands helplessly.

'I'm Suki's new friend. We go everywhere together, don't we, darling?'

Mimi stroked my cheek, and Jeremy smirked. Chrissie scowled.

'How charming,' Jeremy said. 'The sort of girls I like – er, approve of.'

'It's time to eat,' Chrissie butted in, tossing him a filthy look and trying to take my arm. She hissed in my ear. 'What's come over you? What's going on?'

'We'll be there in one moment, Chrissie,' trilled Mimi. 'Suki has something in her eye. But then you'll have to separate us, you know. We are rather joined at the hip, aren't we, darling? Put us next to someone interesting at dinner, won't you? Preferably either side of your gorgeous fiancé.'

Chrissie gave Mimi one of her curt nods, and I started to feel dreadful. I wanted to tell her the truth. She didn't deserve any of this subterfuge. And she certainly didn't deserve that sleazeball of a fiancé.

I started to reply to her, but a very young man with golden curls and a clipboard sidled up to Chrissie and instantly she put on her working face.

'That was quick thinking, but I don't think she bought it, or liked it,' I said to Mimi. 'What are you up to?'

'Your dear little friend needs to know what he's really like. She obviously has her suspicions, and it's not just the sister that she's worried about. Once you and I are unleashed on him, he won't stand a chance.'

Mimi started fussing with my face. Everyone filed past us across the hall and into another cavernous room.

'I told you. She's my oldest friend. I can't do this, Mimi, however badly she wants us to.'

'Explain, or you're fired,' Mimi said. I couldn't tell whether she was joking or serious, but she was still stroking my face.

'I shagged her precious Jeremy at Mikhail's party, for God's sake. I mean, I didn't know it was him until they turned the lights on, but I can't look her in the eye.'

Mimi's finger brushed a strand of hair back under the little velvet cap. She looked down and I realised she was trying to suppress a smile. Mimi's black eyes danced at me and I put my hand over my mouth and started to giggle, too. We had to wait for the giggles to pass.

'Right,' Mimi said after a moment. 'In that case, I will have to take over as his honey-trap. Just when I was looking forward to observing your technique at close quarters. Ah well. Think of this as a freebie and enjoy the show.'

We started to walk towards the dining room.

'Where does that leave me?' I asked and pulled at her hand.

'I guess that leaves you as a free agent, darling,' Mimi said. 'You can simply watch Mimi Breeze in action, and learn.'

It was an hour or so later, when Mimi flicked her tongue at me just before sitting on Jeremy's face, that I wondered how much of 'the show' was for my benefit by then, and how much for his. All through dinner I hadn't quite relaxed for fear that Chrissie would cotton on, realise that I knew Jeremy Hall after all, and make a horrible scene. I knew about Chrissie's horrible scenes. I wanted to tell her everything. I felt a heel, skulking in the shadows, watching her fiancé fall under Mimi's spell.

But what I wasn't expecting to happen at her precious perfume convention was to see the old Chrissie, the Smithson Sandwich, emerging from under the blue eye-shadow. Perhaps it was my presence that encouraged her, or perhaps it was the way everyone else was behaving, but either way I stopped worrying. As the inhibitions fell like so many autumn leaves, so I reckoned the explanations could wait.

Mimi had ignored me throughout dinner, focussing on Jeremy, softening him up for the kill. That was fine by me. A tiny man sitting on my other side, who looked like Hercule Poirot, started to ogle my cleavage.

'I am Jacques,' he announced, in a thick French accent, 'the chief supplier in Paris of perfumes to our beautiful Chrissie.'

Any more of that accent and I would blow my cover by laughing out loud. I willed my new, knowing self to take over. I leaned towards him with my arm thrown over the back of his chair so that my breasts were spread out for him and anyone else to admire. Across the table I watched Mimi's big red mouth moving in flattering, seductive chatter, watched Jeremy's lips part, saliva gathering at the corners as she spoke to him and watched his teeth snap together when her brown fingers stole into his lap and unzipped his flies.

I caught her eye occasionally across the candlelight, then glanced to see if Chrissie had noticed, but Chrissie was already tossing her blonde curls around, flirting outrageously with the golden-haired youth and his friend who were on either side of her. I knew she was good at flirting, but she had a long way to go if she was going to catch up with what Mimi was doing.

I simpered sweetly as the Poirot lookalike started to

stroke my velvet thigh. He leaned hungrily towards me so that his nose was level with my just-covered nipples, and one or two men started craning their necks to see what was happening up our end of the table. I wanted to watch Mimi, but now it was my turn to be distracted. My neighbour lifted his glass to drink and tipped it sideways, spilling white wine right across me so that I gasped out loud. The cold liquid trickled down my throat and droplets seeped between my breasts. The little man flicked out his napkin and started dabbing painstakingly, snuffling his nose between my breasts as he tried to dry me off, edging the napkin under the bodice of my dress and flicking it across my skin. It tickled, starting up little pinpricks of pleasure in my nipples.

He saw me smiling, and allowed his other hand to creep, under cover of my napkin, on to my thigh and started to claw the velvet dress up my leg towards my crotch. His eager groping started to arouse me. I'd become hypersensitive to any kind of touch, I realised, no matter who was touching me. I could make something sensational happen, just by parting my legs a little, letting him push the dress right up, letting him stumble into my warm bush, unearth my secret crack. I felt my head swim a little with the enticement of leading him on, getting pleasure and making his day by letting him finger me.

By losing myself to the possibilities of what the little man could do to me and, by looking suitably demure and keeping my eyes down, I could also see what Mimi was doing. The white tablecloth jerked up and down under Jeremy's plate as she massaged his cock. He gaped helplessly at her, biting his lips to contain the yelp of noisy lust threatening to burst out. Even Jacques stopped short of uncovering my pussy when he saw what was happening to his host, and we all watched silently as there was one final thrust of the tablecloth, Jeremy sank back in his chair and Mimi tilted her head back to lick drips of creamy dessert off her spoon.

'Time for dancing,' called Chrissie, clapping her hands as the conversation threatened to stop altogether. My neighbour removed his hand, leaving my pussy warm with thwarted anticipation, and suddenly dinner was over. Faces calm as if nothing had happened, everyone filed back into the salon and a couple of dark, bearded waiters started gliding about in the shadows with champagne and liqueurs on silver trays.

Chrissie and Mimi ran over to a vast music system in the corner of the room and giggled together as they looked through the CDs. I felt my chest tightening with jealousy. They were both *my* friends, after all. But tonight I wasn't allowed to play with either of them. I snatched a flute of champagne off the silver tray being waved in front of me and watched as Jeremy went up to them. A blast of dramatic Spanish guitar music started. Instantly, Mimi started clicking her fingers above her head. Jeremy grabbed her waist and pulled her across the floor. She snatched up the hem of her dress and started swirling it in a wild flamenco dance.

Chrissie's little face puckered into fury. She watched them with her hands on her hips, chewing her pink lips. I couldn't bear to see her like that. I was about to rush up to my old friend when, as if by a secret signal, my French dinner companion bobbed up in front of me just as the young man who had been sitting next to Chrissie at dinner approached her, kissed her hand and bounced her into an energetic rock and roll.

As they twirled past Mimi and Jeremy, I heard Chrissie shout, 'I've scored the best-looking toy boy in the perfume business!' and it was Jeremy's turn to look furious. Mimi started whooping and writhing round him as the music became more and more frantic, and soon the two couples were separated by their own competing floor shows.

The toy boy, with his blond curls and bright blue eyes, looked rather like Chrissie herself. I wondered if she could see it. Whatever she could see, she obviously liked because she started running her hands up and down his sides as they danced and, after an anxious look towards Jeremy, the boy copied her. Chrissie's black dress was short, unlike most of the other dresses in the room, and was slashed into ribbons that spun away from her legs as she danced, and it soon became obvious that she wasn't wearing any knickers. It was all I could do to stop myself shrieking 'slapper' at her like we used to when we were kids.

Jacques couldn't keep his eyes off her either. He steered me in a sedate waltz nearer to Chrissie, murmuring something about speaking to our hostess, then he let go of me and started to dance with her and the toy boy. Relieved rather than insulted, I backed quickly away, but Chrissie was too engrossed to notice me. She was dancing, opening and closing her knees, wriggling up and down the toy boy's body as if he were a pole.

Jacques went round behind her, planting his small hands on her gyrating hips and guiding her. He was the right height to press his groin right in between her buttocks. I saw her give a little start and glance over her shoulder, then she tilted her bum invitingly against him before grinding her crotch against the toy boy. She was lost in the game, happy to let the two of them push and pull her between them. She was jerking her hips and writhing frantically as if she wanted to go to the loo, and yanking each man against her as she rubbed first her crotch, then her bum, against them.

Mimi and Jeremy had danced into the far corner of

the room by now. It was difficult to see them by the light of one solitary candle. Their flamenco had slowed and they were circling each other slowly like combatants, a few inches apart. Mimi had pulled her dress right up her legs until it barely covered her pubes, and Jeremy was licking his lips, his hands itching to touch her. She continued to twitch herself out of his reach until he grabbed her roughly, his big hands digging into the soft flesh of her upper thighs, and lifted her so that she was wrapped round him. He was big and strong, and carried her like a feather, but he hadn't bargained for her determination. Even in the flickering light of the tall candle I could see her face harden as he tried to take control. She started to struggle, and it was then that she glanced round the room, assessing the scene, and saw me standing by one of the long curtains, watching. Our eyes locked and I held my breath.

Mimi stopped struggling in Jeremy's grip and let herself go weak, and he lowered her to her feet again. She rewarded him by putting her hands on his shoulders. He obviously thought she was going to kiss him because he closed his eyes. But it was me she was looking at. She gave me a sly wink and ran her tongue slowly over her lower lip in a gesture so sensual that I could almost feel her warm, wet lips fastening onto mine, and I gripped the back of a sofa.

Then she pushed Jeremy down until he was on his knees. She hitched her dress up to show him her startling black bush, straddled his head, and pushed herself into his face. I gasped, but no one else appeared to notice. I was aware of one of the waiters hovering next to me. I thought he said something, but I couldn't tear my eyes away from what Mimi was doing. She tensed her legs to angle her goods against Jeremy's mouth, and I saw his tongue come out and start lapping at her, his fingers scrabbling to part her sex-lips and get to the fruit inside.

'Do you think madame la hostess is aware?' a voice asked. The waiter was still beside me, presumably repeating what he'd said before. I didn't look at him, but frowned, as if he'd woken me up. I was so wrapped up in the scene with Mimi. I wanted to feel a wet tongue lapping at me. Her tongue, anyone's tongue. My fanny was hot and prickling with frustration, ignored and abandoned under my velvet dress, while Mimi's was tongued ferociously by the lusty Jeremy.

The waiter pointed and I tore my eyes away from Mimi. On the other side of the room, Chrissie was now tossing herself wildly back and forth between the two men, rubbing herself up and down their groins, her slashed dress giving easy access to her bare, ready cunt. She wasn't interested in taking anything more from them. She was lost in her own abandoned pleasure. Both men were sweating. The boy swallowed hard as Chrissie thrust her hips against him. Jacques looked more composed, a smile fixed on his face. I glanced at his trousers and saw an enormous bulge outlined there. One of his hands was inside, clamped round his penis, bringing it to life while Chrissie parted her legs, wrapped one round the younger man's leg, and swept herself up and down. Her buttocks clenched and her head fell back as she started to thrash wildly against him, her throat bulging as she moaned out loud, 'Somebody screw me, while I'm hot.'

There was an electric silence in the room. All at once she arched herself away from him as her climax overwhelmed her. The boy just stared at her as she started to fall backwards. Another woman had crept up behind him to get a closer look and now, tired of Chrissie's hogging the limelight, she snaked a thin white hand down the boy's trousers and whipped out his fully erect penis. The boy rocked on his heels as the woman pulled him out to his full length, enticing the rounded end of his cock from its foreskin until it stretched out for more. The woman pulled and stroked for a moment or two more, then started to pull him backwards. Most of the other guests formed a circle and closed round the pair of them, clapping and cheering as if they were at a bull-fight, so that they were lost from view.

It was up to Jacques to catch the falling Chrissie. He was a lot stronger than he looked because, as he caught her, he deftly flicked her onto a big sofa, where she fell, still twitching, onto her back, arms and legs splayed open. The little man lost no time. He clambered between her legs, arranged her against the cushions until she was in a suitably inviting position, and then unzipped his black trousers.

'Aren't you tired of watching?' the waiter murmured in my ear.

'I get my fair share of the action,' I replied absently, keeping my eyes on what was going on in the room. 'Sometimes it's a turn-on just to watch.'

Over in the corner, Mimi had Jeremy's hair tangled in her fingers as she kept his head clamped between her strong brown thighs. But they were equally matched as far as control went. Mimi's pelvis tipped and twisted and her long throat was stretched with pleasure as he lapped and sucked at her. His big hands had pulled her buttocks apart and his fingers were probing and prodding inside that dark crack. He must have located his target because the long rope of black hair swung across her back as Mimi, like Chrissie had done, started to buck and thrash against Jeremy's face. I saw flashes of his wet mouth as he tongued and nibbled her remorselessly and finger-fucked the hidden hole of her arse at the same time. She hammered her fists on his back and then she, like Chrissie, was falling, and Jeremy was catching her, and they were in a heap on the floor.

'By the looks of him he thinks he can give her a fucking she'll never forget,' the waiter commented, as Jeremy pulled the collapsed Mimi across the floor towards him. 'But how do you fuck the woman who's already had the best?'

The small man, his dinner jacket still buttoned up, was humping his hostess with vigorous thrusts of his neat bottom, his eyes and mouth closed and silent while her arms and legs waved like tentacles around him and her blonde curls tossed happily against the sofa.

The waiter had melted away again. He'd left his silver tray on the table next to me. I reached for a full glass, and drained it. The music seemed to have faded and the sounds of sexual ecstasy and the applause of the voyeurs clamoured around me. I glanced from one madly rutting couple to the other, two cocks momentarily visible as they drew back to ram again and again in to the two waiting pussies. I felt a weird mixture of randy desire and dull emptiness.

I was off my guard because someone suddenly nudged me from behind, pushing me out of sight into the dark alcove provided by the window seat and the tall curtains. I half stumbled, half fell, with my knees on the window seat and my hands up against the windowpane. Outside the sweeping drive was lit by flickering torches and the moon cast mysterious tree-shadows beyond the ring of light.

'They won't notice we've vanished,' the person said. The heavy curtains fell shut behind him and we were enclosed in a kind of tent, with the windows making a mirror in front of us. The squeals and laughter of the other guests were instantly muffled.

'Shouldn't you be handing round the drinks?' I asked stupidly as a pair of strong arms trapped me in front of a taut body and a warm tongue gave tiny laps at the edges of my ear.

'So I get sacked,' he said and laughed softly, blowing the nape of my neck. 'But I get to screw the horniest person here.'

I tried to twist round to see him, but it was all I could do to retain my balance. The waiter's warm hands stroked over my bare shoulders and spine. I gave up and looked back at the window. The effect of his touch on my skin was mesmerising. His hands came to rest on my waist and I flattened my palms on his hips, pulling his stomach in to my back. We paused, as if waiting for the next step of the dance.

Very subtly, so that I had to concentrate to be sure he was doing it, he pressed his groin against me, moving slightly from side to side so as to edge my butt cheeks open. Then he stopped, only moving his hands up my velvet ribcage towards my breasts. I pulled the focus of my eyes in from the world outside, and stared at our reflection in the window. My eyes were wide and dark, still half hidden by the veil, and he was just a shadow behind me, eyes whose colour I couldn't determine glittering in the half-light.

He leaned over my shoulder, trapping my reflected eyes in his, and then we both watched as his fingers slid easily down the front of my dress in search of my breasts. I held my breath as he drew one out. The air shrank my flesh into little bumps and the rosy nipple sharpened up instantly.

'Juicy as ever,' he breathed, massaging the soft mound

and tweaking the hard nipple with his thumb. I couldn't breathe, let alone ask him what he was talking about. The questions were knocked out of me as he scooped my other breast out of my dress. He started to knead them both together so roughly that I rocked back and forth against him. Seeing my own naked breasts hanging there in the window sent new shocks of excitement through me and I rocked harder against his caressing hands.

As my nipples hardened I felt the thick shaft of his cock stiffen between my buttocks and we swayed together, backwards and forwards, my legs starting to melt apart and faltering on my heels as he continued to flick his fingers across my nipples while grinding his pelvis harder against my bottom until his cock was hard as a rock.

I reached behind and felt it bulging painfully against his tight waiter's trousers. I started to rub myself against the lewd shape, but he bent me forwards onto the window seat so that I was forced to catch my weight with my hands. This way I couldn't touch him, but I could steady my wobbling knees. I was aching and wet with excitement now, and all I could do was watch my shadowy lover as he released my breasts, letting them brush against the window cushion. He pushed my dress up to my waist and my legs trembled even more.

'Like unwrapping a delicious parcel,' he murmured into my neck. So far I had only heard him whisper. 'Do your employers really have a clue how good you are?'

'Who are you?' I gasped. 'How do you know who my employers are?'

'Well, I'd say you've shagged at least one of them already. Mimi, was it? She's on heat all the year round,' he said.

He hooked my French knickers down my legs and

cupped my moist bush. One finger led the way into the wet crack and started circling my wet lips, and I moaned loudly.

'Don't talk about her like that.'

'Not going to deny it, then?'

Two fingers slid up me. My breath blew clouds on the cold windowpane and he held me impaled while he unzipped his trousers with his free hand. I tried to bring one knee up onto the seat so that I could balance myself and turn round, but he simply pushed me forwards so that I fell on all fours, my butt waving naked before him.

My befuddled mind wondered if anyone had missed us. Mimi, perhaps, or the butler rounding up his staff. All it would need now was someone to fling back the curtains to get some air into the room.

My thoughts were snuffed out by the blunt knob of the waiter's cock pushing into the crevice of my bottom. My face was almost crushed into the cushion. I reached up to cup the soft balls dangling beneath the solid shaft nudging into my flesh and they retracted slightly at my touch.

'Let's do it while they're not looking,' he ordered roughly, lifting my hips up. With his fingers still diving into my snatch and his stiff cock probing underneath me, I was more than halfway there, stimulated by everything I'd seen that evening, by the promise of unadulterated lust idling behind me like an engine, and by the constant threat of discovery by an accidental, or deliberate, voyeur.

The thick muscle found its target at last and started to nudge blindly in between my waiting lips. I flung myself greedily on to him. His fingers stayed where they were, plunging in alongside his cock, filling me to bursting point, one or two of them tweaking at my clitoris, playing every tiny part of me.

'If they don't see what you're up to, then you won't get into trouble,' he crooned. I was pinned by his fingers and his cock, helpless. All my thoughts were centred on what he was doing to me. I gave up trying to see his reflection clearly, to make out his features. I should have paid more attention to what he looked like when he was waving the silver tray in front of me. All I could recall was a dark, piratical beard. But who cared about his face? He was inside me now.

But then something caught my eye in the glass. A movement. It wasn't him and it wasn't me. It wasn't coming from inside, either. There was someone outside the window. Looking in at us. Two people, in fact. I could see their faces rising in the moonlight a few inches away from mine and, as I watched with a mixture of horror and fascination, they came right up close and stared boldly in.

'Stop!' I squeaked. 'Look!'

The two spindly lads from the stables, wearing thick jackets, were shivering in the night air, but remained open-mouthed, practically dribbling as they watched what the posh guests were doing inside the Hall.

'Stop?' he muttered, starting deliberately, slowly, to slide himself up me, pushing my face closer to the window as he did so. 'You must be bloody joking.'

They might already have had a good look at Mimi and Chrissie's antics. They ogled me and I gaped at them and, as I worked out what exactly they could see, my shock turned to wicked excitement. I wondered if the waiter could see our new audience. If he could, he didn't care. He didn't alter his rhythm. And I didn't want him to. I wanted my lads to see. Being watched, not by a group of world-weary adults but by a couple of hot-blooded, randy youths was thrilling. They would be able to see my tits dangling out of my beautiful green dress, my hands spread out on the window seat to keep my balance, my body being rocked forwards as the man rammed me from behind. God, they might even know him! He might have arranged to do this, talked about it with them earlier, told them he'd pick one of the randy female guests and fuck her in front of the window at a certain time of the evening so they could see.

'Those boys. They can see us,' I gasped. 'What about those boys?'

'How about we give them a show they'll never forget? You're good at that.'

Their young pricks would be shifting and stiffening inside their grubby jeans. Their hands would be in their pockets, rubbing themselves. They would be muttering obscene comments to each other, but finding it harder to speak as the sight of me and the waiter rutting got to them, made them impossibly horny, and the spunk started rising, ready to pump uselessly over their hands.

The waiter and I were totally locked on to each other now. His cock pushed on up me until it could go no further. I slid down on to him until I could go no further. And then he held my hips totally still, forcing us both to pause again.

'Suki Summers,' he murmured, as we hovered on the brink. I couldn't struggle, let alone demand to know how he knew my name. I didn't want to lose the momentum. He murmured something else, but I couldn't hear him. He pulled out the pins that Mimi had secured in my hair so that it unwound over my shoulders. He stroked it for a moment, smoothing it against my back as if I was a horse, and I felt a jolt of recognition. I tried to focus my mind, but then he started thrusting violently, ramming full length inside me, lifting me off my knees with the force of his thrusting.

'How do you know my name?'

'It's more polite that way, don't you think? Now, just concentrate on the boys all cold and hungry out there. Give them the thrill of their little teenage lives.'

I let myself go limp and managed to find a way to slip my hand down between my legs. The sight must have blown the minds of the young voyeurs outside, and it certainly did the trick for me. His cock jerked faster and faster into my cunt. The rhythm overtook me, overtook us both. Every nerve centred on the desire and pleasure spreading wherever he penetrated, and wherever I rubbed, setting fire to me until finally the ecstasy burst as I came and shrieked and moaned into the cushion.

With two huge thrusts he was juddering to orgasm as well, gripping my hips so as not to slip out of me. His cock stayed stiff as gradually I let him draw out of me. There was another pause, and then he lifted his hands away from my hips, letting me wriggle forwards on my knees, juice running down my thighs, to crumple into a heap by the window

The boys ran off into the darkness, and behind me the waiter pulled aside the curtains. The noise from the other guests spilled into our secret alcove. I sat up, pulled my dress down and turned to face him.

But he had slipped away. I jumped to my feet and hurtled through the curtains after him. Everyone was still milling about as if nothing had happened. More music was playing. I was too confused to make out the individual faces of Mimi or Chrissie in the melee, let alone speak to either of them. I dashed from the room. I didn't want to speak to anyone.

The silver tray was left on the hall table at the bottom of the stairs, with one solitary glass on it. I picked up the glass to take it up to my bedroom, and then I saw, lying beside it, a tiny earring, in the shape of a horse's head.

14

The coldness of the dawn put paid to any more efforts to sleep, and I got up. All night I had heard laughter and music echoing round the Hall. Someone had tried my door several times, but I had locked it. It was out of character for me to be on the fringes of a party, but that night I didn't want to join in. In the few dreams I snatched, all I could see was the waiter's indistinct reflection and his eyes glittering in the window as he screwed me.

I dressed in yesterday's clothes, leaving my velvet finery on the bed. I took my bag and went downstairs. The Hall was silent with sleep, but there were shoes and scarves and even the odd pair of knickers strewn about the corridors and stairs. I remembered that my own magenta knickers would still be in the alcove, where the waiter had ripped them off, but although I searched at every single window in the salon, I couldn't find them.

The early morning air was freezing, and I pulled my camel coat tight around me. I had no idea how I was going to get home, but I wanted to leave, right away. Something about last night's deception made me feel awful. Chrissie was my oldest friend and, through Club Crème, I'd ended up sliding up and down her fiancé's pole. I wanted to speak to her, sort things out, but I didn't know what to say. How could I talk my way out of her inevitable conclusion that my new job had changed me into some sort of boyfriend-stealing bitch?

I wanted to speak to Mimi, too. But I didn't want her

to come marching in to my room and catch me in the middle of escaping.

There was one person I did want to see right now, though. I fingered the silver earring in my pocket and set off towards the stables. As soon as the warm smell of fur and straw and hoof oil wafted over the yard to greet me I felt better. I heard a muffled snort of laughter. I turned, my cheeks burning, expecting it to be Merlin.

But it was the two lads who had stared through the windows last night. They had been a few inches from the action – separated only by a pane of glass. My cheeks burned even hotter. I realised that somehow there was something far more titillating yet embarrassing about being watched by a couple of teenagers than being watched or even shagged by any number of full-grown, hairy men.

The two boys were shuffling across the cobbles, leaning on pitchforks and yawning. They saw me and nudged each other. I blushed scarlet. They looked me slowly up and down. Not that they could see much of me today, swathed in my coat, but still they had the eyes of dirty old men in their young faces, and I felt as if they were stripping me.

I walked as sedately as I could to the nearest stable and started stroking the long face of the big bay horse with a white streak down its nose. More than anything I wanted Merlin to come up behind me as he had last night, disguised as a waiter. I wanted him to decide what to do next. He was usually the outsider looking in and, for a few moments, staring at the sleeping Hall full of hung-over, sated people, I wondered if I was the same.

Seeing Chrissie last night had reminded me who I was supposed to be. The urchin in the ripped jeans – not this sex siren, bringing men to heel with a flick of a shirt button while purporting to be at their beck and call.

And yet I enjoyed being the sex siren. Loved it, in fact. I didn't know if I could turn back to my old sensible ways, even for Chrissie.

As I breathed in all the familiar smells, my heart started thumping. That always happened when I started questioning what I was doing. The horse tossed its head, impatient with me because I had no oats or sugar lumps, and knocked me sideways. I clutched on to the stable door, feeling stupid. In the distance I could hear the hooves of another horse, half trotting, half galloping across the parkland. I changed my mind. I couldn't let Merlin find me here, waiting for him like a love-struck schoolgirl. It was time to go.

I clicked my heels loudly across the cobbles towards the two boys, and pointed to an old horsebox parked nearby. They shrugged, and watched me. I couldn't be bothered to struggle with conversation today, so I just tried the door of the horsebox, which fell rustily open. I lifted my leg to get in, and paused. My coat was undone. They could see the lacy tops of my stockings. If I just parted my legs a little more, it was a struggle to reach the step after all, they could see higher, right up my skirt.

I looked over at them, and winked, then climbed on to the cracked old seats of the front cab. The two lads didn't need inviting twice. They raced over. I crossed my legs slowly, my tight skirt pulled across my thighs, leaving my coat open so that at least they had something to ogle on our journey and, in minutes, we were backing out into the road, leaving the sleeping Hall behind us.

The other horse had nearly reached us, and I noticed that the rider was sitting like a cowboy, legs straight in the western-style saddle. We had nearly passed him before he frowned over at the horsebox and saw who was rattling out of the gates. My heart started racing again as I saw who it was. He wheeled his horse in front of us, putting his hand up as if we were Bonnie and two Clydes escaping from a bank raid with the booty.

'Shit. We're in trouble now,' muttered the boys. They licked their hands and looked lively as their boss approached the lorry.

'Kidnapping Miss Summers?' Sir Simeon enquired coolly. The boys shifted about anxiously on the seat. 'I'm not sure that's allowed.'

'I asked them to take me to the station, Sir Simeon,' I spoke up for them.

'Well, we'll swap. You boys take the horse. I'll take the girl,' Sir Simeon said, dismounting stiffly.

The three of us sat blankly in the cab, watching him. I realised that with his bad leg the only way to ride was western style, with his legs straight in long stirrups. It suited him. In the cold morning light he looked ruddy and bright-eyed, his eyes accentuated by a thick blue sweater. He wore leather chaps over his cream cords to protect them from the inevitable sweat and grease of the saddle. I couldn't help admiring his elegance even when he was dismounting from a horse. The intriguing lord-of-the-manor style was every bit as irresistible as his son's contrasting, Mexican-bandit style.

'I said, you take the horse!' Sir Simeon repeated loudly, rapping on the door.

The boys scrambled out without even looking at me, and Sir Simeon hoisted himself up into the driver's seat. The horsebox was still vibrating as its ancient engine idled, and I watched his strong fingers as he wrestled to get the gear stick into place.

'Can you take me to the station?' I asked, as the lorry lurched into first gear.

'Certainly not. It's breakfast time.'

'If you don't mind, I'd like to go back to London. I had a bit of a jolt last night. Jeremy Hall's fiancée is my oldest friend, Chrissie. She knows that I had an interview back in October with Club Crème but she has no idea that he's a member. She doesn't know that her perfume convention was organised by the club. And she most certainly doesn't know what goes on there.'

Sir Simeon's laugh came from deep down in his chest. He stepped on the accelerator and the horsebox coughed its way towards the house. 'I'm aware of the poor woman's ignorance,' he said. 'But she knows all about it now, you can be sure of that. And if she does mind about it, that's not our problem. It's not up to us to chastise scoundrels like Jeremy Hall. It's only up to us to take care of our members when they're away from home. Cosset them. Offer them succour. You know the drill.'

'Don't get me wrong,' I said. 'On the whole I absolutely love what's been going on – what I've been doing at Club Crème –' I stopped, remembering what he'd been doing to me that very first night in the bar, '– but I never intended this to be a permanent position, and it nearly got me into serious trouble last night. Chrissie will never speak to me again when she finds out.'

'Let me tell you, young lady, that you are tailor-made for this job, and you've only just begun. All the members love you. The word is spreading via the grapevine. We've never had so many applications to join the club. You can't possibly let little concerns like an old school friend stop you in your tracks.'

All the curtains were still drawn at the house. We creaked to a halt round the side and Sir Simeon turned the full force of his eyes on me.

'I can't be as blasé about this as you,' I said and squirmed in my seat. 'And I still think I should reconsider my position.'

'It's too early in the morning to be so formal. I'm more

than happy to consider your position, but not in the way you mean. Look at you, Suki. Even sitting in a smelly horsebox at six in the morning, you still can't help oozing it, can you?' He hauled on the handbrake, then slid his hand easily off it onto my leg. 'Legs akimbo like you're posing for a lingerie catalogue ... no wonder those poor lads were practically blowing a gasket.'

He was right. My legs may have been demurely crossed, but my coat was thrown open and my skirt was hitched right up to my crotch. The triangle of my pubic hair was clearly visible between my thighs. In the haste to get away from the stable yard I'd forgotten that I'd lost my knickers.

'I only wanted them to give me a lift,' I mewed weakly but, as Sir Simeon raised one cynical eyebrow, I couldn't keep the grin off my face. 'I thought an eyeful would do it.'

'They'd have driven you to John O'Groats with that on offer,' was his rejoinder, as he cast his eyes to my crotch, 'and I'm not letting such a treasure slip through *my* fingers, either. But first things first. What did I say earlier about breakfast?'

Before I could protest any further he had marched me through the silent house and into a small study that smelt of lavender and French polish. The walls were painted a soothing dark green and were lined with books. There was a large desk in the window and an old leather Chesterfield sofa beckoned me from beneath a stunning portrait of a dark-skinned woman with waist-length black hair and Cherokee cheekbones. She was lying naked, one hand thrust between her smooth legs, her other arm flung over the arm of what looked like the very same Chesterfield sofa. The décor was very similar to some of the rooms at the club.

I went across to sit down and, as my eyes shut, it felt as if I was sinking forever into the enveloping leather.

Then came the strong aroma of coffee wafting in my nostrils, too tempting to ignore. Who was bringing me coffee in bed, I wondered blearily. An irate Mimi? A livid Chrissie? An off-hand Merlin? I sniffed the coffee for a moment, unwilling to come to, but then I opened my eyes blearily. I wasn't in bed at all. A big white bowl of coffee and a buttery croissant were on the table in front of me. They blurred out of focus as I closed my eyes again, thankful that Mimi and Chrissie and Merlin hadn't discovered that I was still here, slumbering in the master's study.

'Don't go to sleep again, Suki. This is too good an opportunity to miss.'

I forced my eyelids apart. Sir Simeon was sitting in a big armchair opposite me. He'd taken off the jumper and was wearing a denim-blue shirt open at the neck. I thought of all the other guises I'd seen him in: the tramp shuffling through the hall at the club; the businessman in his suit and tie, calmly taking me from behind; the smart spy in his long coat and trilby.

I imagined the shirt and countrified cords were his usual look, but I could have been wrong. This could be yet another disguise. And Merlin was pretty nifty at changing his look to suit his surroundings too. They were a pair of chameleons. This morning Sir Simeon looked ridiculously youthful and virile, lord of all he surveyed and lord especially of me. He pushed the coffee across the table.

'What do you want me to do?' I asked nervously, sitting up and shaking my hair out of my eyes. He was, after all, my boss. 'I imagine you've kept me here to do something for you.'

'Oh yes, I want you to do something for me,' he said. 'It's not fair that everyone else, including my wayward son, keeps getting to taste you, Suki. It's time I exercised my rights over you.'

'*Droit de seigneur*, do you mean?' I asked cheekily. I remembered the medieval term. I'd always thought the idea of the lord of the manor having his wicked way with any wench he chose was dead sexy. And in some ways that was how it had been with the prince. Perhaps Merlin also.

'A modern version,' Sir Simeon was saying. 'Nowadays you have the choice to refuse, which those poor milk-maids and shepherdesses didn't. But I'll take advantage of you anyway.'

The laugh was rumbling up from his chest again. I was starting to feel horny at the thought of him taking me by force, but I felt compelled to deflect him, not show him I was that easy.

'Mimi will never forgive either of us,' I warned him, sitting up and trying in vain to pull my skirt down. It would have been simpler just to take it off. I tried to get a grip on the bowl of coffee, but my fingers were shaking. No one else had this effect on me, I thought crossly. Hot coffee slopped over my fingers. I tried to lift the coffee bowl to my lips to hide my face, but it tipped danger-ously to one side and I let it go. I started crumbling the croissant instead.

'That tactic won't distract me, Suki. Mimi is my employee as well, don't forget. It's not up to her what I do.'

'She's not just that. She's your mistress, isn't she? I saw her with you, in your flat in London.'

'Did you now? Exciting, was it? What were we doing, exactly?'

He wanted me to confess to being a voyeur, the dirty

sod. His eyes flashed but I couldn't tell if it was amusement or anger. I picked up the croissant and held it like a gun towards him.

'You were in front of your fire. I saw you from the club penthouse, that's all. When I was at Mikhail's party. Merlin was standing by the window all night, and I wanted to see what he'd been looking at.'

'What did you see, my peeping Thomasina?'

He was standing up now, coming round the coffee table towards me.

'Nothing,' I answered, slightly shakily. 'It's none of my business. But Merlin can't have been very happy by what he saw.'

'That serves him right for being where he's not welcome,' Simeon snapped. 'I'm sure whatever mischief we were getting up to, you've done with him. Lucky devil. So you see, we're all even.'

'Except we're not even at all,' I retorted, 'because, in the end, she and I are just your wenches.'

I was halfway to my feet now. Simeon pushed me into the soft leather of the sofa and I fell back again, dragging him with me. In falling, I yanked him towards me and felt his weight crushing me. I lifted my hands, trying to get a grip on something, and my fingers caught round the back of his head. I froze at the intimate touch of his thick hair and tried to twist away, but his face was close. I could smell faint cigar smoke and the scent of some bespoke eau de cologne, no doubt purchased in Jermyn Street. My lips slid against his, and then he was biting my mouth. I was too shocked to move. I was in awe of him, and yet I wanted him. I forced myself to wait and see what he would do.

I realised I was struggling to breathe, suffocated by the sudden ferocious desire rocketing through me. He was heavy lying on top of me. It was intoxicating, but it was also squeezing the life out of me. I didn't want real life to come crowding in, let alone the party of guests who would be waking upstairs, but I needed to get him off. With a huge effort I twisted away from under him and tried to stumble to my feet, but he caught me round the middle, slamming me back across his knees.

'Where are you going, my pretty maid?' he enquired, whisking my coat off. 'Because I was planning to have you for my breakfast.'

'Here? Now?' I whined. 'They'll all be awake soon.' I gasped and wriggled, suddenly becoming as helpless as the proverbial milkmaid. I glanced across the room. 'Anyone could barge in looking for you.'

'Who cares? They'll either run a mile or else stay for the show, if they've any taste. That doesn't bother you, does it?' he asked. He could tell I was still tense. 'It's a bit late to come over all shy with me, Miss Summers.'

He had my tight T-shirt up over my head before I could stop him, and tossed it on to the floor. He paused when he saw that I was wearing the magenta corset and, as always, I preened with satisfaction at the sight of my own breasts cupped in my carefully chosen underwear.

'I'm not shy,' I whispered, fighting the urge to undo the corset for him.

'Mimi said you had amazing taste in lingerie,' he said. 'She was surprised, considering the orphan Annie act you tried on with all of us at first.'

'That wasn't an act.'

I looked down, jealousy elbowing my lust aside. I didn't want to think about Mimi at this precise moment, for God's sake. His fingers traced the seams and embroidery of the garment, felt the delicate cups holding my breasts, but avoided touching my skin. My nipples pricked up. My tight skirt was rucked up round my hips.

The expanse of white flesh at the top of my thighs gleamed out from the silk stockings, spread on either side of his legs, inviting the eye up to delve into the shadows of my sex.

'You know she's touched me?' I said. So much for not thinking about Mimi. 'She took me in hand. Literally. She fingered me. Like this.'

I slid my fingers down between my legs. I was being purposefully provocative. For a moment his blue eyes rested on my face, then he looked down. I shifted to part my legs a little more, and edged my fingers into the auburn curls. I held my breath to stop myself gasping out loud as they grazed the hidden clit.

'And who can blame her,' he said quietly, unzipping my skirt.

'Mimi did this to me on my first day working for you,' I repeated myself stubbornly. 'She finger-fucked me in her house, and kissed me, with tongues, and I enjoyed it. How does that make you feel?'

'It makes me all the more determined to have you again myself, Miss Summers. Save you, and her, the bother of sisters doing it for themselves.'

I couldn't believe how cool and cheeky he was. Nothing fazed him. He was snatching me from under Merlin's nose as calmly as he had snatched Mimi. No wonder Merlin was always so angry. But it only made me want Sir Simeon all the more. The resistance had ebbed right out of me.

Sensing this as clearly as he would sense fear in one of his horses, Simeon suddenly hoisted me off his knee and ripped my skirt off, then thumped me down again and started to unhook the corset. The daylight coming through the window was harsh and bright now, leaving nothing to the imagination. He lifted the corset away and my freed breasts tumbled heavily forwards.

'No arguments now, eh? Fight gone out of you?'

'It's too early in the morning to fight. Anyway, look at me,' I said, and we both looked down. I was naked apart from my stockings and boots. I was straddling his knee, and he had one arm round my waist to stop me moving. He caught one bouncing breast with his other hand, and he was pulling it towards his face. I was sitting on his thighs, my fingers still poking and prodding inside my warm, wet lips, even though he couldn't see what I was doing.

'And you're not going to try running away again?' he asked.

'I've nowhere to run to,' I replied.

The potent mix of awe and desire was crushing me. I couldn't run away because my legs would collapse beneath me. As if he knew what I was thinking, he let go of my waist, inviting me to try to run, but then he started fondling my breasts and, pulling me towards him, he bit hard on one nipple, then the other, sending shocks of desire straight to my cunt.

I pushed myself hard against his face, grabbing his hair and angling my nipples brazenly into his mouth, scraping them against his teeth, pulling back, muffling his cheeks and ears with the warm mounds as if to drown him.

'That's good. Because no one ever runs away from me,' he said calmly, and the arrogance only fired me up even more.

I rose up on my knees. My moist sex stuck to his trousers for a minute, the tiny curls caught on the fabric, tugging the tender skin before letting go. I wanted to be higher up than him, feel his head burrowing in between my breasts. He was hurting me now, biting and nibbling, as my nipples stretched taut like arrowheads. They felt hard yet sensitive, feeling the pain yet relishing the pleasure. My hips started to gyrate automatically; the female instinct that kicked in during arousal.

I wriggled my buttocks backwards, still leaning my torso against his face, and scrabbled for his zip. I felt him tense and, for a moment, his mouth relaxed on my nipple, but I got my hand firmly inside his trousers, then pulled them down until my fingers landed on his waiting prick.

'Not even Mimi?' I challenged him, egged on by the sudden vision I had of him having sex with her in her big white house, rolling across the white carpet, her big brown nipples dangling over him, his cock ramming up inside her . . .

His penis jumped in my hand. I tilted my pelvis in answer, teasing him with the moist prize of young pussy. Even I wasn't so cruel as to prolong the proceedings for too long and I gently guided his cock until it rested just inside me. Even then, I thought about Mimi. I liked her. More than liked her. But now we were in competition for this guy and his son. The fighting spirit made my whole body pulsate with longing.

'I warn you, Summers. Don't get smart,' Sir Simeon went on. 'I'm capable of anything if I'm roused, particularly to anger.'

'I'd like to see you roused. But you wouldn't hurt me, Sir Simeon,' I mocked softly. 'You want me too badly.'

Instead of waiting, relishing the suspense, I let myself drop, driving myself on to his cock. He kept his fingers on my nipples, rubbing and pinching, but he pulled his mouth away, and I could feel his breath hot on my throat.

'I won't be spoken to like that, Summers. You are a dirty little bitch, Summers, and you're asking for it.'

Then we were growling and swearing like old foes going into battle, both bucking furiously against each other. I gripped him with my thighs, thrusting my hips against him, cramming him in, grinding right down to the very base so that he filled me with all those solid inches of rock-hard, thrusting cock.

Each time we pulled back and slammed against each other we became more violent, and I cried out loud as I felt him hitting the G-spot. Time was running out.

'Go on, then,' I taunted him. I had no idea where this all came from. 'Show me what you're like when you're roused. Show me how cheeky I've been, before they all walk in and see us.'

I couldn't hold on much longer. I was arousing myself to a fever pitch. I clawed at my clit, lewdly frigging myself to egg him on further, giving him the treat of his life. This was my first proper time with him, and very likely my last, and I wanted it to keep going as long as possible. On the other hand, I couldn't stop the flow. I could tell from the sounds around the house – clattering of pans in the kitchen, plates and cutlery being laid out in the dining room – that we were no longer alone and, any minute, a butler or someone would come knocking at Sir Simeon's door.

'I warn you, Summers,' he started to growl, but there were other sounds coming from him. Up until now he had kept himself in check but there was a low, surprised groaning which I guessed signalled his approaching climax. His head fell back against the sofa and he stared at me, his eyes clouding over, frowning as if this wasn't what he expected, and I rode him for all I was worth, moaning in my own exquisite pain as I started to come and, as the climax broke over me and his eyes flickered, I leaned over and kissed him again, licked his lips, flicked my tongue over his teeth, sucked his tongue as it slipped into my mouth. He strained up against me, his mouth warm and fixed on mine, and I felt him pumping his juice into me. I squeezed every drop and held it there. I didn't want it to ebb away because then it would be gone for good.

There was a sharp rapping at the door and we jerked apart. We stared at each other, trying not to laugh. I gripped him inside me as hard as I could. His penis twitched once, twice, then started to slip out. I twisted away from him, grabbed my clothes and turned my back. The daylight and the rapping had knocked sense into us. Our mingled juices dripped down the insides of my legs as I zipped my skirt back up. My nipples still tingled as I pulled the shirt back on. I couldn't relax until I had buttoned my coat up, run my fingers through my hair and taken several more breaths.

Then I turned to look at Sir Simeon. Thank God, he'd done up his trousers and was sitting there calmly as if we'd just had a business meeting.

'Come in,' he called. The butler entered and glanced immediately at the magenta corset slung over the arm of the Chesterfield. His face didn't flicker. He picked up the crumbled croissant and the untouched coffee. We must have looked a picture. Me standing over Sir Simeon as if I'd just been telling him off, him sitting on the sofa rubbing his bad leg, cool except for his burning eyes.

When the butler had gone, Sir Simeon stood up and went across to his desk.

'Still determined to leave?' he asked, waving the MG car keys at me. 'Even though the party carries on tonight? Even though you're the best we've ever had?'

'What do you mean, the best? Employee or lover? For Mimi or for you?'

'Both. All of it. She'd agree with me. She's wild about you. We all are. Don't go, Suki. The Club Crème needs you.'

I couldn't help snorting. 'You make me sound like the cavalry,' I said.

'Not that the cavalry arrived in a little old MG, but if you'll stay, there'll be more than car keys on offer.'

His back was to the window, so I couldn't see the expression on his face. I hoped he was desperate for my answer to be yes, and reluctant to show it.

'Let me go back to London,' I said, catching the keys as he threw them at me. I was equally desperate to have him again. 'And then I'll think long and hard about staying on at the club.'

'Fine,' barked Sir Simeon, once more the lord. Then he turned and threw something which landed softly on my shoulder. I hooked my fingers into it. It was a sliver of magenta satin. The lord looked haughtily down his nose before his cheekbones lifted in unmistakable amusement. 'But don't forget to take your knickers with you.'

15

All roads seemed to lead to Club Crème. I got back to my accomdation and changed in to my one remaining set of jeans and a sweater, but I was restless. I paced up and down for a while, debating what I was going to do about my immediate future. Then I pounded back down the stairs and out to where I'd parked the MG.

I walked up the anonymous alley and into the elegant hallway, still not entirely sure what I was going to do or who I was going to do it to. At first I thought the building was deserted, but then I heard the low voice of Miss Sugar speaking to someone in the office. I peered round the doorway. Miss Sugar was alone. She was speaking, but on the telephone. And she wasn't her usual composed self. Not in the least. I dodged back out of sight.

For a start her feet were up on the desk like she didn't give a damn. Her habitual long grey skirt wasn't pulled demurely to the ground, but crumpled up round her knees, and her thighs were swathed in sheer black silk. I had never seen further up than her ankles. She had incredibly long slim legs that were waggling slightly as she spoke, as if she wanted to take flight at any moment. She had always looked so contained before, as if she was set in stone, like a ballerina striking a pose. I couldn't peel my eyes away from this new Miss Sugar, who had all about her the definite air of imminent debauchery.

With each twitch of her legs her skirt fell further away from any pretence of modesty, and now I could see the definite promise of white flesh gleaming at the top of her leg. She was wearing stockings, not the matronly tights I would have expected.

She hadn't seen me, and I stood in the doorway, silently staring at her. One long white hand was writing something down on her usual memo pad as she spoke, and I realised, to my relief, that despite her languid pose she was actually speaking in her normal clipped, formal voice.

'And after you've checked in with us here at the club, you would like me to accompany you to the opera? In a private box?'

She put the silver pen down and took her glasses off. She tapped her fingers on the pad as she listened to the phone. Then the idle fingers of her hand landed like delicate insects on one exposed knee and started walking up and down the narrow bone. She banged her knees together, then slowly let them fall sideways. Her fingers started stroking up her own silky thigh.

'I'd be delighted, Mr –'

She yawned, a wide, insolent yawn which displayed her pearl-white teeth and her red throat. Believing she was alone, she made no effort to cover her mouth and, in any case, both her hands were occupied.

I had trouble stifling surprise rising up as I watched her, but I didn't want to interrupt her. This was riveting. A whole new side to Miss Sugar, going about her business unobserved. Or so she obviously thought, judging by the way her hand was creeping up under her skirt now, pushing it back, right up her legs, so that I could see the suspenders and the forbidden slice of white flesh which led my eye straight to – a knickerless groin.

I always like the feel of silk or satin or cotton, however flimsy, brushing against me – that's if I remember not to lose my knickers in country houses – but Miss Sugar obviously had other preferences. The stark contrast between her governess-stern exterior and the fact that she wore no knickers was startling, and devastatingly sexy.

What had I expected her to wear? Old lady's frilly bloomers? I hadn't expected anything because I hadn't given it any thought, but now I couldn't take my eyes off her.

I looked up at her face, seeing it as if for the first time. She hadn't quite finished the yawn because her mouth was still open. The tip of her tongue flicked a couple of times across her lips, and her big pale eyes watered slightly. The sudden question popped into my mind: did Mimi know about Miss Sugar's rejection of knickers? Did Sir Simeon? After all, they were like a little family before I came along. A small hard nugget of curiosity started nagging at me. There was still so much I wanted to know about Club Crème and all who sailed in her.

I wanted Miss Sugar to see me watching her, tell me what she was doing, what was going through that head of hers. I wanted to know how intimately Mimi knew this other employee. Another rival for her affections, I now realised. I remembered Mimi saying something about there being more to Miss Sugar than met the eye. And of course Miss Sugar had been around for a long time before I showed up.

'Yes,' Miss Sugar said suddenly and loudly into the phone, startling me so that I fell back against the door-frame. 'We absolutely specialise in escorting our members out and about if that's what they want.'

She tipped her head back and laughed – a laugh which started out as a filthy guffaw. She hastily lifted it up the scale so that it finished as a more ladylike tinkle, but the damage was done. I wondered what the uptight client at the other end was thinking. But I was fascinated. I looked at Miss Sugar through new eyes. Her hidden, filthy laugh. And now, her exploring, private fingers, stroking lovingly and definitely over her pubes, celebrating the lack of knickers as she conducted the phone call. She looked as if she shaved, the scattering of hair over them was so pale.

She slid down slightly in her swivel chair as she listened to more outpourings from the hapless client and twisted the chair from side to side. Her feet up on the desk slid further apart, the pointed boots splayed outwards across the files and papers.

'Right. So we'll see you this evening. A few more details, please, before we ring off.'

It was like listening to one half of a dirty phone call. Miss Sugar closed her eyes and lifted her skirt right up to her waist. As an afterthought she put the phone on 'conference' mode, and a man's voice, young, hesitant and breathless, started to speak.

'It's my wife. I have to get away from her. Just for one night, every so often. She's frigid, you see.'

'Oh, my word. I didn't mean those kind of details. But do go on, if it helps,' she said.

She was still rocking her chair from side to side. Her knees were slack now, open on the edge of the desk. Her hands were busy, one smoothing up and down her flat white stomach, little finger tickling meditatively into her navel, the other fiddling, not quite delving in, but hovering around the two secret lips of her sex.

'I have to fantasise to get any relief,' stuttered the man after a few false starts. 'I can't live without sex forever. I'm only young.'

'And what exactly do you fantasise about? If you want to share that with us – me,' Miss Sugar asked tentatively.

No wonder she knew everything about everyone. She had her style down to a tee. The secrets were pouring out of him now and she was loving it. Two fingers were crooked like horns over her pubes, going to pin back the soft pussy lips. My throat was tight as I watched her milking the poor man's story for her own pleasure. I had a feeling that if she knew that she, in turn, was being watched by me, she would be turned on even more by the thought.

'A threesome?' He sounded as if he was asking her permission. Any minute now she would crack a whip. 'You know. Two women. Crawling over me. I suppose crawling all over each other as well.'

'Perfectly normal fantasy,' she said in her most reassuring voice. 'And healthy.' I could hear a bubble of mirth in her voice. 'And what sort of women do you fantasise about? Businesswomen? Sophisticated women or simple girl-next-door types?'

At this she splayed herself open so that her dark red slit was suddenly, dramatically exposed. Miss Sugar's hips tilted slightly, raising herself in the chair. I was fidgeting now, wanting to copy what she was doing. The little movements, the arching, tilting, all helping to accentuate the tension, the anticipation – a curious solo game of offering and denial, since it was her own hands that she was playing with.

I leaned against the doorframe, my own arousal weakening me. Outside it was getting late, the day dark and cold. Rain was beginning to fall in earnest in the dingy alleyway, darkening all the windows. The only light in the office was the pool cast by Miss Sugar's angle-poise lamp, shining directly on to the action of her hands and her hungry snatch.

'It doesn't matter, so long as they are as different as possible from my wife!' spluttered the poor man, making both me and Miss Sugar jump out of our trances. 'Women who love sex, in other words.'

'And how would you feel,' said Miss Sugar in her

smoothest, poshest voice, 'if you met such women in real life?'

There was a strangled sob at the other end of the phone. Miss Sugar's throat was extended with amusement and pleasure. A vicious little smile stretched her lips as she listened. If only the poor man could see the effects his story was having.

'I'd think I'd died and gone to heaven,' the man said, regaining his composure. 'But for now all I have to fall back on is my new membership of your club. I need to spread my wings, have some adventure. And I've been told that you are the best.'

'Rest assured of that,' Miss Sugar responded hoarsely, her hands frantic now as they sought their pleasure. 'All your dreams will come true if you join Club Crème. We are constantly gratified by the reports we have of our popularity – a source of endless satisfaction to our members. I know we won't disappoint.'

Her fingers started pushing roughly, brutally, into herself, even as she was still speaking. Her knees were opening and closing, her feet kicking papers and pens off the desk as she rocked herself more violently in the chair, biting her lip, not being gentle at all but giving herself a real seeing-to, her arm flexing back and forth into the secret folds of her groin almost as if she was punishing herself, knocking herself backwards in the chair, then regaining composure and pulling herself back towards the desk so that she could balance.

Her buttocks were half rising off the chair as she started what I assumed was the onset of her climax. I rubbed myself against the doorframe, desperate for some friction to ease the ache between my legs.

The doorframe was hard and unforgiving, but I wedged it between my legs, so that the wooden edge bit through my jeans and my knickers, into my hidden fanny, and, like Miss Sugar, I wasn't gentle. I wanted to keep up with her, relieve the mounting tension down there as quickly as possible. I had tried to resist, told myself this was another woman pleasuring herself, and not of any interest to me, but I seemed to be in a constant state of semi-arousal these days: men, women, older gentlemen – I was turning into a wanton slut!

And now here was Miss Sugar, offering the possibility of more stimulation than anyone else, revealing a whole new side to her demure demeanour.

'I hear you have a magnificent staff. I'll look forward to seeing you tonight, then?' The voice at the end of the phone needed an answer.

Miss Sugar answered, with one last thrust of her fingers over her clit she flung herself backwards in the chair and it wheeled away across the floor. She had to shout to make herself heard.

'Oh yes. Yes, yes, yesss.'

I was half laughing, half shuddering my small, wet climax against the doorframe as I heard her hang up and let out a long sigh of satisfaction. She paused in her chair with her back to me, then spun herself round to face the door. Her legs were stretched out in front of her, her hands still buried between them. Her eyes without the glasses were huge and glazed, as if she'd been sleeping.

'Ah, Summers.' She sighed out my name in another yawn, pulling her skirt down in a lazy fashion. There wasn't a trace of embarrassment on her solemn features. 'What are you doing here?'

'I could ask you the same question,' I replied, stepping into the room and dropping my bag noisily on the floor. 'Bringing yourself off while talking to a new member! Whatever next?'

'Bringing myself off *with* a new member, perhaps?' she said. She raised her eyebrows suggestively, and I found it was me who was blushing. 'Do you think we should find out if *he's* the one with the magnificent staff?'

I let out a yelp of astonished laughter, and she inclined her head, pleased with her joke.

'It always turns me on,' she said, smiling. 'They ring up, all royal and polite with their enquiries about the club, and they tell you their lives are dull and sad, and yet after some gentle prodding they give you all the gory details, and their lives aren't dull and sad at all.'

'You give good telephone, that's why,' I joked. She nodded vigorously, lowering her feet to the floor and standing up.

'So why are you not at Symes Hall?' she demanded, back to schoolmistress mode, and I sat down meekly in the chair in front of her.

'I couldn't hack it. Turned out Mr Hall's fiancée was one of my oldest friends. I didn't put two and two together. She'd never told me his surname and she always calls him Jeremy. Avril called him Jez.'

Miss Sugar pulled out a fresh file, ready to fill with tonight's new member and his details. 'So you didn't enjoy yourself at the Hall? Nothing interesting happened while you were there?'

I grew hotter and shifted in my seat. I had a feeling that if I told her I'd screwed both Merlin and his esteemed father, Miss Sugar would go mad. And I wanted her on my side for a little longer.

'I came here today to hand in my notice,' I said instead. 'I think I've gone as far as I can go in this job.'

'What on earth are you talking about?' she said briskly, flipping over a couple of sheets in the file as if I had just told her I'd chosen some controversial new linen for the bedrooms. 'You've only just started.'

'Seriously, Sugar. I feel as if I'm being sucked into this

place. I had lots of future plans when I came for that interview. I never intended to stay forever.'

She picked up the silver pen and tapped it against her teeth for a moment, studying me.

'You'd be making a big mistake leaving here. You've a great future ahead of you. Right here. Or so I'm told,' she said. She patted her hair and folded her feet neatly underneath her chair. I was flattered. I expected her to try to dissuade me, but she simply changed the subject. 'Now, I need you to help me out tonight. With that new member.' She jerked the pen towards the telephone. 'Then make your final decision, if you must, tomorrow.'

'Oh, I don't know,' I mumbled, trying to see the file she was now making notes on. She whisked it playfully away from my scrutiny. 'I feel I ought to put some distance between me and the club immediately before I'm completely trapped.'

'Don't be so dramatic,' she chided, and I sat back. It was oddly comforting to be ticked off by her, I realised. I wondered if, in fact, good old Miss Sugar already knew what I'd been up to. I studied her again and, with a shock to add to my earlier surprise, realised just how attractive she might be underneath that pale hair and ghostly expression.

I wrenched my mind away from the memory of her secrets and the streak of folded red flesh I'd spied, and spread my hands in protest.

'I love the job, Sugar. In fact, that's the trouble. I love it too much. I'm not used to feeling like that. It scares me. You all scare me.'

'So you keep saying,' she sniffed, slapping the file shut. She glanced at the clock, which said well after five. 'But the others aren't here right now. I am. And think of the overtime you'll earn if you come with me tonight. Looking at you, I can't believe some more cash won't come in handy. I'm in charge while they're away, and your resignation hasn't been accepted. So I'm telling you to get dressed.'

'What shall I wear?' I gave in.

'Oh, come now, do I have to make all the decisions for you?'

'Yes,' I said, hanging my head meekly. 'I'm no good at this kind of thing. I still need to be told what to do and what to wear.'

She clicked round the desk, her face relaxing visibly as she sensed she could start ordering me about.

'Do you have any idea how much Mimi spends on dressing her employees? Image is everything. And I just happen to have something here that might suit you. We don't have much time. You could put it on now.'

She dipped her hand into a large bag beside her desk and drew out a diaphanous white Ghost dress and some silvery sandals. The dress looked impossibly creased to me, but she shook it out in such a way that instantly it floated through the air, ready to wear.

'Do you ever chill, Sugar?' I asked, taking the dress and holding it against me. Instantly I felt beautiful and floaty myself. She had chosen well. 'I mean, don't get me wrong. I like the way you order people about. It makes me feel secure; like you're my governess. But you're not really Miss Prim, are you? I mean, talking about people being left to their own devices . . .'

She took the dress off me, jerking her head stiffly to indicate that I should take my baggy old sweater off. I pulled it over my head then started to tug at my T-shirt.

'That's right. Everything off,' she ordered. She wrenched the T-shirt off before I could protest, and then I was standing in front of her in my underwear.

'What about this?' I teased, twirling around in the way I'd been taught to model the swimsuits, jutting out my hips and pulling back my shoulders, staring down my nose at her as if I was at the end of a catwalk. 'This is quality stuff. Or would you like me to take this off as well?'

Miss Sugar licked her lips and stood still for a moment, then reached out and took a corner of the lace that bordered the breast cups of the cream basque I was wearing and fingered it thoughtfully. Her cold fingers very faintly brushed the plump skin of my breasts, and goose pimples came up at the touch. Then she pushed me gently so that I had to give her another twirl.

'Yes. No. This will do perfectly,' she said. She seemed to be out of breath and stepped back from me hurriedly. She went back behind the desk and started to pack up her briefcase. 'You were going to say something? About people being left to their own devices?'

'Forgotten already?' I teased, easing on the silvery sandals and strutting round the office still wearing only the basque. I didn't want to put the dress on until the last minute. 'I meant, I know what you do to yourself when you think no one's looking. Frisking yourself when you're talking to clients on the phone.'

Miss Sugar paused with her back to me, and I wondered if I'd gone too far. She was quite capable of slapping me if I wasn't careful. Then she buttoned up her coat, picked up her briefcase and walked calmly towards the door where I had hovered a little while ago, watching her.

'It doesn't trouble me what you've seen. I've done nothing wrong as far as I can see. Perhaps if the phone was one of these new-fangled video phones it would be even more fun.' She gave a little shrug, a tight smile stretching her mouth as she glided out on to the landing. 'But we all have hungry cunts tucked away in our drawers, don't we, Summers?'

I nearly choked with surprise, and found that I was the

one folding my arms defensively across my bulging cleavage as I stood half naked in front of her. I nodded sheepishly.

'I have to go and change,' she said. 'Don't bother to return home. Just meet me at the opera house in an hour.'

'I'm looking forward to it,' I whispered, as she clicked up the stairs to her room. And I meant it.

16

It was good to be part of a swirling, anonymous crowd again. It reminded me of arriving in a strange city for the first time. London still felt strange to me, even though I'd been back for a couple of months. There was still so much to discover. Yet again an inner voice told me to put my travelling plans on hold.

The fragile dress alternately brushed over and clung to my body as I took the bus up Piccadilly. I had grabbed a long scarlet coat that was hanging in the office to keep me warm. One of Mimi's, I assumed. I reckoned I'd be in trouble if she found out but that only filled me with a jittery excitement as I drew the borrowed velvet folds round me and hurried into the foyer of the opera house.

I couldn't see Miss Sugar anywhere. For a few minutes I allowed myself to be jostled and pushed by the crowd. The scent of expensive perfume wafted in the air and, for a moment, I was reminded of Chrissie. I wondered what was happening at Symes Hall. To distract myself from the meshed images of Sir Simeon and Merlin, not to mention Mimi and Jeremy, Chrissie and her golden-haired toy boy, and Miss Sugar frisking herself in her swivel chair, I tried to plan what I would say to Chrissie when she came back to London. Meanwhile, I searched the crowd, expecting to see Miss Sugar in her long grey coat.

The bell rang to announce the performance and every-one surged into the auditorium. There was hardly any-one left. I remembered that Miss Sugar had mentioned an opera box when she was on the telephone. I followed the signs towards the boxes as the lights went down and one or two attendants frowned at me as they wheeled away trolleys stacked with half full glasses of champagne and canapés.

All the box doors were closed. Except one. I tiptoed over and peered in. There was a row of people sitting at the front of the box, already peering through their opera glasses at the stage. On a little chair in the back corner I could see the outline of a man, sitting alone.

'Go in, quick,' a voice hissed behind me. My velvet coat was pulled off and I was pushed inside. Someone rustled about, closing the door. We were all sealed inside the warm gloom of the box. I could see only a ghostly figure, also wearing a white dress, flitting towards the man in the corner and sitting beside him. A long white arm beckoned me to follow just as the overture started up below us, and I realised who it was.

I could get used to this life, I thought, as the first act burst into life and carried us along on a tide of colour and rich vibrating voices. Under cover of the music, Miss Sugar was leaning towards the man and occasionally whispering. Once or twice she gestured towards me, but I kept my eyes firmly forwards, determined to enjoy the evening's entertainment. Coming to the opera was her idea. Let her do all the work.

'This is my friend Suki. I hope you don't mind her gatecrashing your box, Johnny, but as I told you, she was desperate to see this production,' Miss Sugar was saying to the man as the lights eventually went up for the interval. Actually, she was purring at him.

I turned and, as I did so, she wound one arm round my neck and pulled me right across her body to introduce me to her new companion. I concentrated on the warm glow of a new challenge stealing through me as I cast my eye over our new member. I'd been right about his voice on the telephone: he was very young indeed – an endearing mixture of cocky and cute. Not much over twenty. Much younger than the other men I'd met so far, in fact.

So much the better, to get Sir Simeon and Merlin out of my head.

Our Johnny had the scrubbed blond looks of a man fresh out of an all-male college and a hunky body trussed up awkwardly in a dinner jacket. Was his wife blind as well as off sex?

'Enchanted,' he said, his voice catching nervously.

I caught Miss Sugar's eye. She raised her eyebrows at me; her version of a wink.

'Where are my manners?' I tittered, reaching to shake hands with our man. 'I work with Miss Sugar at Club Crème. I'm sorry. I didn't catch your surname.'

'Neither did I,' giggled Miss Sugar. 'I was so wrapped up in listening to you on the phone earlier, I quite forgot to ask.'

I sat up to look at her properly and could hardly contain my amazement. The dress she was wearing was not only white, it was an identical Ghost dress to mine. Her pale gold hair, instead of being scraped back in its usual bun, fell in gentle waves around her face like a flapper girl. She had told me to wear my hair loose, too, and she wore the same startling shade of scarlet lipstick as mine.

'I don't mind you gatecrashing at all,' he said and coughed, looking from one to the other of us. The expression in his face changed rapidly from mild awkwardness to frankly open lust. 'How could I mind two such gorgeous creatures dropping into my lap like this?'

Miss Sugar tipped my face up and kissed me full on the lips.

'We're like sisters, aren't we?' she crooned, still holding my face close to hers.

'You certainly look as if you could be,' Johnny agreed, shifting out of his seat so that the one on the far side of him was vacant. 'Now, Suki, why don't you come and sit beside me? Then I can be a thorn between two roses.'

Miss Sugar dug one sharp fingernail into my ribs. I stood up obediently and tried to step past her, but I stumbled in the narrow gap between the seats and fell forwards, virtually straddling Miss Sugar. I grabbed the back of her chair to steady myself so that my arms fell on either side of her head. I paused deliberately. The game was beginning.

'Whoops! Lost my balance,' I said, giggling softly, smiling a big red smile at her. She smiled back, and slid her hands up my legs to my hips, pulling me down on to her knee. I hesitated, then spread my legs a little further, settling down. Johnny rubbed his hand across his mouth, staring at us, but we carried on looking at each other. I'd thought seeing her frisking herself in the office was revelation enough, but seeing Miss Sugar as an almost transparent beauty who you could blow over like a feather, was something else.

Somewhere behind me I thought I could hear the other people at the front of the box also shifting about, trying to see what was going on. But any minute now the lights would be dimmed again, and we'd be alone with our victim.

'Has Mimi seen you dressed up like this?' I asked Miss Sugar without really thinking. 'Or have you been hiding your light under a bushel all this time?'

'Of course she's seen me dressed up,' she sniffed, a hint of the normal personality appearing. 'I've been doing this job as long as she has. You're the newcomer around here. Just remember that.'

I leaned over so that my breasts were nearly in her face. Her fingers tightened their grip on my hips, and then she couldn't resist lowering her gaze to take in the valley of my cleavage, just inches away.

'And I've already proved myself as indispensable. Just remember that,' I replied. Then I raised my voice so that our companion would be bound to hear me. 'Do you think we should let Johnny get on with his opera in peace? There's plenty else we could be getting up to . . .'

'I say, girls. You both look a little . . . frisky,' Johnny said. He cleared his throat again and, very slowly, we turned our heads to look at him. He was sitting on the edge of his seat, wiping sweat from his brow. 'How about we split from here and go somewhere more private?'

'We were forgetting ourselves. Sorry,' said Miss Sugar, pulling me closer so that my groin was up against her stomach and her cheek was pressed between my breasts. 'It's just that we haven't seen each other for ages, have we, Suki? And I missed you.'

She nuzzled her nose in between my breasts and I gave an involuntary shiver. Of surprise or pleasure I wasn't at first certain, but I was sure of one thing: the little slick of wetness I felt as she licked the warm cleavage was not for Johnny's benefit. He couldn't possibly have seen.

'I could hold you all night, Sugar,' I said and giggled again, wriggling as her hands edged up my sides and she drew herself away from my breasts with a soft shake of her head. 'But as we're here as guests, I think we should take up Johnny's kind invitation to stay in his box and catch the rest of the show, don't you?'

'Oh, no. I think we've already outstayed our welcome,' Miss Sugar started to protest. I could tell that her plan was to leave the theatre as Johnny had suggested, and get on with this blatant seduction scene somewhere more private. I could tell he was itching to leave as well. But I had another idea.

'This way we can enjoy the show *and* look forward to some fun afterwards,' I insisted.

I slid off her knee as I spoke. The lights were going down for the second act. The people in the front of the box were reluctantly turning away, putting the opera glasses up to their eyes. I pulled my dress right up my thighs and stepped over Johnny's knees so that I was on his other side. I pretended to stumble again, falling onto his lap as I turned to sit down. He held my arm to steady me. A gentleman, I noted. His other hand was buried in his lap, clutching his groin. Just as I had thought – he was already turned on.

The music in the second act was even more rousing than in the first, and it meant that no other noises could possibly be heard. I didn't want to wait until the end, or until we left the theatre, I wanted to get to work right away. Not just for Johnny's sake but my own as well. This latest adventure with Miss Sugar had blown away my cares. Acting with her as part of a duo was going to be far more interesting than I'd anticipated. My 'professional' self had taken over. And I was going to enjoy it.

As the music and voices on the stage joined forces and swelled out around us, I pushed my seat right back against the wall of the box, pretending to be a little restless. All that charade of climbing over everyone's knees was unnecessary. There was plenty of room at the back for us all to stretch our legs, and any other part of us.

I glanced across at Miss Sugar. She glanced back, frowning a question. I hadn't worked it out myself and, after all, she was technically the leader on this occasion, but on impulse I jerked my head at our victim and then pushed my forefinger in and out of my mouth. It was hard to see clearly, but I was pretty certain I could see her dip her head in agreement. The first step of our campaign was decided.

I fell back in my chair and leaned my elbow casually on the back of Johnny's. I crossed my legs languorously, allowing the white dress to slide up my thighs. Despite the cold weather I had left off the stockings. Easier access, I thought, and giggled to myself as I swung my foot and absently stroked my thigh. A fluttering started up in my stomach. I made a mental note to stroke myself more often. As I watched my own hand, just letting the music rise and fall around me, infiltrating my senses, I realised how clever Sugar had been to make us wear white. In the theatrical gloom we both glimmered like phantoms.

I glanced down and saw that Johnny's hand was still resting in his groin. It wasn't moving, but he was watching my hand as it moved up and down my leg. The other people in the box sat rigidly a few feet away from us, facing forwards. Miss Sugar appeared to be awaiting my first move. I couldn't do anything too full-on or too obvious given the surroundings, but there was another way of warming the guy up ...

My hand paused on my leg, then I let it lift and land on his nearest thigh, where I continued the stroking motion. He shifted slightly in his seat and spread his legs apart, shoving his chair backwards across the floor. I was twisted awkwardly now as I stroked his leg. I slithered off my chair and knelt between his legs. I didn't dare try to see what Miss Sugar thought of this tactic; nor Johnny, for that matter, in case they tried to stop me. I was on a mission.

A soprano solo sang her tragic heart out on the stage,

accompanied by a growing crescendo of strings. I unzipped young Johnny's trousers. Still no resistance. I eased my hand inside his flies. The fluttering in my stomach grew stronger as I felt the warm nest of fur and then the long, thick shape nudging into the palm of my hand. I could feel heat pumping out of it as I could feel heat spreading in my own groin.

How I'd changed in the last few weeks, I thought, as I wrapped my fingers around his sizable cock and felt it jump in my hand. I was greedy for this. The thought of a big hard dick at my disposal, ready to penetrate any part of me I chose or demanded, was like a drug as I pulled his flies wide open.

Perhaps all this wanton behaviour really had become my speciality, as they were all suggesting. Certainly it knocked any other ideas out of the ring. What had I been thinking, considering leaving this world of opportunity, this parade of upper-class men just gagging for my favours? I realised I had almost come to expect a scenario like this to unfold. I had come to expect untrammelled, uninhibited sex to occur whenever I was within two feet of something red-blooded and wearing trousers.

In a theatre full of people there was just me, him, Miss Sugar's eyes watching, and the music providing its own sensuous backing track.

I bent my head until it was buried between his legs. His hands, relieved of any effort, pulled my hair out of my face so as to clear the way. As always, the touch on my hair turned me on even more. I tried to see the extent of his tackle, but it was too dark. I would have to do all this by feel, but I was good at that. I could smell the manly sweat and the hint of spunk and now his penis was nudging into my face, prodding its blunt end into my cheekbone. I let it rest there, then tipped my face so that the plum end slipped stickily into my mouth.

Johnny tensed backwards, perhaps with shock at how quickly I had taken control. Remember he's young, I told myself. Had his wife's thin lips ever clamped over him like this? If not, he had a lot to learn. I smirked to myself. What role was I playing, now? His schoolmistress?

I followed the jerking backwards of his body with my mouth so as not to lose track of him. As far as this particular activity was concerned, no one had taught me. This was the first time I'd given head. And yet it, like everything else, was proving to be as natural to me as breathing. They should call me Madame Summers.

His hands were tangled in my hair. I gripped the tops of his legs and kept the moist tip of his penis firmly in my mouth. I doubted he would want to pull out. His cock was too busy jumping over my tongue, rudely thrusting at the warm wetness. Sure enough he relaxed again. I congratulated myself, tipped myself forwards and opened my jaw wider so as to envelope him more fully. He was engorged now and huge. To stop the size of him gagging me I pushed the thick shaft back a little with my tongue. That closed my lips round his length and I automatically sucked it back into my mouth.

His penis stiffened and swelled even more as I started to suck on it. Now I could taste, as well as smell, his clean skin mixed with the sweet salt of the droplets edging through the slit. He couldn't help thrusting against the roof of my mouth. His hands started to guide my head slowly but firmly up and down, and that relieved the pressure of him in my throat. As my mouth slid up and down, I nipped the taut flesh, straining to avoid biting too hard. He pushed in more urgently, spreading his thighs further to get a better angle.

Suddenly, I felt a pair of hands behind me, pushing my dress up. They wrinkled the flimsy material around my waist, paused, and then started stroking the inside of my thighs. The fluttering in my stomach had long since tightened into an expanding knot of lust.

It was all I could do not to clamp my jaws down and bite Johnny as something warm and wet replaced the exploring fingers and started licking up the inside of my thigh, flicking from one leg to the other. I stopped tonguing Johnny's prick for a moment, but he laced his fingers behind my neck to keep me there. My lips nibbled their way right down to the rigid base of his shaft. But the other invisible tongue was licking me again. The invisible mouth was lapping up my leg and, with an expert flick, Miss Sugar's tongue made contact with the surface of my tender pussy lips.

My head was spinning with the unexpected pleasure, and my instinct was to close my legs to the tickling touch, but Miss Sugar wouldn't let me. Instead, she held me firmly in her cool fingers and spread my legs further apart, then brought one hand up to spread everything open. Then her tongue was back again.

I strained myself greedily towards the mouth and fingers probing at my cunt. She was licking my clit now – right on the button. A woman was licking me out. This was another amazing first for me. Writhing with Mimi that first morning in her house, letting her finger me to climax, had been a sensational taster, but this went several steps further. And Miss Sugar struck me as an expert.

I wondered vaguely, as the sensations attacked me from all sides and the music on the stage below our box seemed to gather in volume, several voices joining in a frantic chorus, whether Sugar shouldn't be pleasuring Johnny in some way, rather than caressing and licking me. But then perhaps the sight of her tonguing me from behind would excite him, if he could see what was going on.

I thought I must be drowning her tongue I was so wet. At the same time I ached to take Johnny's big cock in there as well, engulf it in my moistness. Take them both in. Take everything in. I wanted to lie back and let Johnny fuck me, let Miss Sugar lick me to madness. As if reading my mind, the firm tip of her tongue twirled more definitely at my clitoris, flicked across it several times and started to encircle it. I started to jerk frantically. I couldn't help nipping at Johnny's penis so that he groaned out loud. She might as well have applied an electric probe when she tapped at that tiny bud. I didn't know what to do with myself. Luckily Johnny withdrew, allowing the tip to play around my lips while he started to massage his balls.

Meanwhile, Miss Sugar had closed her lips around my clit and was sucking mercilessly so that tiny ripples of fire followed her tongue. The flicking of her tongue was building up the pressure. I started to push myself against her face, trying to open my legs wider to get the full benefit of her wickedly clever mouth and teeth and tongue.

The music had gone very quiet, the strings shivering as some new tragedy was awaited, or a new death enacted on the stage. I panicked for a moment. What if the lights went up? But perhaps that was Miss Sugar's problem, not mine. Anyway, the shivering of the strings set the hairs on my neck on end.

All three of us had paused, but now Miss Sugar dipped her head between my legs to savour my juices once more. Johnny rammed his fat cock back inside my mouth. I didn't want to suck any more, I wanted to fuck, but at the same time I wanted to grind myself into Miss Sugar's face and capture the mounting ecstasy. She had stopped circling my clit and her tongue was now pushing into my snatch, flicking from side to side.

Surging towards the edge now, I licked and gobbled on Johnny's dick. It quivered and strained against the roof of my mouth, and my tongue traced the ropey veins along its thick shaft.

As I sucked, hot pleasure radiated outwards. Sugar was lapping hard now. One finger, then another, inserted themselves inside me. I was torn between the two conflicting demands: wanting to thrash wildly into her face and wanting to suck Johnny off to a climax he'd remember for weeks. My cunt was filled with her jabbing fingers and the relentless sliding of her tongue.

It seemed that we were all working at the same pace because, as I was about to abandon Johnny's pleasure for the sake of my own and started to tilt and buck my hips wildly at Miss Sugar, Johnny's cock suddenly stiffened, extended for what felt like another couple of inches, and then pumped once, twice, straining and knocking my head back. My mouth slid violently up and down his shaft as he came and hot spunk shot into my throat.

Down on the stage the principals and chorus held their final notes, and the orchestra worked itself up to its finale, cymbals clashing and every instrument singing as loudly as the conductor would allow.

I held Johnny tightly inside my mouth until he had shot his load, then wriggled frantically against Miss Sugar's face as her tongue and her fingers worked me to my final frenzy and my body shook at last with an exquisite, drawn-out climax. As I shuddered to calmness, Miss Sugar licked the cream from me as if she were a cat, and then she patted me on the bottom to tell me to get up, quick, off the floor.

The audience rustled its approval, and then the applause started. I fell into my seat, gasping for breath as I pulled my virginal dress down over my knees. Johnny zipped up his flies, puffing his boyish fringe out of his eyes and trying to look cool. I reckoned Miss Sugar and I had taken him on to a whole other plane of experience.

On the other side of Johnny, Miss Sugar was touching the ends of her hair back into place, her white dress and her white features already rearranged into perfect, almost steely composure. The lights went up, but the applause continued, and all three of us raised our heads to rejoin the real world.

'Bravo, Suki,' said Miss Sugar.

The row of people in the front of our box was leaning against the balustrade, backs turned to the stage and the auditorium, not even pretending any more. They stared with open admiration and astonishment from one of us to the other, the two women with huge, yearning eyes, fanning themselves with their programmes, the two men clapping our performance with glittering, lustful eyes and frankly drooling mouths.

'As for you, Miss Sugar,' I said, actually batting my eyelashes. 'Talk about dark horses.'

Outside in the chilly street Miss Sugar and I stood close together as the well-dressed crowd surged round us. Our box companions turned out to be wealthy American business associates of Johnny's. They followed us down the stairs, pressing business cards and mobile phone numbers on to us, even begging us to go with them then and there to their rooms at the Ritz. I was tempted. I was on a roll.

But Miss Sugar had other plans. She invited our new friends to try out the club tomorrow. Then she wound her arm round my waist and said pointedly, not looking at them but deep into my eyes, 'Because we're keeping things intimate tonight, I think.'

They waved their hands about and nodded, the men clapping Johnny on the back as if he was some kind of hero. Miss Sugar and I stood as still as statues, wrapped around each other, the vestal virgins.

'Whatever we do, I need to do it soon, Sugar,' I told her under the hubbub. 'I'm dripping for more. For God's sake, I haven't come yet. I'd like to take him home. I'm horny as hell. He's so young, Sugar. So ripe ...'

Once again her filthy laugh was surprising coming out of that fragile face. She pulled me closer, her lips brushing my cheek. 'You don't need to convince me what we need to do, Summers. It's all planned. That was only a taster of things to come.'

Johnny saw the Americans into their limousine and came back to us. He squared his shoulders slightly nervously and said, 'So where do I sign?'

17

Johnny left Miss Sugar's attic bedroom, speechless with
exhaustion, as dawn broke. We had sucked and seduced
every last drop out of him, and out of each other. Miss
Sugar and I barely said goodbye to him, we were still so
engrossed, but much later we had fallen asleep, tangled
in the sweaty sheets on her enormous mattress.

I drifted off into that wonderful post-orgasmic high,
imagining his cock thrusting into me, the scene running
past my eyes again and again as if it was on film, his
energetic, boyish hips jerking their rhythm for hours, in
no hurry to come a second time, delaying his pleasure so
that he could keep fucking me while Miss Sugar writhed
over my face just in front of him.

The knocking on the door awoke me. I twisted and
turned on the bed, totally confused. Miss Sugar had gone,
as had my silvery sandals and my white dress. There
was a long white envelope on the pillow next to my
head. There was more knocking. Sugar must have forgotten her key. Or this envelope. I grabbed it and stumbled
off the mattress, totally naked. I flung the door open,
expecting, hoping, it was Sugar, come back for more.

'Good morning, Suki. I'm so glad you're still here. I'm
getting a little tired of your disappearing acts.'

Mimi stood there, elegant and cool in a chocolate-
brown leather miniskirt, high spiky knee boots and a
soft cream cashmere jumper. Her skin was warm and
brown, her eyes flashing fire as she glanced at my naked
form. I wondered if she could tell how bruised my whole

body was after the rough sex of last night, delivered by her prim assistant. Mimi's mouth tilted at the corner as she put a hand on to my bare shoulder and steered me back into the flat.

'Mimi. I thought you were Miss Sugar come back for ... I mean, I thought you were still at Symes Hall,' I said as I cast about for something to cover myself. The only thing between my bare skin and the outside world was the envelope, but Mimi wasn't looking at me. She was peering around the room as if looking for something.

'Which is where you were supposed to be,' she said. 'But I think you've become a little too comfortable in your new vocation, or perhaps we've given you your head a little too much. Not only do you come back to London before we've given the word, but you borrow my velvet coat, as well, and nearly cause a disaster.'

She glanced down at the rumpled bed.

'I'm sorry,' I said sheepishly. Mimi had a knack of making you feel like a million dollars one minute and no better than a worm the next. 'I couldn't stay there. I couldn't risk Chrissie finding out the truth about why I was there. It would be the end of our friendship. Sir Simeon knew I was leaving. But I should have told you and I'm sorry. And about the coat ... I grabbed the first thing I could find in the office because I needed it for the theatre last night, so I'm sorry for that, too. But we were working, Mimi. After a fashion.'

I was jibbering. Stop it, I told myself. Anyone would think you were still a novice.

'So I understand. I'm still your boss, Summers, even if I haven't been around much. In fact, I was in two minds about keeping you on after you did a runner. But then again, I do appreciate why you had to leave that particular party and, luckily for you, I've already read Miss Sugar's report on your performance last night. You've earned yourself several gold stars for your ... assignation with young Johnny Symes. Not bad, considering you planned that to be your last evening as the club's housekeeper.'

Mimi came towards me and nodded at the envelope. I looked at it, and saw that my name was typed on it, no doubt by Miss Sugar's careful fingers. It was full of fifty pound notes. I really was rolling in money now.

'Johnny Symes?' I croaked, as if he'd jumped out of the envelope. 'That big, blond chap was a Symes?'

'A cousin. They come in all shapes and sizes, that family,' Mimi said airily. 'Merlin takes after his mother, as you'll have seen from the portrait at Symes Hall. Little Johnny is from Sir Simeon's side.' She shrugged. 'I must say I didn't know he existed until this morning. Little chancer. Thought he'd suss out his uncle's club by using the tradesmen's entrance, as it were. He pulled the wool over everybody's eyes, didn't he?'

'You mean it was all a trick? He's not got a frigid wife? He's not married?'

'None of the above. He's still wet behind the ears. Only just started his first City job this autumn.'

'What did Sir Simeon say?' I asked, blushing furiously.

'He made some comment about you working your way through his entire family tree, but if Johnny can rope in some of his wealthy clients and colleagues to join the club, so much the better.'

'I didn't set out to work my way through them. Oh, I'd better get dressed,' I mumbled hopelessly, casting about for my clothing. But I had gone straight to the theatre from the office last night, leaving everything there. I had nothing, not a stitch, to put on. I sat down. My body and head were pounding and I knew I looked like shit.

'It's a shame to cover that delectable, bankable body,

but yes. You should get dressed. Here. I brought you these,' Mimi said briskly, handing me yet another shopping bag. 'I guess you'll need something to wear out in the street when you go back to that dreadful bed and breakfast, won't you? That's if you won't let us keep you captive here, naked and beautiful, forever?'

'I need to speak to you, Mimi. You said I meant last night to be my last night as your housekeeper. So you've obviously heard that I've decided to leave.'

'So I understand. But luckily I've made a decision of my own which will alter your decision, I'm sure of it. But first things first.'

She swiped the envelope out of my hand and walked over to a cabinet by the window. I glanced up at her long legs and generous hips walking about in the huge airy bedroom which a few hours earlier had seen me and Miss Sugar climbing all over young Johnny, vying with each other as to who could surprise him the most, shocking him as we took turns in pinning him to the bed and sitting on his swollen prick.

When it was my turn I had dangled my tits in his face, swinging them back and forth across his nose and mouth, pulling away, showing him how I caressed them myself, tweaking the red nipples until they stood out like acorns, then lowering them down towards his mouth. I had shouted with pleasure as he had tentatively started to suck first one, then the other.

'I've never met a girl who liked her tits sucked,' he had murmured, licking at my nipple as if it was an ice cream. 'This is heaven.'

'You have to learn to take it slow,' Miss Sugar had said and pushed Johnny aside, whispering something to him. She had wriggled down in his place on the bed and I had crouched over her, desperate to have his cock in me, but my pussy dripping its sticky honey instead over

241

her flat, white stomach. I had hovered for a moment, looking down at her stretched beneath me like a sacrifice, and then she had pulled me down so that she could take my tits and brush them across her closed eyelids.

'What are you doing, Sugar? What about Johnny? He's the member –'

'This is for Johnny as well as for me,' she had replied. 'This is our special floor show.'

My nipples had sharpened as she had caressed the rounded flesh of my breasts with the merest butterfly touch, caressing with her fingertips, her eyelashes, even her hair. I had realised I was holding my breath as I waited for her to leave off the feathery tickling, to take the nipples into her mouth and for her woman's lips to fold round them, and I had concentrated on the novelty of seeing her lying beneath me, wanting me.

'OK. Now show him, Summers. Show him how good we can be.'

Her lips had parted and her expert tongue had flickered out, just touching one burning tip before flickering in again. I had moaned out loud, trying to contain my frustration.

From behind me, Johnny had spread open my still raised buttocks. He had parted them with eager fingers, and had paused. Miss Sugar had nodded at him. He had prodded his knob into the warm, dark crevice inside my cheeks. He had let it rest there for a moment. I hadn't helped to guide him in. I had been intent on hanging between him and Miss Sugar, letting them each take whichever part of my body they wanted the most.

'Can I join in, now?' he had said again, his knob leaping impatiently.

'This is all for you, Johnny,' Miss Sugar had said quietly. 'Take what you want. It's all part of the service.'

Johnny had groped his way in, feeling the moist

warmth inside my bush, then finding and parting my pussy lips. He had shoved a finger roughly inside me then had followed it instantly with the length of his prick, knocking me forwards and therefore closer to Miss Sugar's teasing mouth.

'I'm in,' he had cried, grunting with triumph. 'God, I never guessed the club was this good. No wonder it's such a well-kept secret.'

As he had rammed himself inch by inch inside me, Miss Sugar's fingers had clawed harder and harder into the two breasts dangling above her face, until darts of indescribable ecstasy sliced down my body to where Johnny was starting to yank me against him. Miss Sugar had latched on to one breast as it kept whipping out of reach, biting on to it hard so that I had yelped out loud. The two of them had gone into overdrive, competing to pleasure me the most.

As Johnny had plunged deeper inside me, and Miss Sugar's hands and mouth had caressed me more frantically, I had wanted to complete the circle, do my bit. As the two of them had pummelled me between them, I had lifted one hand and tentatively cupped the mound of Miss Sugar's bush.

'I want to feel you, Sugar,' I had gasped. 'I want to please you.'

Mimi waited as I replayed last night's scenario in my head. I looked up at her now, watching me from the window, and I was convinced she could read my mind. She was the first woman who had touched me, after all. I had wanted to finger her, that first morning in her white bedroom, but she had fingered me instead, to a quick, shattering orgasm.

And Mimi's first lesson had obviously stayed with me because last night I was ready to do it all again with Miss Sugar. I had imagined her sex to be cool and dry, like her outward appearance, but as soon as my finger-tips brushed over it, it was as if it were a second mouth, waiting to suck in my fingers.

'Feel free, Suki, feel me, deep as you can,' Miss Sugar had said as she raised herself off the bed, still licking my nipples, so that my fingers slipped easily inside. I had been astonished to find that far from being cool and dry she was hot and wet in there, ready, excited to fever pitch by my touching her like that. I had felt powerful, but I had also felt that yet again she, like Mimi, was educating me.

'Feel me, Suki,' Johnny had echoed. 'Feel me ramming it into you. That's what you really want, isn't it?'

There had been a delicious tension in me then. I had enjoyed the pretence that I was torn between them, but I wasn't torn at all. They were both going to satisfy me. I had plunged three fingers inside Miss Sugar, letting my thumb trail behind until it caught the little nub of her clitoris, and then, as if I'd been doing this all my life, I had rubbed and plunged, grinning to myself as I had seen her writhing and bucking on my hand just as I had been writhing and bucking on Johnny's prick.

'Me first,' Miss Sugar had moaned.

'No, me first. I'm the member. You're here to please me!' Johnny had yelled.

'I'm ready,' I had gasped, 'so shut up, the pair of you, and do it.'

The big wave had been building inside me, my moaning had seemed to trigger the other two to their own climax, so that we had rocked and writhed and pushed and groaned, until one by one we had come, and soon we had all been a sweating, dripping, pumping heap and had fallen on to the tangled sheets as the first pink finger of dawn had edged between the chimney pots outside and had poked nosily at the window.

I folded my arms around my body, holding the memory of the night's amazing activities. I could hardly believe we'd done it.

'I need to shower, Mimi, before I put these on,' I said.

'Be my guest. You look totally shagged out. But could you just come here first? I want to show you something.'

I wrapped a fake fur throw from the sofa round me and stood up. As I came towards Mimi I looked past her out of the window and saw that Miss Sugar's room had the same view enjoyed by the penthouse. Looking straight into Sir Simeon's flat.

'Oh, we know Miss Sugar watches us when we're in his flat. We always leave the blinds open,' she remarked casually, taking a tiny camcorder out of the cabinet and squinting down its viewfinder. 'But as I think you've gathered, it's not straight sex that Miss Sugar is really interested in.'

'I thought she worshipped Sir Simeon?'

'Don't we all, darling?' she cooed, tucking my bed-tangled hair behind my ear. I flushed. 'Sir Simeon's the man who came closest to converting Miss Sugar to heterosexuality. Her initiation, when she joined the club, nearly did it. But it looks like you've set her back on her Sapphic trail again.'

'What did you do to her at her initiation? You said you practically had to tie her down?'

Mimi sat back on the windowsill and crossed her long legs.

'It wasn't up to me. I wasn't keen on the experiment. I liked her the way she was. But as this is a club for men, it made sense to at least show her what sex would feel like with a man. So we showed her what sex would feel like with *two* men, just to make sure.'

'Oh, Mimi. That's cruel,' I said. I felt sorry for Miss

Sugar, remembering her lips and fingers probing my female bits with such delight.

'Cruel? Some might say it was extremely generous of us all. After all, it was Sir Simeon and Merlin who initiated her. What could be nicer?'

I pulled the fake fur closer round my shoulders. At that moment I couldn't think of anything nicer.

'So we got her on the floor between the two of them –'

'When? At her interview?'

'Yes. As soon as she told us she was gay. There was no point wasting time, was there? We got her on the floor between the two of them, and she went down on Merlin while Sir Simeon shafted her from behind.'

I gulped.

'To be honest it was more of a competition between the two of them,' Mimi went on, half to herself. 'They're always feuding, you see.'

'Yes,' I replied sharply. 'Feuding over you, Merlin told me.'

Mimi waved her hand dismissively. 'Childish nonsense. They're about to learn that I don't belong to anybody. They wanted to send me out of the room, but I refused. I had to be there to coax her in case she bottled out, but in the end there was no need. She was lapping it up. Literally.'

I giggled and Mimi flashed me a big smile.

'They got her on all fours between them, and Merlin sat in front of her and opened his trousers. It's beautiful, isn't it?' she asked.

'What?' I said.

'Merlin's cock. The colour of *café crème*, wouldn't you say?'

I spluttered again, torn between girlish amusement and furious jealousy that the gorgeous Mimi had shared the same cock; felt it slipping up her as she thrashed about with him on an antique bed in Paris, perhaps, or rutted in the back of Merlin's battered truck.

'And it might as well have been something edible because she took it perfectly happily into her mouth. I think she reckoned she was getting off lightly, not having to go the whole way. Giving Merlin a blow job was the easy option, or so she thought. It didn't compromise her lesbian preferences, but then she didn't bargain for Sir Simeon coming up from the rear. He reckons it's better that way the first time. A woman might be overawed to see that someone as impressive as him is fucking her.'

'That's true,' I said. 'But then he's not everyone's boss, is he?'

'That's how it feels, when he's around. That he's the boss. Don't you find that?'

Mimi's smile was still there, but I couldn't tell if she was testing me or genuinely sharing confidences with me.

'Go on about poor Miss Sugar,' I said obstinately.

'She had Merlin up to the hilt, as it were, and then Sir Simeon sat behind her and gripped her hips, pulling her in to him with his knees. He may have a bad leg, but he's strong. He can still tame nervy horses, you know.'

'And nervy women.'

We both laughed.

'She was busy with her head in Merlin's lap, and I don't think she knew what was about to happen. Simeon just lifted that prim little skirt of hers and slipped it in to her. Merlin held her head, guiding her mouth up and down his cock to distract her. He was trying hard to keep his face straight, too, not show his father that he was losing control. She must have been doing a good job. Simeon's good at keeping his own face straight, as well. It was like looking at some curious tableau. Their arms were working, pulling her back and forth between them, but they sat bolt upright, no expression on their faces, as always in competition not to be the first to lose it. So when they came, they each let out no more than a kind of quick grunt, and let her go.'

'And how did she feel about that?' I asked, trying to imagine Miss Sugar's neat clothes all dishevelled, her mouth wet with Merlin's spunk, her knees red with carpet burn, her vagina aching from the deep thrusting of Simeon's cock.

Mimi laughed and opened the double doors of the cabinet to reveal a small television.

'She was her usual self. Got up, brushed herself down, pinned her hair back in to place and said that although they would never change her, she trusted she had got the job.'

'She's amazing.'

'The feeling's mutual,' Mimi replied thoughtfully. 'She's already reported to me about last night. She thought you were both simply, and successfully, putting a new member through his paces. But there was more to what she said about you. I've never seen her quite so ... besotted before. Not quite herself. I must say, a girl could get jealous.'

'So what was it you wanted to show me?' I asked. I was getting stiff, perching awkwardly on the sofa.

'Well, in all the excitement of last night, and getting down to the office on time this morning – she's always dead on time – she'd forgotten to collect, let alone file, the evidence, so I thought I'd come and see everything for myself.'

'Besotted? Evidence? Can't this wait? Mimi, I really need to talk to you ...'

'Hush, Suki. Hush.'

Mimi came and sat beside me on the sofa and flicked

the remote. All at once, picked out in sharp focus and with the jazz backing track we'd put on when we got in from the theatre, were Johnny Symes, Miss Sugar and me, butt naked on the bed. So it wasn't only my memory or my hazy dreams. There really was a film of what happened. There was Johnny, slamming his buttocks up and down, my legs wrapped round his waist, my back arched as he fondled my breasts and Miss Sugar, wriggling and gasping as she lowered herself athletically over my face. Then there was the second, third, fourth position.

And then there was me and Miss Sugar on our own. My tongue, flicking up into her pale blonde bush, her sex wide open for all to see.

Mimi glanced at me, that big smile cracking open her face.

'What have we here?' she wondered aloud, settling herself back on the bed and crossing her long leather-clad legs. I tried to stand up but she put one hand on my leg and pushed me back down beside her. 'This looks like action well beyond the call of duty.'

I waited to feel the blush rise from my toes upwards but it didn't. I looked at the television screen and, instead of embarrassment, I sizzled with the remembered thrill of excitement. And it was made all the more acute by the fact that Mimi was sitting beside me, watching the scenario as well.

There was Miss Sugar, totally naked, on all fours on the bed and me, also naked, kneeling behind her. Of Johnny there was no sign, and there was very little sound apart from the muted music in the background. As the camera rolled, Miss Sugar glanced over her shoulder at me, and I slapped her hard on the rump so that her whole body arched up like a cat's. Then she let her head sink down into the bank of pillows at the other end of the bed, while I let my head sink into the shadowy valley between her thighs. My tongue was out, long and pink, and I was flicking it up her legs and in to the crack of her butt. At the same time, my fingers dug in to the soft flesh, pulling her apart.

Sugar was like the sort of lithe, white animal that lives in the snow. Now her small, firm breasts jutted out in the soft light of the candles lit all around the bed, her head thrown back as she rammed herself into my face. I pulled back, and you could see my mouth glistening wet with Miss Sugar's juices. I licked my lips slowly, my eyes burning with wicked adventure, then I wrenched Miss Sugar's legs further apart, pulling her labia open so that I could nuzzle my way in. She yelped and jerked violently, and I slapped her again before lapping at her hot slit like a cat – fast, furious, nipping and licking.

Mimi jabbed at the pause button, capturing the moment just before Miss Sugar came, ramming and writhing into my face, her sweet juices trickling out of her and on to my waiting tongue. I couldn't take my eyes off the screen. The tip of my tongue was trapped between my teeth as I remembered how it had felt, licking her in the candlelight, my own fanny still glowing with the violent screwing I'd demanded from Johnny, my mouth savouring the taste and smell of another woman's body.

'How did you know?' I asked in a quavering voice, as Mimi finally took the video out of the machine and put it in her handbag.

'Part guesswork, part intimate knowledge of how Miss Sugar operates when she's in charge. She couldn't possibly have let the evening end without initiating you fully into her own tastes. She's a bit of an evangelist when it comes to women. She wants to convert them all. Sir Simeon and Merlin failed dismally to swing her.

Women are definitely her thing. And that includes you, it seems,' Mimi replied. She chuckled, stood up and pulled me to my feet, than handed me the envelope. 'Overtime. You certainly earned this money, but you could earn even more if you play your cards right. Get dressed. I need to talk to you.'

I laid the clothes out on the bed and couldn't help a rush of greedy delight at the soft feel of the brown leather in my fingers. As well as the beautifully tailored trousers and the pointed ankle boots I had worn before, Mimi had thrown in another tight-fitting T-shirt, this time the same cream colour as her sweater, and a long leather coat.

'I look like you,' I remarked when I was dressed.

Mimi looked up.

'That's the idea,' she replied, patting the seat beside her. 'The transformation is complete.'

'What do you mean?'

'Apart from the fact that those clothes do wonders for you, my ugly duckling, we have standards to keep up. Let's just –' she took my hair in her hands, pulled it off my face for a moment, then let it fall in ringlets '– no, let's just leave it loose today.'

I sat beside her and breathed in her musky perfume.

'I meant it, Mimi. I don't think I want to work for you any more.'

'I heard you the first time, and that's fine. You won't be working for me,' she said, sitting back comfortably and pulling the red velvet coat on to her knees. 'Let me show you why I was so anxious when I found you'd taken my red velvet coat last night.'

She pulled something out of the pocket of the coat and waved it in front of me.

'An airline ticket,' I muttered stupidly. 'One way to New York.'

'That's right. I'm starting a new Club Crème – a quintessential English venture with a French name to attract our American friends.'

'I can think of some takers straightaway,' I said, thinking of last night's opera companions. 'Johnny Symes has some very willing American associates.'

'There you are, you see. Ideas just come pouring out of you,' she said. She tapped the ticket against my cheek. 'I was going to talk to you about this at Symes Hall, Suki. Which reminds me ... your friend Chrissie wants to see you. That was some party.'

I stood up and walked over to the window. Sir Simeon's flat was extremely tidy. More than that. It was empty.

'One thing at a time, please, Mimi. Of course I'll go and see Chrissie before I leave. I owe her a huge apology. But I can't think about that now. What's Sir Simeon doing, removing all his stuff? It looks like he's left his flat.'

'Yes. He's moving in to my house. He'll be looking after it for me while I'm gone.'

'He's not going with you?'

'I'm the cat that walks alone, Summers. Rather like you. And I intend to keep walking. But I haven't finished what I wanted to say to you. You've changed since you came to work here. Or perhaps it's the real you.'

'I've overstepped the mark, I know. I've been carried away. That evening in the club bar, Mikhail's party, meeting Geoffrey Grey on the London Eye,' I said. I hung my head, trying to look ashamed. 'But I can't apologise for it, Mimi. All that debauchery, all that sex, all that exhibitionism – I've loved it.'

'I don't want you to apologise for it,' she replied, those fingers stroking my cheek. 'That's not what I'm getting at. All that sex, all that energy, you really have no shame, do you? Even the spying and the secret rendezvous ... You've emerged in the last couple of months as a force to be reckoned with, Summers. Everyone thinks so. You've blossomed, further than my wildest dreams, and that's saying something. I thought you'd be hot, but not this hot. There's no stopping you, is there? Insatiable doesn't touch it. And they want more of you.'

'I don't understand.' I frowned, sitting very still so that she wouldn't move her fingers away. 'I thought I'd gone way beyond my brief as housekeeper. Then again, I've never been entirely clear what a housekeeper is supposed to do. I mean, I've been screwing the members. I even screwed my best friend's fiancé.'

Mimi's laugh gurgled for a while, increasing so that she laughed out loud when she saw my worried face. 'Wake up and smell the pot pourri, Summers! Club Crème is absolutely flourishing, mostly thanks to you. And the hilarious thing is you don't even realise it. We've got more members than we can handle. So here's our pro-posal, and we need an answer straightaway. We want you and Miss Sugar to take over the management. We want you to keep it small and discreet, but keep those members queuing.'

I looked up at her, a dirty grin spreading across my face, my whole body puffing up with pride and excitement.

'Does that mean I can choose the cream of the crop?'

Mimi tried to look disapproving, but then her black eyes glittered and she leaned close. I breathed in her sexy scent, half-closed my eyes. She stuck the tip of her tongue out and swiped it across my lips.

'Why do you think I've enjoyed this job so much, Summers? You can lick the cream, that's why. Whoever and whenever you like.'

18

'So you're going to be a tycoon.'

Chrissie was prowling round the penthouse apartment, running her fingers up the chrome banisters of the stairs, pinging the spotlights which dangled down from the ceiling on bendy wires, opening and closing the doors of the enormous walk-in wardrobe.

'I told you I could put down roots,' I replied, pouring out some champagne. I could get used to this. I *was* used to this. Chrissie shot me a look and came over to get her glass.

'It was a close call, though, wasn't it? You nearly bailed out and scarpered abroad again without telling me. And I nearly didn't find out that Jeremy was a member of the same club where you went for that strange interview. Just think. You could have met each other, without knowing you had *me* in common.'

Now I *did* go red. This was close to the knuckle. But for a quirk of fate it could have been me bent double over a bar stool with Jeremy rogering me from behind on that very first night at the club, not to mention Mikhail's party. But that would be too much information even for this new, relaxed Chrissie.

'I thought you'd hit the roof when you saw me at Symes Hall,' I said. I spoke quickly to cover my embarrassment. 'I should have been in touch with you weeks ago, told you about the new job. I'm sorry about that. But it's not my fault Jeremy was keeping things from you. So how are things between you two?'

'Never better, as it happens. The Ugly Sister has been dispatched, and we're as much in love as ever.'

Chrissie tossed her yellow curls and crossed her legs with a satisfied swish. I didn't quite share her confidence. Avril Grey had the tenacity of a terrier with a rabbit. I doubted very much that she would go quietly.

'That's great,' I said heartily, casting about for a change of subject. 'And how's golden boy, the lad from the perfume convention? Has he recovered from your assault on him at the party?'

'He didn't know where to look when I next bumped into him,' Chrissie tittered. 'But I soon told him where to look. I reminded him that the label "superior" only applies to me when I'm at work. But he's getting cocky now. He's started taking liberties even when I'm on the shop floor.'

'Liberties? You sound as if he's nicking the custard creams without asking. What liberties does he take on the shop floor?'

'He's really turned on by touching me up when I'm wearing that hideous uniform. Puts his hands right up my turquoise skirt. Sometimes when there still cus-tomers to be served.' Chrissie tweaked her tight jumper down over her hips in imaginary protest.

'This is all such a relief,' I said and sighed, pressing my glass against my cheek. 'I didn't know how you'd take all the revelations – how some of the members like to use the club, what Jeremy likes to do – and especially some of the things I've been required to do. But how come you're so mellow about it?'

'That Mimi Breeze.' Chrissie shook her head and chuckled. 'She could charm the pants off a monk. She talked to us the day after that wild party and told us how wonderful you are and how many of your clients end up thanking her and her team for what they've done. How could I possibly mind my Jeremy belonging to such a smart club? She's amazing. I could fancy her myself if I was that way inclined. I expect you'll miss her.'

I nodded. So Mimi hadn't explained things at all. Chrissie had been given a carefully edited version of what *exactly* her beloved future husband had been up to at the club. And I wasn't about to enlighten her.

I glanced round the apartment. I still couldn't believe my luck. I'd just snapped my fingers, and now this was to be my new home. After our discussion about my future, Mimi had marched into the bed and breakfast with me, settled my bill, asked me which room at the club I would prefer and installed me in here without a quibble.

'Mimi's been a kind of mentor to me, and I will miss her, yes. She's brilliant and captivating. But if I'm going to make a go of this, and not be tempted to rush overseas again, I need to stand on my own feet. And there's always Miss Sugar.'

'Who?'

'My partner.' I felt my cheeks warm up at the thought of it. 'My partner in crime.'

Chrissie gave a little cough and put her glass down on the glass-topped coffee table.

'I've been thinking, Suki. Do you think you might be wanting any other partners?' she asked. I knew what that mewing voice meant.

'You mean you'd like to come in with us?'

'Well, to tell you the truth, I'm dead jealous of the way you've landed this plum role after such a short time back in London, scruffy urchin that you were! I'm sure it's because of my borrowed suit that you got the job in the first place.'

'It took more than a borrowed suit to get and keep my

job. Do you really see yourself doing what I do, Chrissie?'
My voice was soft and low, something else I'd learned
from Mimi when she wanted to make herself perfectly
understood. 'You reckon you could really run an establishment like this? Fold the towels, arrange the flowers,
invent new cocktails, take the members' money, even
field their personal phone calls? Keep them happy.
Understand them. Shed all judgement. Be at their beck
and call night and day.'

'You're failing dismally to make it sound anything
other than great fun. Remember, I spend all day spraying
perfume onto people's necks and listening to their mari-
tal woes. If you can do all that . . .'

'Anything you can do, I can do better? Is that it?' I
asked. I was failing dismally to conceal my irritation.
'You think it's just a walk in the park, this job, do you?'

'I think it must be a breeze. Yes.'

There was a pause, and then we both realised the play
on words. Her lips twitched and so did mine, and with a
huge sense of ice breaking, we started to laugh. I poured
out some more champagne.

'OK. Let's go back to your idea,' I said, thinking fast. 'I
think we could use you in the business, yes, but not in
the way you meant.'

'All ears, darling.'

'Your perfume department. A hotbed of confidences.
Women, wives, mistresses. You can recruit for us. Not
that we have problems with publicity, but it's word of
mouth we rely on, and your perfume department would
be an ideal starting point. Not to mention all those
conferences you go on.'

'Yes, but this is a club for men, Suki. What use would
all my duchesses be to you?'

I opened the door of my apartment and ushered her
downstairs. As we passed the smaller of the two drawing

rooms I noticed that two of my favourite club members had just arrived. Geoffrey Grey and Merlin Symes were planted on either side of the fireplace. I pulled my stomach in, feeling the kiss of lace underwear on my breasts and the sharp tweak of the matching thong pinching up my crack.

Chrissie was still on the stairs, her head snapping right and left, marvelling at the beautiful decor, her hand extended to open all the doors.

'Not in there,' I said, kicking the drawing room door shut. 'There's some heavyweight board meeting going on.'

In the office, I sat her down at my desk and showed her the proofs of a slim new brochure.

'It's only at the ideas stage, but this is what I want to do. I want to start up a club, just like Club Crème, but for women. If you were involved in our publicity, perhaps we could call it Perfume Place. Women can come here, escape their home lives, husbands, boyfriends, bosses, and be cosseted and flattered, just like our members are here. And you can be our founder member.'

As Chrissie started looking through the brochure, Miss Sugar glided in to the office. She was still dressed in her usual pallid grey, but there was something jaunty in her step and a very faint tinge of pink in her cheeks. She raised her eyebrows at the sight of Chrissie sitting at her desk.

'I want you to talk Chrissie through our new venture,' I hissed at her. 'Avril Grey's prepared some draft copy, but don't for heaven's sake mention Avril's name to Chrissie. Just sell the idea. Can you spare me? I've got some members to attend to.'

'Would that be flaccid members?' Miss Sugar retorted in a rare moment of jest. The high notes in her voice suggested that she'd scored last night. 'Or full-on, filled-up members?'

'What do you think, Sugar?' I retorted, nudging her in the ribs.

She stuck her chin in the air and advanced upon Chrissie with a greedy glint in her eye.

I couldn't wait to get to the red drawing room. I had decided to make this my unofficial, personal domain, and members could only enter if they were personally invited. I kept the decor as it had always been. Old fashioned, welcoming, intimate. Dark red walls, kilim rugs, low-slung sofas and mirrors everywhere. A carved table laden with wine bottles. Dim lighting. A set of French doors led out on to the glassed-in patio shared by all the downstairs rooms. Already the layout of these downstairs rooms had given me an idea for a fabulous party.

'Gentlemen,' I said, sweeping in and at last feeling like the mistress of the house. I wondered if I could ever truly emulate Mimi's style. 'How lovely to see you both. I was hoping you'd be here again soon.'

'We wanted a piece of you, lady, before you get too grand with all this new responsibility.'

As always Merlin sounded cool and a little disdainful. He was trying to bring me down to earth as if I still had dung on my boots, but I noticed that he'd scrubbed up for the trip to London. He was wearing black jeans and a pure white shirt. His hair had been cut short so that I was shocked to see the boyish bareness of his neck and ears. He looked unutterably tasty.

'I'll never be too grand for you, Merlin. I mean, Mimi was never too grand, was she? Not in the sack, I mean.'

'Mimi's gone now,' he growled. I kept myself from smiling. It was so easy to rouse him to anger, and so easy to quell it again. And he was right. Mimi had gone. And with her had gone the competition. Much as I loved her, I wanted Sir Simeon and Merlin to find a new woman to fight over. And I intended to be that woman.

'Hey, you two, stop fighting,' Geoffrey Grey protested, wiping his glasses and putting them on again to silence us. He, too, had scrubbed up. He had shaved, which made him look younger and cleaner, and his tawny hair, which had not been cut, matched the soft tweed suit he was wearing. His brogues were polished so that I could see the reflection of the firelight dancing on the leather toes. 'It suits you, the new position. You look sensational, Miss Summers. Very regal. What's your secret?'

'This place,' I said, and meant it. I walked over to the drinks table and picked up a cold bottle of Chablis. I even moved differently now, shoulders back, tits out, hips swaying. It was the clothes, the shoes and the new status. 'It's not like coming to work. It's like having a party every day. And now I'm managing the club, well, the sky's the limit.'

'If you don't mind, Miss Summers,' Geoffrey said, coughing politely as he took a tall glass of wine from me, beaded with cold. 'We don't particularly want a party tonight. We came here for some peace and quiet, didn't we, Merlin?'

'After the week we've had on the Continent buying more horses for Symes Hall, we just need some TLC,' agreed Merlin. The callous edge to his voice was gone at last. He slumped back in his chair, his blue eyes half closed. I could tell he was tired. The pair of them were at my disposal.

I walked over to the main door and locked it. I didn't bother with the patio door. Then I put on a CD. A cool, sexy sax pierced the silence. The two men remained seated, one in each big armchair, and looked at me expectantly.

'Then peace and quiet is what you'll get,' I murmured, returning to the fireplace and staring at myself in the huge mirror. I pressed my hot cheeks, then started to undo the pearly buttons which ran down the front of my long black dress. 'And special treatment, too, if you obey the rules.'

The first few buttons revealed the deep cleft of my cleavage, the rounded shapes of my breasts illuminated by the firelight and a couple of low lamps. Then I unfastened some more until I reached my legs, where the dress fell open anyway. I held the dress closed for a moment, clinging for a few more seconds to my new, domineering image. I held my breath. Then I opened the severe dress and let it slide down. I wriggled my shoulders free and there I was, standing in the firelight in just my black lace bra and stockings. The wisps of material held my breasts up firmly, yet the pattern traced around the dark red nipples, accentuating them with the delicate design.

'We said peace and quiet, Suki,' whimpered Geoffrey Grey.

'Tough,' I replied.

I flicked open the front hook of the bra and let my breasts drop heavily forwards. Geoffrey Grey groaned. Merlin grinned, stroking his shadowy upper lip. He stretched his long legs out in front of him.

I took my breasts in my hands and started to knead them, gently at first, then more firmly. This was going to be my own floor show. Just having the two men sitting there in my little red room, rigid with expectation, was enough to excite me. They were going to watch, and then they could fight over me if they chose. I knew which one I preferred, had preferred all along, and probably he knew it. I knew which long, hard cock I wanted plunging into me soon, soon.

'You've come a long way, Miss Summers,' remarked Merlin, shifting in his seat. 'You only do it in threesomes, now?'

'A third party always adds spice,' I responded. I sighed, dancing slowly round. 'It's something I've learned. It's something I'm going to enjoy again, and again, and again. Just watch me.'

A great surge of hot lust pounded through me as I made myself that promise. The music wound around us all, and I caressed my breasts more passionately, swaying and letting my hair swing down my back. The touch of it on my skin reminded me of Mimi stroking my hair, sorting me out, transforming the ugly duckling, as she called it. If only she could see me now.

I let myself relax, enjoying those eyes on me. 'You're getting hard watching me, aren't you, boys?' The heat curled up from my cunt.

'Geoffrey, would you mind?' Merlin leaned across to his friend. 'This one's for me.'

I curled one arm under my bouncing breasts to keep them raised, my hand fondling and squeezing the yielding flesh and, with the other hand, I tweaked the diamanté-studded thong sideways to show them my waxed pubes. I still wasn't used to the stimulation of wearing a thong, let alone one with little studs inside as well as out, which constantly rubbed and tickled my tender crevices as I moved about.

'I make the rules at this club,' I said. 'And I say Geoffrey stays.'

I stepped across to Merlin, placing one foot on either side of his long legs and tilting myself towards him so that my crotch was up against his face. His hands stroked up the back of my stockings, tickling the skin behind my knees. He knew my weak spot. I pushed my velvety pussy lips against his face and felt his breath blow across the bare skin. I started to sway my hips again, into him and away, unable to stop myself moving in a way that matched the desire pulsating through me.

'Whatever you say, Madame Summers,' Merlin muttered. 'But I'm going to have you first.' He grasped my buttocks, digging his fingers into them, and pulled me against his mouth. I heard Geoffrey groan again. I was so horny already that when Merlin's tongue snaked out and touched my clitoris I let out a loud groan, as if answering Geoffrey, and ground myself against Merlin's mouth.

Then, with a superhuman effort, I stepped away again. 'You must learn to take turns, Merlin.'

I swayed round to face Geoffrey. He was down on the floor on all fours like a dog, right behind me, virtually snarling, his face nuzzling up against my thigh. I spread my legs on either side of his head and pushed myself into his face. He opened me up without waiting, stared greedily at the pink, then it wasn't his tongue but his teeth that nipped sharply at my clit.

I jolted with surprise as Geoffrey's teeth started to work me into a frenzy. I was losing control after all. So who was I going to have first? Who was going to do it the best? It was their fight, if they wanted it. I was just the prize. I reckoned Merlin would be beside himself now, but that was all the better. The more they were revved up, the more explosive our lust would be. I shivered with pleasure at how easy and how instant it all was. But it mustn't be so easy that it was over before it began.

'Slow down, Geoffrey,' I said.

I stepped away from Geoffrey's busy mouth.

'High and mighty all of a sudden. What are you playing at?' he grumbled.

I kept one hand on my breasts and the other cupped between my legs. I forced myself to keep my fingers still in case I flicked the button way too early. Then I lowered myself to the floor. I spread my arms in a kind of welcoming gesture and lay back on the blood-red rug.

'Not high and mighty at all,' I whispered. 'As low down as you want.'

The two men were crawling all over me immediately, stroking and kissing up and down my prone body, pulling my legs apart. I got ready to feel someone's tongue, but then one of them brought my hands up roughly above my head and tied my wrists with a tie. I rolled and twisted as they manhandled me, still biting and licking, one of them coming up the inside of my thighs with his mouth, the other kissing my neck, pulling my hair out of the way, then moving down towards my breasts, heaving them up so that my taut nipples were tilted skywards. I wriggled and squealed, already twitching with my approaching climax, imagining myself floating above the scene, watching the fantasy. I wondered how long I could hold on for.

'I want you both!' I exclaimed suddenly, struggling to sit up and give myself more authority, but one of them just pushed me down again. 'I want to feel you both inside me. Now.'

'She thinks she can order us about, but of course she can't. It's only Suki Summers, after all.' It was Merlin talking, with all his old arrogance. 'She's tied up and she's lying down. So who's the boss now?'

'Right,' said Geoffrey Grey uncertainly, 'if you're sure you didn't tie it too tight, Merl? Oh, but she's gorgeous. Let me go first.'

'Be my guest. You already are, after all,' Merlin said. He was enjoying himself. 'I'll wait, Geoff. Believe me, it'll be worth waiting for.'

I opened my eyes and took the weight of Geoffrey's big body as he lay down on top of me, breathing heavily. He pressed his mouth onto mine and kissed me long and hard, then he pushed my legs further apart, and eased himself up inside. I loved knowing that once again I had two men on the go. I wondered what Merlin thought, watching his friend plunge his huge cock deep inside me, my tits bare and swollen, my mouth open with ecstasy. He was up close to the action this time. Rather different from watching at Mikhail's party.

'She's wet, see, and welcoming. There won't be anything left for you,' Geoffrey gloated. I wrapped my legs round his waist as he started to thrust. I didn't want Geoffrey to suspect anything, but I was keeping myself back for Merlin. I kept my mind on Geoffrey, but trained my thoughts on those few sensational times with Merlin: on his father's bed, in the wood, at Chrissie's party in the big house with those lads watching through the window. I kept my mind on those images, but with every fibre of willpower I stifled the urge to let the waves of my own climax break, especially when Geoffrey was thrusting harder and harder to reach his goal, slamming into me as he gave in, biting my neck as he groaned my name.

My body already ached and felt deliciously bruised. I was light-headed and dizzy, not sure how long I had been aching like this, who was there, or who was watching me.

Merlin was pulling Geoffrey off me. Geoffrey swore and swung round as if to punch Merlin, but Merlin was too fast. He ducked, and simply pushed Geoffrey over.

This was a real test for both men, I realised. But I couldn't let this opportunity go. I wanted Merlin. Then I wanted his father. Then I wanted Merlin again.

'The tomboy turned trollop,' Merlin murmured in my ear, smoothing his hands slowly up my sides, pushing my breasts together, letting them bounce. He darted his head down and caught one nipple in his mouth, biting it hard, sending sharp messages of desire through me as such biting always did. I trembled with the mingled pain and pleasure. Keeping his teeth round the burning bud, he raised my buttocks towards his groin, bending his head so that he could still bite my breasts and aim the tip of his cock towards my wet, waiting hole.

'Just fuck me, Merlin,' I growled.

'Such language coming from the manager,' he sniggered. 'OK, tomboy. I'll fuck you.'

His cock seemed even larger than I remembered. It kept on growing as first the bulbous tip, then the first rock-hard inch crept into me, pulling out again to tease me, and then he was grinding in a little bit more, teasing, probing, nudging in and around my aching pussy, testing, tasting, exploring.

'Just look how she drops all that dominatrix stuff when she's getting a good shafting,' he said to his friend. 'I can't let this golden opportunity pass me by, can I? Let's see how long we can draw this out, eh?'

My breath was jagged now. Merlin was inside me, letting go of my breasts, his face hanging above mine, diamonds of saliva gleaming on his lips in the firelight as he arched his back to thrust the entire length of his incredible cock in to me, and started to speed up the jerking of his buttocks.

My arms were tied above my head, but I could still move, and I pressed my thighs hard against his hips, pulling him out of me so that he faltered momentarily then I fell with him and, as soon as we started pounding together, I felt the ecstasy gathering into a point, ready to explode, and the cool, sardonic Merlin disappeared and it was just the two of us groaning noisily on the rug. He pulled out slowly and thrust back in once, twice, and then my whole body convulsed and I knew he was climaxing too, his cock was pumping in to me, my insides were gripping him like a tight glove, squeezing every second of pleasure until the pleasure rippled, burst and faded.

'Untie me please, Merlin,' I ordered shakily, when I could get my breath. I drew my knees up to my chest, feeling the sticky fluid slicking across my thighs. 'The night's still young. There's plenty more where that came from. But I can't entertain the pair of you if I'm all trussed up like this.'

'No,' taunted Merlin, sprawling back against his armchair. 'I like you just the way you are. Helpless and naked. Not the grand lady boss now, are you?'

'And you haven't changed a bit either,' I snapped, twisting my wrists to see if I could loosen the knots. 'Still the stable lad underneath it all, aren't you? And there was me thinking how grown up you look this evening.'

'Guys, guys, we've just had a great time,' stuttered Geoffrey, starting to get off the floor. 'Let's not argue. Come here, Miss Summers. I'll sort you out.'

'Don't you dare, Geoff,' ordered Merlin, not budging.

'I can always call Rick,' I warned, hoping that they would let me. Rick the barman was always in the background. His mysterious, slightly menacing presence was always watching, whatever I was doing. The thought of getting him to join us was suddenly very tempting.

'Untie her, Merlin,' a voice boomed across the room. 'This isn't a dungeon.'

So much for me being the boss. The three of us were

on the floor, scrabbling for our clothes as Sir Simeon darkened the doorway from the patio.

'Miss Summers,' he continued quietly, stepping over us to unlock the other door, 'a word.'

19

I stood in front of Sir Simeon like a naughty schoolgirl in front of the headmaster. He had kicked Merlin and Geoffrey out of the room before I could protest, and they were waiting for me in the bar like sulky boys.

I was still in sexed-up mode. I tried to conjure up the image of Sir Simeon's cock thrusting inside me, his face loosening with ecstasy, his voice cracking with climax – anything to lighten the situation, but his face gave nothing away. It was as if each time I wanted to charm him, I would have to start from scratch.

'Merlin is best off in the country, don't you think?' he said, picking up a photograph that I'd placed on the table next to the fire. It showed me on my favourite Arab mare a few years ago, my hair and her tail streaming out in a dramatic sunset and the great pyramids in the background. 'He has a job to do down there, after all. I don't think London is the place for him.'

'He's here as my guest, Sir Simeon, as well as being a member of the club,' I replied airily, putting one hand on my hip, determined to regain my cool. 'And he's going to find it very hard to stay away. I think he blends in very nicely, actually.'

'Blending in isn't exactly what he came here for though, is it?'

'In the end they all come here for the same reasons,' I replied, perching on the arm of the opposite sofa. I nonchalantly fastened a couple of buttons on my dress. 'You know that's why this place has become so successful.

Since Mimi put me in charge and you announced you were taking a backseat, I've taken it upon myself to run it exactly as I please. And exactly as the members please, of course.'

He leaned back in his chair and tapped his fingertips. He was wearing a dark-navy suit with a very subtle pin-stripe. The white cuffs of his shirt emphasised the brown skin of his wrists and hands. He could be a politician or an off-duty judge.

'I fully supported Mimi appointing you as her successor,' he said. 'But I still have the power to sack you if I choose. As far as Merlin is concerned, I'm telling, not asking. And if you're not careful, Miss Summers, you could ruin years of careful planning on my part. I don't want Club Crème, or this new club you're launching, to get a reputation.'

'Too late, Sir Simeon.' I came and sat beside him. 'It already has a blistering reputation. A far more exciting reputation than it had when I came here. There's no going back. Not unless you want to close it down altogether. And I'm not about to let that happen over a stupid family feud.'

He stroked one finger thoughtfully along his upper lip. I kept my eyes steady on him as I slowly crossed my legs. I could feel the spunk sticking my pussy lips together, smell the tang of raw sex wafting through the hastily fastened buttons of my dress.

'I can see there's no arguing with you,' Sir Simeon remarked after a pause. Across the patio, we could hear male laughter in the bar as Rick the barman tossed his cocktail shakers. Like that naughty schoolgirl, I was itching to be dismissed so I could get back to my mates.

'I'm afraid that's right, Sir Simeon. I'm having too much fun. I'm determined to make a success of this club, in my own sweet way.'

'What a lot you've learned in so little time,' he murmured, still studying me. I kept very still on the sofa beside him, and breathed in his faint cologne. 'I didn't spot this ruthless businesswoman tucked away under that old beret. I didn't see the dominatrix busting out from that ill-fitting polyester suit, either. But I did see the foxy little minx!'

'But do you like what you see?' I asked softly, adding seductress to the list of my new skills. His jacket opened over his pale pink shirt as he stretched one arm along the back of the sofa. His stomach was flat and toned underneath that shirt. Those arms were strong and persuasive, I knew.

'Mimi's an expert. Like me, she spotted your potential, and she was so right. This job has opened you up. Like a flower. And now look at you.'

'What do you see?' I was bristling at the idea that Mimi had somehow shaped me. If there was some truth in what he said, it didn't matter now. Mimi wasn't in charge here any more. I was.

'A devastatingly sexy girl-woman. Half scruff, half sophisticate. I'd still like to see you naked in the hay one day.'

He extended his leg with a very slight grimace and I remembered that, despite the stony, unbending exterior, he had at least one weakness. There was a silence between us, broken only by the clattering of pans in the club kitchen. I sat up straighter.

'How about naked right here, right now?'

Sir Simeon laughed then, his blue eyes genuinely amused. His arm slid off the back of the sofa and gripped my shoulders, pulling me towards him until my face was a couple of inches from his.

'You should know by now I prefer the element of surprise. And anyway,' he said and glanced scornfully at my lovely kilim rug, 'someone's been here before me. It will have to be some other venue. I'll find you when I want you.'

Battle was drawn after all. I felt dizzy with the wealth of choices spreading out before me. The debonair aristocrat in front of me, his devilish son a few feet away in the bar and a posse of others both tasted and waiting in the wings. My wings.

I jumped to my feet. 'If that's it, Sir Simeon, I have a club to run.'

'I haven't finished with you yet,' he objected mildly, as I marched towards the door and held it open.

Very slowly I did up the other buttons on my dress so that I covered up again. Respectability itself. I ran my fingers through my hair and smoothed it over my shoulders.

'I'm sorry, Sir Simeon, but tonight is our first school dinners night. That's why the club is full to bursting. I have to go and put the finishing touches to our menu.'

He stood up as well, straightening his tie as if we actually *had* been conducting a board meeting.

'And what's on the menu, apart from the staff?'

I smiled mysteriously and wagged my finger at him.

'That's easy, Sir Simeon. It's toad in the hole.'

LOOK OUT FOR THE ALL-NEW BLACK LACE BOOKS – AVAILABLE NOW!

All books priced £6.99 in the UK. Please note publication dates apply to the UK only. For other territories, please contact your retailer.

MIXED SIGNALS
Anna Clare
ISBN O 352 33889 X

Adele Western knows what it's like to be an outsider. As a teenager she was teased mercilessly by the sixth-form girls for the size of her lips. Now twenty-six, we follow the ups and downs of her life and loves. There's the cultured restaurateur Paul, whose relationship with his working-class boyfriend raises eyebrows, not least because he is still having sex with his ex-wife. There's former chart-topper Suki, whose career has nosedived and who is venturing on a lesbian affair. Underlying everyone's story is a tale of ambiguous sexuality, and Adele is caught up in some very saucy antics. **The sexy *tours de force* of wild, colourful characters makes this a hugely enjoyable novel of modern sexual dilemmas.**

SWITCHING HANDS
Alaine Hood
ISBN 0 352 33896 2

When Melanie Paxton takes over as manager of a vintage clothing shop, she makes the bold decision to add a selection of sex toys and fetish merchandise to her inventory. Sales skyrocket, and so does Mel's popularity, as she teases sexy secrets out of the town's residents. It seems she can do no wrong, until the gossip starts – about her wild past and her experimental sexuality. However, she finds an unlikely – and very hunky – ally called Nathan who works in the history museum next door. **This characterful story about a sassy sexpert and an antiquities scholar is bound to get pulses racing!**

PACKING HEAT
Karina Moore
ISBN 0 352 33356 1

When spoilt and pretty Californian Nadine has her allowance stopped by her rich Uncle Willem, she becomes desperate to maintain her expensive lifestyle. She joins forces with her lover, Mark, and together they conspire to steal a vast sum of cash from a flashy businessman and pin the blame on their target's girlfriend. The deed done, the sexual stakes rise as they make their escape. Naturally, their getaway doesn't go entirely to plan, and they are pursued across the desert and into the casinos of Las Vegas, where a showdown is inevitable. The clock is ticking for Nadine, Mark and the guys who are chasing them – but a Ferrari-driving blonde temptress is about to play them all for suckers. **Fast cars and even faster women in this modern pulp fiction classic.**

BONDED
Fleur Reynolds
ISBN O 352 33192 5

Sapphire Western is a beautiful young investment broker whose best friend Zinnia has recently married Jethro Clarke, one of the wealthiest and most lecherous men in Texas. Sapphire and Zinnia have a mutual friend, Aurelie de Bouys, whose life is no longer her own now that her scheming cousin Jeanine controls her desires and money. In a world where being rich is everything and being decadent is commonplace, Jeanine and her hedonistic associates still manage to shock and surprise. Will Sapphire remain aloof, or will she be drawn into games of depravity and deception? **Another wildly entertaining story from talented erotic author Fleur Reynolds.**

Published in October 2004

BEDDING THE BURGLAR
Gabrielle Marcola
ISBN O 352 33911 X

Maggie Quinton is a savvy, sexy architect involved in a building project on a remote island off the Florida panhandle. One day, a gorgeous hunk breaks into the house she's staying in and ties her up. The buff burglar is in search of an item he claims the apartment's owner stole from him. And he keeps coming back. Flustered and aroused, Maggie calls her jet-setting sister in for moral support, but flirty, dark-haired Diane is much more interested in the island's ruggedly handsome police chief, 'Griff' Grifford. And then there's his deputy, Cosgrove, with his bulging biceps and creative uses for handcuffs. There must be something in the water that makes this island's men so good-looking and its women so anxious to get their hooks into them – and Maggie is determined to find out what it is by doing as much research as possible!

MIXED DOUBLES
Zoe le Verdier
ISBN 0 352 33312 X

When Natalie Crawford is offered the job as manager of a tennis club in a wealthy English suburb, she jumps at the chance. There's an extra perk, too: Paul, the club's coach, is handsome and charming, and she wastes no time in making him her lover. Then she hires Chris, a coach from a rival club, whose confidence and sexual prowess swiftly puts Paul in the shade. When Chris embroils Natalie into kinky sex games, will she be able to keep control of her business aims, or will her lust for the arrogant sportsman get out of control?

Also available

THE BLACK LACE SEXY QUIZ BOOK
Maddie Saxon
ISBN O 352 33884 9
£6.99

- What sexual personality type are you?
- Have you ever faked it because that was easier than explaining what you wanted?
- What kind of fantasy figures turn you on – and does your partner know?
- What sexual signals are you giving out right now?

Today's image-conscious dating scene is a tough call. Our sexual expectations are cranked up to the max, and the sexes seem to have become highly critical of each other in terms of appearance and performance in the bedroom. But even though guys have ditched their nasty Y-fronts and girls are more babe-licious than ever, a huge number of us are still being let down sexually. Sex therapist Maddie Saxon thinks this is because we are finding it harder to relax and let our true sexual selves shine through.

The Black Lace Sexy Quiz Book will help you negotiate the minefield of modern relationships. Through a series of fun, revealing quizzes, you will be able to rate your sexual needs honestly and get what you really want from your partner. The quizzes will get you thinking about and discussing your desires in ways you haven't previously considered. Unlock the mysteries of your sexual psyche in this fun, revealing quiz book designed with today's sex-savvy girl in mind.

Black Lace Booklist

Information is correct at time of printing. To avoid disappointment check availability before ordering. Go to www.blacklace-books.co.uk. All books are priced £6.99 unless another price is given.

BLACK LACE BOOKS WITH A CONTEMPORARY SETTING

☐ SHAMELESS Stella Black	ISBN 0 352 33485 1	£5.99
☐ INTENSE BLUE Lyn Wood	ISBN 0 352 33496 7	£5.99
☐ A SPORTING CHANCE Susie Raymond	ISBN 0 352 33501 7	£5.99
☐ TAKING LIBERTIES Susie Raymond	ISBN 0 352 33357 X	£5.99
☐ A SCANDALOUS AFFAIR Holly Graham	ISBN 0 352 33523 8	£5.99
☐ THE NAKED FLAME Crystalle Valentino	ISBN 0 352 33528 9	£5.99
☐ ON THE EDGE Laura Hamilton	ISBN 0 352 33534 3	£5.99
☐ LURED BY LUST Tania Picarda	ISBN 0 352 33533 5	£5.99
☐ THE HOTTEST PLACE Tabitha Flyte	ISBN 0 352 33536 X	£5.99
☐ THE NINETY DAYS OF GENEVIEVE Lucinda Carrington	ISBN 0 352 33070 8	£5.99
☐ DREAMING SPIRES Juliet Hastings	ISBN 0 352 33584 X	
☐ THE TRANSFORMATION Natasha Rostova	ISBN 0 352 33311 1	
☐ SIN.NET Helena Ravenscroft	ISBN 0 352 33598 X	
☐ TWO WEEKS IN TANGIER Annabel Lee	ISBN 0 352 33599 8	
☐ HIGHLAND FLING Jane Justine	ISBN 0 352 33616 1	
☐ PLAYING HARD Tina Troy	ISBN 0 352 33617 X	
☐ SYMPHONY X Jasmine Stone	ISBN 0 352 33629 3	
☐ SUMMER FEVER Anna Ricci	ISBN 0 352 33625 0	
☐ CONTINUUM Portia Da Costa	ISBN 0 352 33120 8	
☐ OPENING ACTS Suki Cunningham	ISBN 0 352 33630 7	
☐ FULL STEAM AHEAD Tabitha Flyte	ISBN 0 352 33637 4	
☐ A SECRET PLACE Ella Broussard	ISBN 0 352 33307 3	
☐ GAME FOR ANYTHING Lyn Wood	ISBN 0 352 33639 0	
☐ CHEAP TRICK Astrid Fox	ISBN 0 352 33640 4	
☐ THE GIFT OF SHAME Sara Hope-Walker	ISBN 0 352 32935 1	
☐ COMING UP ROSES Crystalle Valentino	ISBN 0 352 33658 7	
☐ GOING TOO FAR Laura Hamilton	ISBN 0 352 33657 9	

☐ THE STALLION Georgina Brown   ISBN O 352 33005 8

☐ DOWN UNDER Juliet Hastings   ISBN O 352 33663 3

☐ ODALISQUE Fleur Reynolds   ISBN O 352 32887 8

☐ SWEET THING Alison Tyler   ISBN O 352 33682 X

☐ TIGER LILY Kimberly Dean   ISBN O 352 33685 4

☐ COOKING UP A STORM Emma Holly   ISBN O 352 33686 2

☐ RELEASE ME Suki Cunningham   ISBN O 352 33671 4

☐ KING'S PAWN Ruth Fox   ISBN O 352 33684 6

☐ FULL EXPOSURE Robyn Russell   ISBN O 352 33688 9

☐ SLAVE TO SUCCESS Kimberley Raines   ISBN O 352 33687 0

☐ STRIPPED TO THE BONE Jasmine Stone   ISBN O 352 33463 0

☐ HARD CORPS Claire Thompson   ISBN O 352 33491 6

☐ MANHATTAN PASSION Antoinette Powell   ISBN O 352 33691 9

☐ WOLF AT THE DOOR Savannah Smythe   ISBN O 352 33693 5

☐ SHADOWPLAY Portia Da Costa   ISBN O 352 33313 8

☐ I KNOW YOU, JOANNA Ruth Fox   ISBN O 352 33727 3

☐ SNOW BLONDE Astrid Fox   ISBN O 352 33732 X

☐ THE HOUSE IN NEW ORLEANS Fleur Reynolds   ISBN O 352 32951 3

☐ HEAT OF THE MOMENT Tesni Morgan   ISBN O 352 33742 7

☐ THE WICKED STEPDAUGHTER Wendy Harris   ISBN O 352 33777 X

☐ DRAWN TOGETHER Robyn Russell   ISBN O 352 33269 7

☐ LEARNING THE HARD WAY Jasmine Archer   ISBN O 352 33782 6

☐ VALENTINA'S RULES Monica Belle   ISBN O 352 33788 5

☐ VELVET GLOVE Emma Holly   ISBN O 352 33448 7

☐ UNKNOWN TERRITORY Annie O'Neill   ISBN O 352 33794 X

☐ VIRTUOSO Katrina Vincenzi-Thyre   ISBN O 352 32907 6

☐ FIGHTING OVER YOU Laura Hamilton   ISBN O 352 33795 8

☐ COUNTRY PLEASURES Primula Bond   ISBN O 352 33810 5

☐ ARIA APPASSIONATA Juliet Hastings   ISBN O 352 33056 2

☐ THE RELUCTANT PRINCESS Patty Glenn   ISBN O 352 33809 1

☐ HARD BLUE MIDNIGHT Alaine Hood   ISBNO 352 33851 2

☐ ALWAYS THE BRIDEGROOM Tesni Morgan   ISBNO 352 33855 5

☐ COMING ROUND THE MOUNTAIN Tabitha Flyte   ISBNO 352 33873 3

☐ FEMININE WILES Karina Moore   ISBNO 352 33235 2

☐ MIXED SIGNALS Anna Clare   ISBNO 352 33889 X

☐ BLACK LIPSTICK KISSES Monica Belle   ISBNO 352 33885 7

☐ HOP GOSSIP Savannah Smythe   ISBN0 352 33880 6
☐ GOING DEEP Kimberly Dean   ISBN0 352 33876 8
☐ PACKING HEAT Karina Moore   ISBN0 352 33356 1

BLACK LACE BOOKS WITH AN HISTORICAL SETTING

☐ PRIMAL SKIN Leona Benkt Rhys   ISBN 0 352 33500 9   £5.99
☐ DEVIL'S FIRE Melissa MacNeal   ISBN 0 352 33527 0   £5.99
☐ DARKER THAN LOVE Kristina Lloyd   ISBN 0 352 33279 4
☐ THE CAPTIVATION Natasha Rostova   ISBN 0 352 33234 4
☐ MINX Megan Blythe   ISBN 0 352 33638 2
☐ DEMON'S DARE Melissa MacNeal   ISBN 0 352 33683 8
☐ DIVINE TORMENT Janine Ashbless   ISBN 0 352 33719 2
☐ SATAN'S ANGEL Melissa MacNeal   ISBN 0 352 33726 5
☐ THE INTIMATE EYE Georgia Angelis   ISBN 0 352 33004 X
☐ OPAL DARKNESS Cleo Cordell   ISBN 0 352 33033 3
☐ SILKEN CHAINS Jodi Nicol   ISBN 0 352 33143 7
☐ ACE OF HEARTS Lisette Allen   ISBN 0 352 33059 7
☐ THE LION LOVER Mercedes Kelly   ISBN 0 352 33162 3
☐ THE AMULET Lisette Allen   ISBN 0 352 33019 8
☐ WHITE ROSE ENSNARED Juliet Hastings   ISBN 0 352 33052 X
☐ UNHALLOWED RITES Martine Marquand   ISBN 0 352 33222 0
☐ LA BASQUAISE Angel Strand   ISBN 0 352 32988 2
☐ THE HAND OF AMUN Juliet Hastings   ISBN 0 352 33144 5
☐ THE SENSES BEJEWELLED Cleo Cordell   ISBN 0 352 32904 1

BLACK LACE ANTHOLOGIES

☐ WICKED WORDS Various   ISBN 0 352 33363 4
☐ MORE WICKED WORDS Various   ISBN 0 352 33487 8
☐ WICKED WORDS 3 Various   ISBN 0 352 33522 X
☐ WICKED WORDS 4 Various   ISBN 0 352 33603 X
☐ WICKED WORDS 9 Various   ISBN 0 352 33860 1
☐ WICKED WORDS 10 Various   ISBN 0 352 33893 8
☐ THE BEST OF BLACK LACE 2 Various   ISBN 0 352 33718 4

Please send me the books I have ticked above.

Name ....

Address ....

....

....

....

Post Code ....

Send to: Virgin Books Cash Sales, Thames Wharf Studios, Rainville Road, London W6 9HA.

US customers: for prices and details of how to order books for delivery by mail, call 1-800-343-4499.

Please enclose a cheque or postal order, made payable to Virgin Books Ltd, to the value of the books you have ordered plus postage and packing costs as follows:

UK and BFPO – £1.00 for the first book, 50p for each subsequent book.

Overseas (including Republic of Ireland) – £2.00 for the first book, £1.00 for each subsequent book.

If you would prefer to pay by VISA, ACCESS/MASTERCARD, DINERS CLUB, AMEX or SWITCH, please write your card number and expiry date here:

....

Signature ....

Please allow up to 28 days for delivery.